Also by John F. Rooney
Nine Lives Too Many
The Daemon in Our Dreams

THE RICE QUEEN SPY

a novel by

John F. Rooney

Senneff House Publishers
Fort Lauderdale, Florida

Senneff House Publishers
P.O. Box 11601
Fort Lauderdale, FL 33339
www.senneffhouse.com

This book is a work of fiction. Names, characters, places, and
incidents either are products of the author's imagination or are
used fictitiously. Any resemblance to actual events or locales or persons,
living or dead, is entirely coincidental.

Copyright © 2007 by John F. Rooney

All rights reserved,
including the right of reproduction
in whole or in part in any form.

Manufactured in the United States of America

ISBN-13: 978-0-9752756-6-5
ISBN-10: 0-9752756-6-6

The Cover Painting is by Steve Walker.
It is called "Man of Flowers," 1997 and is acrylic on
canvas, 48" x 36". Steve's wonderful works can be
previewed on his website: www.questart.com.

Cover design by Kevin Stawieray

Inside book design and formatting by
Dawn Von Strolley Grove

1

"Faggot. Queer. Cocksucker. Asslicker. Pervert. Poof. Homo. Bloody scum. Shitlicker. Ass reamer. Sodomite. Sissypuke. Bloody cunt. You are nothing but a fucking faggot."

In a converted farmhouse a crude, potbellied, choleric inquisitor leaned over his hapless victim spouting a stream of invectives and spurting intermittent spittle.

Five miles away, a car was headed toward the farmhouse. The black Bentley limousine, late sixties vintage, rolled through an English countryside with a patchwork of fields and plots. Heading north from London, the car threaded its way through frequent hedgerows.

As the car went down a hill, it was out of sight momentarily, then magically it reappeared. The road was narrow, and when another car came along in the opposite direction, both vehicles had to veer off to the verges.

The Bentley, in an area with few farmhouses, outbuildings, or other structures, rolled along at a stately pace, almost as if it carried a member of the Royal Family. Occasionally, sheep and cattle would look toward the car, but they could hardly be less stirred. Their mouths were too busy chewing the sparse winter plant life.

It was a gloomy December afternoon in 1973, an overcast day that made the countryside even more desolate. The trees were bare of their leaves. Some skittish birds were put to flight by the approaching vehicle. Wintry gusts of wind caught clumps of dead leaves and sent them scuttling by the roadside.

The driver sat up tall, back ramrod straight, almost at attention. He had a martial bearing; rather a sergeant major look about him, a burly man who had the appearance of being a driver cum bodyguard, a "don't dare mess with me" sort of bloke.

The passenger, a distinguished-looking executive type,

wore a topcoat that covered his black pinstripe bespoke suit. He, too, had that military posture that must have come from a stint in the service, but he had the attitude and bearing of an officer while his driver was of the non-com variety.

The man ensconced in the rear seat was in his mid-fifties, his hair largely turned to gray. A handsome man, a successful looking man, but a man who at present looked worried and disconcerted. From a folder embossed with an official government seal, Sir Charles Monmouth pulled a large photograph of a man also in his fifties, a man he knew well, and it was strange looking at the photo as if he had never seen the man before. Perhaps because the man in the photograph was, in a sense, a condemned man.

The man in the photo was Philip Croft. Sir Charles, deeply troubled, would stare at the photo and then look out at the bleak countryside. The photograph was of a man who looked quite ordinary, nondescript, unprepossessing, a man who looked as if he could fade into the background. He looked like the sort of ordinary man Alec Guinness might play in a movie in the role of a nobody, a man of no importance. The man who was an inconspicuous clerk, the man who wasn't there.

But if one looked closer, something about the eyes and the mouth said, no, this was a sly one, a bright one, a man with a sensibility who had deep layers beneath the deceivingly ordinary exterior. The eyes and lips revealed a slight grin, a merriment and an intelligence that was there for those people who took the time to get to know him. Sir Charles was one of those who wasn't taken in by the man's seemingly ordinary looking features. Philip was a friend of long standing.

The car continued moving along the deserted country road until it reached a narrow lane bridging off the main road. It drove slowly down the lane and came to a fenced off section with a gate. Beyond the gate was a battered old van. A man, again a person with military bearing, stepped out of the van, went to the gate, and dragged it open. The Bentley drove through. The gatekeeper nodded and casually touched the brim of his cap. The car continued up a lane overgrown with trees and brush.

The Bentley approached a very large rambling stone building that could have been an outsized farmhouse or the dormitory of a school. There was nothing captivating, manorial, or impressive about the structure. It looked institutional and purposeful. The car came to a stop in front of the building. The driver quickly alighted and opened the door for his passenger.

Sir Charles stepped out of the car, nodded, managed a weak smile and said, "Thank you, Gregory." He headed for the main door of the building. His eyes traveled to a second floor window with wooden shutters tightly closed over it. Before he got to the door, it was opened by a bulky weight-lifter type who ushered him in.

On the second floor of the building, which was called the Terminal, even someone hard of hearing could have discerned the shouting coming from behind a closed door. Words and phrases were spat out at three second intervals: "Faggot. Queer. Cocksucker. Asslicker. You are nothing but a fucking faggot."

A ten-second pause and then the invective stream resumed. "Pervert. Steamer. Poof. Poofter. Homo. Bloody scum. Shitlicker. Ass reamer. Sodomite. Sissypuke. Bloody cunt."

Sir Charles heard the deep male voice thundering as he walked down the second floor hallway. He was led into a darkened room that had a one-way glass that gave voyeurs a view of the brightly lit room next door. The lit room's windows were shuttered so that no outside light could enter. Floodlights on the ceiling transformed the room into a stage setting. What he saw made him shudder because he knew this was the prelude, the prefatory interlude before the Grand Guignol indignities began.

As he entered the room, he heard the loud, deafening male voice again intone, "Faggot. Queer. Cocksucker. Asslicker."

Blackout curtains prevented any outside light from getting into a sparsely furnished room. The bright overhead lights illuminated a room with three occupants. Seated at a pine table was Philip Croft, a mild-mannered, bespectacled, gentle man, aged fifty-eight. He wore a brown woolen tweed suit, a vest, and loosened tie. He was unshaven and looked very tired and worn.

Standing to one side of the table was Sergeant Whaley, a large man just turned thirty-five, six foot-two, balding, with a coarse, ruddy face, a belly bloated from too much beer and spirits, a nose with the boozer's telltale veins flaming. He was in shirtsleeves, no tie. On the other side of the room, seated, was Trimmer, another big man, but in fairly good shape, athletic, younger than Whaley.

Whaley stood above Croft, leaning over, face close to Croft's, threatening, menacing, spitting out his invectives as he yelled at his set intervals, "You are nothing but a fucking faggot. Pervert . . ."

As he spat out his epithets, his spit landed on Croft, who lowered his head to avoid the spittle. He stared down at the table, exhausted, humiliated, seemingly defeated.

Croft could smell last night's alcohol, his fetid breath.

"The British intelligence service does *not* need another bloody pervert. One more fucking spy poof, and we'll be the laughing stock of the world. Right, Trimmer?"

Trimmer quickly acquiesced. "Right, Sergeant Whaley. Enough is enough."

Whaley laughed scornfully. "We might as well be known as the gay intelligence service with all of you pansies flouncing around."

Philip did not answer. Whaley was trying to bait his suspect. Subtlety was not one of his strong suits, and compassion was alien to him.

"Croft, you're another of that cozy Cambridge bunch. God, the number of you from that bloody bolshie nursery. Burgess, Maclean, Kim Philby. God knows how many others."

There was still no answer from Philip.

Whaley was winding himself up, his face turning redder, unable to pace himself in an interrogation. Go for the throat first and fast. The element of surprise had served him well in his old hand-to-hand combat days, but now it only served to make him apoplectic and decidedly impatient for results.

Whaley, reddening, shouted, "I was addressing you, Phyllis Poofter, Esquiress. Miss Croft, Queenie dear, I am addressing YOU."

Philip's quiet voice could hardly be heard. "Sorry, I didn't hear the question, Sergeant Whaley. Your shouting has made me temporarily deaf. Your voice does have a tendency to carry. God knows what the neighbors will think."

"There are no neighbors hereabouts the Terminal, Miss Croft, as you well know."

"Oh, that's right, we're in that farmhouse in the middle of nowhere. One of those safe houses you trainers were always going on about."

Was it foolhardiness, bravery, or a masochistic streak that made Philip talk back to his brutalizing interrogator? Or deep down was it Philip Croft's link to an older generation where members of Whaley's class did not address people in Philip's strata in a demeaning manner?

Philip squirmed in his chair. He grimaced in pain. There was obviously some physical problem tormenting him as he sat through the interrogation.

Whaley continued on the warpath. "Mr. Croft, never mind the impertinence, the snide remarks. You are in shit up to your armpits. Stay alert. Do you realize the harm you have done to your country?"

Philip sat up straight. "I have never harmed my country. I would never think to do so. I love my country as much as any patriot. As much as you, I dare say."

"Croft, while you were under the carpet or in the closet, or doing your cottaging, what information were you giving away with the blow jobs and the reaming? You were selling out your country for a bit of cum, weren't you? Thinking with your cock rather than your brain, I dare say. On your knees in some common W.C., eh, Croft?"

"I've told you over and over. I have always been loyal to Her Majesty's government."

"Faggots always lie."

"I would rather die than betray my country or anyone in the service. I would never shop anyone. I was a patriot before you were born."

Trimmer was trying to follow this colloquy. He was the good soldier and did what he was told. Sergeant Whaley was of the old school. The sledgehammer approach. It wasn't for Trimmer to interfere. He just sat and watched and occasionally cringed.

Whaley bulled on, shouting, having no trouble playing the bully, "One question here before this august body is your perversion, your homo tendencies."

"I haven't denied being gay."

Whaley leaned over with his face mere inches away from Philip's. This proximity was distasteful to Philip. He leaned away from him, but this emboldened Whaley and he maintained the closeness.

"How many times in some fleabag hotel did you whisper our bloody secrets to one of your faggot chums?"

Philip was emboldened now. His voice grew louder, more determined. "I've told you I admit to being a homosexual. I've come to a point in my life where I no longer wish to deny my sexuality."

"All very well, Miss Croft, the poofter, but we need you to spell out your sexual indiscretions. Dates, times, places, companions. Yes, especially your sex partners."

"I couldn't possibly do that, even if I wanted to."

"Think about it. Names, dates, places. Think about your fellow agents who aren't around anymore because of you."

"I never compromised anyone's safety in my life."

Whaley backed away from the table and motioned to Trimmer. Trimmer stood. They went to the corner of the room, and Whaley conferred quietly with him. Philip rested his head on the table.

Whaley was sweating. He whispered to Trimmer, "I'm

getting sick of this shite. I'm going to check the observation room. I'm sure there's somebody there. Be back in a bit."

Louder, he growled, "Got to wet my whistle. Take a pee."

Whaley left the room. Trimmer went forward and sat opposite Croft whose head rested on his crossed arms. In his mind, Philip Croft was already back reliving his past.

2

It was an excruciatingly hot humid day in Singapore. Philip had willed himself back to the past, to happier times, anywhere away from this horror, this dank room reeking of sweat, stale beer, and tobacco. He was using a technique he had been taught in refresher courses at the Depot, the training school for his Intelligence Service. The recent trainers, indeed one of them had been Whaley, had told the students that when being interrogated they should will themselves back to better times, fond memories, bright periods in their lives.

Philip willed himself back, back eighteen years before the interrogation.

A younger, more vital, more virile Philip was with a vibrant young man named Tom, Singaporean, possibly Peranakan, Straits-born Chinese, that combination of Malay and Chinese that often produced very exotic handsome men. The two men were laughing.

The sun was bright, startlingly bright, searing white light that made one squint. He and Tom were in the whitest of white shorts and polo shirts. They were carrying tennis rackets. God, that sun was so blinding. Tom clapped his arm on Philip's shoulder as they enjoyed a joke together. They were entering the Raffles Hotel.

Around them at the entrance were a line of rickshaws with their cadaverous coolie pullers. A bicycle loaded with a high pile of bales rolled by. People were walking in and out of the hotel amid street noise and street theater. The doorman, a huge turbaned Sikh gave them a pleasant greeting. Tom, often demonstrative, again put his arm around Philip's shoulder as they entered.

In the lobby they passed the Writer's Bar and the Tiffin Room. (Fasten on details, the minders had said. The more you recreate the happier moments, the less substantial will be your present horrors.)

Philip's mind did a quick dissolve to a room in Raffles shortly after their lobby entrance. In times like this, you wanted a memory stream that brought back the best of times. Nothing grim, nothing sad or gritty.

Philip and Tom were embracing in a hotel bedroom with plantation shutters on the windows, a ceiling fan, rattan furniture. There was a look of supreme happiness on Philip's face. Sun flooded into the room. Both were stripped to their undershorts. Philip could even now feel the stirrings of an erection as he had then.

The spell was broken. Whaley strode back into the room. He said something to Trimmer. Philip shook his head, looked around. Whaley approached the table. Philip gazed off into space. Trimmer stood to the right, fiddling with a tape recording device.

Whaley licked his lips. Perhaps he had stolen time for a quick drink. A bottle hidden somewhere. He resumed his tirade. He started to talk more quietly now, ruminatively, almost as if he were talking to himself.

"You gents, you swells, your kind always were the precious ones, the agents. You had the glamour jobs. You were the bloody fuckin' glory-seeking caseworkers running your networks. Even in the field you had others to do the dirty dangerous work so you wouldn't soil your precious soft hands or get bloodied."

Whaley had his hands on his hips, lecturing Philip, talking partly for Trimmer's benefit.

"You had the posh educations, sat drinking your pink ladies in Berne or Lisbon."

He addressed Trimmer. "Miss Croft here spent years in Switzerland in the big war. Of course it were neutral so our friend here didn't have to worry about the bombs falling. Trimmer, me lad, did you ever get to see Switzerland?"

Trimmer answered dutifully, "No, Sarge, I wasn't one of the lucky ones."

Whaley began again, addressing Philip. "Getting posted back to London so you could go to your clubs. Meet at the Savoy and talk over your bloody exploits and go to your Sunday afternoon tea dances, poncing around."

Philip had to rearrange himself in the chair. His ass was burning. He looked up at Whaley. "Sergeant, I am in great pain on my backside. I need medical attention."

Whaley ignored Philip's pleas and continued his ranting. All of the injustices *he* had suffered. "We couldn't even pee where you peed. Blokes like me and Trimmer here. We weren't good enough for you until and unless you got in some scrape where you needed muscle instead of manners."

As he spoke, it was obvious that Whaley was the pub blowhard who talked to hear the sound of his pontificating, self-inflating voice.

Whaley was also talking for the benefit of the man watching the interrogation from the darkened room next door. While he was out of the room, one of the minders had alerted him to Sir Charles's presence in the watching room.

Sir Charles, still standing, followed the interrogation from the other room. Whaley was disgusting to him. A brute, a bully, a petty tyrant who was probably a necessary evil. Willing, as he himself said, to do the dirty jobs like this one.

Philip pleaded. "Sergeant, I am in pain. It is . . ."

"When you needed to be pulled out of one of your screwups, we were the ones who had to come in and change your nappies, clean up after your mistakes and incompetence."

Philip raised his voice. "Whaley, for God's sake, I need to see a doctor. I am . . ."

"We were the bloody peons that trained you, wiped your arses, cleaned up your messes, did all the dirty little deeds' eh, Trimmer?"

Trimmer, on cue, chimed in, "Yes, all the crap details."

Philip cried out. "Sergeant Whaley, I am in pain. I . . ."

Whaley continued, his voice louder, drowning out Philip and ignoring him. "We were the ones that pulled the hours and hours of surveillance, the shite work.

While you were sleeping with your rent boys . . ."

"There were no rent boys."

Whaley was on a roll. "We were the ones in the bone-chilling cold winter nights or the shitty rain watching some bloody flat all night."

"I know that. We all appreciated your . . ."

"Standing in doorways, scrunched down in draughty lorries, trying not to look out of place in hotel lobbies and tea shops."

"No one denies your patriotism and devotion to the service," gasped Philip, "Is my loyalty in question just because I'm gay?"

"To give you some credit, Croft, I remember once not too many years ago when you were in a hand-to-hand refresher course I was running. For a poof, you were very good. Quite wily, tricky. And much stronger than I thought you'd be."

Philip was using his memory, his willpower, to blank out Whaley. His mind went back to an earlier time. This time his memory chose, nay imposed, an unpleasant time. A time of danger and crisis.

He had supervised the building of a tunnel under the Berlin Wall. It ran under the headquarters of the East German secret police where the Brits could monitor their activities and listen to bugs planted in their offices. The tunnel had been discovered. It was night.

Claus, a radio operator, and a younger Philip were running for their lives in an earthen tunnel. Each had a small flashlight, Philip a drawn automatic. Behind them were Russian troops with dogs. The soldiers had submachine guns and carried flashlights.

"Schnell! Schnell!" Philip cried out to Claus.

The advancing Russians' machine gunfire thundered in the enclosed tunnel. A sudden cry. The radioman was hit. He slumped to the ground, his hand grasping his leg. Philip spun around, took aim and fired a clip of bullets at the advancing soldiers. There were screams. Two of the Russian soldiers were downed.

Philip grabbed the radioman under the man's armpits and dragged him through the tunnel. Behind them came shouts, a burst of gunfire and with it a great deal of earth collapsed in from the roof and sides of the tunnel. Philip's face was stretched into a grimace of exertion as he dragged his comrade. Half carrying, half dragging, Philip pulled him to safety into the Western zone.

Back in the interrogation room, a quick burst of intense pain shot through his buttocks. He cried out to Whaley. "I'm in terrible pain."

He might as well be talking to a stone, a block of wood.

Whaley smiled, saying, "Now we have to dig out the fairies in the garden. We have to follow the trail of black slime that leads to you filthy slugs."

"This pain is . . ."

"We have to spy on the spies and catch them with their trousers down and their pricks up. There are so many of you bloody ponces that they ought to call it the Queen's Intelligence Service for queens. My God, where did all you fags come from?"

"Sergeant," said Trimmer, "perhaps it was all that caning they got in their boarding schools."

Whaley answered, "Their very private public schools? Being a sissy fag is a bloody epidemic among the upper classes."

"Please let me see a doctor, for God's sake." Philip's voice was louder now, pleading.

Sir Charles, watching from the next room, was wincing. He dared not interfere at this point. He'd have to endure this for a time, but it made him very uncomfortable. He despised Whaley for the bully and sadist that he was. He thought, *God, we stoop so low in what we do. Each day we seem to lose a little more of our humanity.*

Whaley was getting his kicks out of this. "Them, the people like Croft here, were so used to getting caned and plunked in public schools that they became perverts. Either taking it or giving it up the bloody arse."

Philip tensed himself as a stab of pain ran through his body. "Sergeant, my . . ."

"Yeah, I know your bloody arse is sore. As well it should be considering the things you and other poofs do with your arses."

Then Whaley was weaving another strain into his litany. "God, how do you all keep going? Mincing in an out of drawing rooms, balancing tea cups on your knees."

Philip knew he should be still but couldn't resist showing some defiance to this clod. "Sergeant Whaley, wouldn't it be rather difficult for us to mince in and out of drawing rooms with those teacups stuck to our knees?"

"SHUT YOUR BLOODY FUCKIN' MOUTH, CROFT."

He stood menacingly over Philip, his fists clenched, holding himself back from pummeling him. He cooled off after pacing the floor and taking a few deep breaths. Then he continued with his catalog of injustices.

"Your kind got the credit, the glory. We got the shit. Your kind were pensioned off. We were made redundant. Some of your sort got knighted, got Queen's honors. We got shunted into the back streets to become security guards at Paki markets . . ."

Trimmer was energized, ". . . Or night watchmen."

Whaley nodded at Trimmer and turned back to Philip. "Over and over again, we got the shite jobs. Little thanks we got for digging up your slimy secrets. You and your kind keep the class system going. The workingman slips onto the dole. Your class goes to vesper services at St. Paul's."

Philip whispered, "Please let me see a doctor."

Whaley persisted, "You live completely apart, no workingman's pubs for you. Maybe the occasional posh gay bar with your ponce fellows. You even attend the Queen's chapel. Her Majesty and the Queen Mum are surrounded by poofs."

Whaley needed a break. He headed for the door, opened it, but couldn't resist some parting shots. "Right now I'm going to the loo to pee—unless you'd care for a golden shower. Are you one of those, too? Do you like leather and rubber?

Denim? Or is it a kimono for you? I've heard a chink or a slant-eye catches your fancy. Bloody hell. We know that you have a large gang of gay friends in Asia. You've built up your own gay network there."

Philip wondered who had supplied him with this information. Had they spied on the spy? Of course they did. It was par for the course.

Sergeant Whaley looked at Philip in disgust and left the room, slamming the door.

Philip was glad to be rid of him even if were only for a short spell. He muttered, "Blowhard."

Trimmer, alone with Philip, was politer, quieter, more subtle, seemingly more compassionate. Now he felt free to speak up. "Sir, in your experience you may not know people like Sergeant Whaley as well as you think you do. They can get very nasty."

"Why is my backside so sore? I think I should be given an opportunity to see a doctor. I am in great pain sitting here."

Ignoring Philip's entreaties, Trimmer continued, "Or maybe you really don't understand Whaley's type. The lengths they'll go to. I've read your file. You were brought up in a good home, distantly related to the Scottish aristocracy."

"Very, very distantly related, I'm afraid. Quite distant from the money."

Trimmer's voice was calming, persuasive, confiding. "You went to good public schools, was sent up to Cambridge, had good A-level results, scholarships, well-placed friends, joined private clubs."

"My family was never that well-off. I had to earn almost everything for myself."

"I don't think you ever really hung around the pubs, got to know the ordinary common man, the Whaleys of this world. Have you ever played darts, snooker, raised a few pints, sat in the stands at football?"

"Aren't you just echoing the same things as your partner? My lack of affinity for the man in the street? I thought it was good interrogation technique for you to take an entirely different tack."

"Sarge's kind is the one you read about in the papers, the football hooligan that tears up a pub and bloodies some poor lout just for the fun of it. His kind loves to see others suffer."

"Then why does the service tolerate him or his ilk? I know why. Because he'll do what the bosses don't have the stomach to do. A football hooligan given official sanction, encouraged to let go and be the complete brute."

"That's our Sergeant Whaley."

"Then more's the pity for us to use the worst types we can find from under the rocks."

"Blokes like Sarge catch a homosexual in a cottage situation and beat the shit out of him. He can be wickedly nasty when he sets his mind to it. He is a complete faggot hater. He's my mate, but he can go daft when a gay is around."

"And you, Trimmer, you're not like that? You're a truly liberated man who tolerates all manner of human behavior and homosexuality?"

"I believe in live and let live."

"Trimmer, the nasty brutes like Whaley don't exist in a vacuum, you know."

The telephone on a table in the corner rang. Trimmer answered it.

"Yes, I understand. I'll tell him."

Trimmer replaced the receiver and returned to the table. He spoke quietly to Philip. "Sir Charles Monmouth is here in the building. He wants to see you. I've heard you're old chums. You were at boarding school and university together, weren't you? Part of the old boy network."

"Yes, a year apart at school."

"If you can't tell us anything, then come clean with him. He's your own kind."

Philip didn't answer. He dropped his head onto his crossed arms. He didn't want to see his boss, the chief of MI6, here under these circumstances.

3

Sir Charles Monmouth walked into the room. He didn't want to be there, didn't want any part of it. What good did it do? Philip, he knew in his gut, wasn't a traitor. Sure he was a poof; Sir Charles had suspected as much for years.

Impeccably dressed, something of a dandy, Sir Charles was a tall, distinguished looking man, the high-level bureaucrat, or successful business executive. A man normally full of self-confidence, self-satisfaction. A man to be reckoned with. Not at this moment. He had a defeated look and posture to him. He glanced over at the wall with the glass knowing that Whaley would be spying on him just as he had spied on Whaley.

Sir Charles had only recently been appointed head of the British foreign intelligence section. He approached the table and looked down at Philip, whose head was still bowed down on the table. At first he reached out with his hand to establish some human contact, but then drew his arm back, pursed his shaking lips. His voice was soft, apologetic.

"Philip, how are you, old boy? I can't tell you how dreadfully sorry I am about all this."

Philip looked up. His expression didn't change. No smile of greeting or even recognition.

"Is it morning, afternoon, or evening?" asked Philip. "They've taken away my watch. And someone has curtained off all the windows. Like a blackout in the Second War."

"It's just past noon. How are you bearing up?"

"What day is it? They don't let me sleep, Sir Charles."

"It's Friday."

"My rear end is frightfully painful. I seem to have an infection or something. I really should see a doctor."

"You look exhausted."

Philip was very tired. He seemed to be drifting off into

some other state. "I think I need a doctor to look after . . ."

"I'll order that a doctor examine you."

"Why have they chosen to go after me? Why me?"

"Part of the old regime's paranoia, I'm afraid. But you must realize they initiated this before I took over the reins. Once these purges get rolling, we can't stop them, I fear. These witch hunts take on a life of their own."

"So many purges, so many scapegoats. The years are strewn with victims, walking wounded. When will it ever end, do you suppose?"

"Philip, we've been through some very tough times together. The real war, the Cold War, the conniving, the power plays and the double dealing by the cousins."

"Yes, we've seen it all."

Sir Charles stood behind Philip momentarily. Then he circled around the room as they talked. He was restless, nervous.

"Philip, you must know that the knives are drawn. They're looking for blood again."

"They're always looking for blood. *They*. Always *they*. Who are these *they* everyone refers to? Aliens from another planet?"

"It's the new regime fighting the old. This time, Philip, what they really want are carcasses. You've got to tell the minders everything."

"But why did I become the target?"

"It's a different world now. The Russkies are getting more belligerent. Our American cousins are always on us about moles and leaks and holes in the system. In the old days, we covered up too many indiscretions, but now we are in the public spotlight. Everything is a sieve these days. Leaks, rumors, investigations."

"All my life I've been told *they* don't want us to walk on the grass, to go wading; *they* want us to go to church. *They* . . . *they* . . .*they*. *They* shake *their* heads and purse *their* lips, and say no, no, no. *They* try to destroy your very being. *They* tell you to dance with the girls. To be straight. To marry. To not rock the boat. To not go off the deep end. To not dare be or act like a fairy."

"Philip, listen to me, I think . . ."

Philip interrupted him and plowed on, desperate to be heard and understood. If this man wouldn't listen to him, no one in the organization would. They were from the same old school, the same class.

"Sir Charles, from the moment they brought me in for questioning, I admitted my sexual proclivities."

Philip started to raise his voice, almost shouting. "I am and always will be, forever and a day, now until eternity, a bloody queer. But not a bloody traitor!"

"Philip, please."

Sir Charles's face was suffused with deep emotional anguish. Philip was so concerned about his own situation that he was unaware of Sir Charles's mental state or reactions. It was obvious that Sir Charles was wracked by his own demons. For him, this was far more stressful than just the interrogation of a casual friend.

Philip cried out, "It was time for me to come out of the closet, out from under the rug. From the first hour I was here, I have admitted I was a homosexual, albeit a barely practicing one."

Sir Charles tried to reassure. "You've gone through hell here. You've . . ."

"I have never, on my honor betrayed any secret, compromised any operation, revealed anything to anyone about my work. Why should I? I loved my work."

"You were good at what you did, Philip."

"In thirty-six years with the service, I never associated with anyone other than Oriental boys who were only interested in a few pounds, or a dinner, or an evening's entertainment. Young chaps who genuinely liked an older man. They hardly knew enough English for me to get them to bed. It was all gestures and sign language."

"Philip. . . ."

"Sir Charles, pardon me, let me finish. I have nothing to tell other than I sought a few moments of pleasure with some Asian boys. I was and am what is called in gay life a rice queen. I have never had sex with a Caucasian in my whole life."

"Philip, you needn't . . ."

"I loved only Oriental lads. They weren't aware of or interested in what or who I was professionally. They wanted a bit of comfort, of love, of sex—the same things I wanted."

"God, Philip, please . . ."

"I wanted to caress and hug them and disappear into another, kinder world for a few fleeting moments. I've lived with the deepest secret of all, my own sexuality, for years."

Philip stood up for the first time in hours, stood to face Sir Charles in his attempt to convince him. "My God, Charles, if homosexuals cannot be expected to keep secrets, who in this whole world can be expected to do so? Most homosexuals hide their very being for most of their lifetimes."

"Philip, what we need now is your cooperation to clear up some matters."

Philip, dispirited and exhausted, sat down again, realizing the pain as he did so. He went on talking, unaware that Sir Charles himself seemed haunted by his own inner turmoil.

Philip's voice was lower, more resigned. "When you lie and cover up the essence of your being, it's child's play to hide state secrets. Being secretive is what we are all about. We queers are born for subterfuge. Many of us marry, and even our spouses and children never suspect. Deception becomes our way of life."

"Philip, you know yourself that these minders can be vicious, nasty. When you came in here several days ago, they gave you an injection."

"Yes, I know, in my buttock. It is very, very sore. Painful like an enormous boil or carbuncle."

"For God's sake, cooperate. We've been friends for years. Please give them what they want before they turn vicious."

"I have nothing to give them."

"They wanted you to admit you were gay, and you did so. And now they want . . ."

"I am not a turncoat."

"Philip, it's not you they want. They don't really think you would betray your country or the service."

Sir Charles poured a glass of water from a pitcher on a table against the wall and set the glass in front of Philip, who merely stared dumbly at it.

"Let me go, and let me out of the service so that I can get on with my life."

"It's not as easy as all that, Philip."

"What then?"

"They want you to shop a couple of people. Give them the names of a few queens in the service. Pick out a few names that everyone knows about anyway. That's what they want, all they want."

"Names? What names? Traitors? I know no traitors."

"For God's sake, Philip. Not traitors. Queers, queens. Men, or women for that matter, in the service who are homosexuals or lesbians or thought to be."

"Charles, listen to me! I don't know anyone who's gay in the service. How could I? I've only gone with an occasional Asian boy."

"Some names. Names!"

"Why would I associate with gays who are looking to pick up Caucasians? I don't go to gay bars or gay parties in England. I'm not interested in white men."

Sir Charles looked aghast at Philip, finding it difficult to believe that Philip could hold such views.

"Caucasian men repel me with their big noses and ears, their hairy skin, their terrible manners and their smell. Swigging beer all day. Those horrible fetid beer farts."

Even Sir Charles managed a smile at this. "Oh, for Christ sake, Philip, Asians don't fart?"

"Only dainty, sweet smelling little puffs."

"Philip, you *are* a hopelessly romantic rice queen." He took a long breath. "Please give them some obvious names."

"Charles, they'll have to kill me here and now. I have absolutely nothing to tell them."

"Philip, you and I know the names of some obvious queens in the service. Everyone knows them. It would be giving away nothing they don't already know."

"If everyone knows them, and if you know them, then you give their names. Just because some people act effeminately doesn't mean they are homosexuals. Do THEY think it takes one to know one?"

"The names have to come from you. Give them the obvious."

"I know less about gay life in Britain than any straight man. All of my British gay friends are rice queens in Asia, and none of them was ever stupid enough to be connected with the service. I realize now that I should have gotten out years ago before I became entrenched."

"You were one of our most important operatives. Berlin, Lisbon, Geneva, Hong Kong, Tokyo. They didn't come any better than you. The best of the best."

"And what am I now?"

Sir Charles walked to the table across the room. Philip rested his head on his crossed arms, daydreaming to escape the horrors of the present. He was willing himself into kinder, pleasanter times, times of love and sexual fulfillment. Anywhere but the horror of the present.

4

It was again a bedroom in Raffles in Singapore on an afternoon in 1955. Bright cleansing light flooded a room with a whirring fan, big wicker empress chairs, a large bed, and colonial style rattan furniture. Light was streaming in through open French windows. Beethoven's "Fidelio" played very softly in the background.

A younger Philip entered the room, age forty. He was nude. He walked over to the wide windows and gazed out, his well-shaped buttocks glistening with small droplets of water from the shower. He reached down, picked up his drawers from the floor and pulled them on.

A young bare Tom entered from the bathroom. He strode toward Philip. His body, his walk, his attitude permeated the room with what was for Philip his Asian sexuality and sensuality. He was hairless except for a small area in the genitalia. His body was perfectly formed, not muscular, but strong and lithe. He smiled at Philip. Philip glowed.

"I love these old colonial hotels," said Tom. "Style, grandeur, elegance, and a certain taste of decadence. Very British. Very colonial."

The two embraced and kissed. Philip caressed the young man's body. He enjoyed the feel of the silky skin. He enjoyed looking at him. He gently fondled Tom's penis and testicles.

Tom, in a very proper, posh British accent, said, not meaning a word of it, "Enough of that, sir. Let us have some decorum here, especially in these storied precincts. I can just imagine the old days when this hotel was frequented by Joseph Conrad, Somerset Maugham, and Rudyard Kipling. Perhaps even Noel Coward, eh, what, old chap? The atmosphere in these places is infectious. A Singapore sling for lunch, my love?"

"Yes, Tom, dear."

"That would be lovely. And some fresh strawberries and cream."

"Thomas, I love you because you are so boyish, yet so masculine. And you're more British than the Brits themselves."

"Thank you, my lord and master."

Philip caressed the right nipple on Thomas's flat chest, then leaned over to kiss his chest. His hand had gently stroked Tom's penis so that it became aroused. Tom gave him a fervent kiss.

"Later, my darling," said Tom.

Tom donned his shorts. He put his hand up to his ear and said, "I notice that you seem to have found Beethoven being broadcast by some station on your radio. Is it *Fidelio*?"

"Yes, marvelous of you to recognize it. I've been quite lucky today. Earlier they played *The Eroica*."

"Beethoven is a favorite of yours, isn't he? And Wagner, too?"

"I love them both. When I was quite young, my father had a customer who gave him oodles and oodles of Beethoven and Wagner recordings as payment for a bill. I used to play them on the gramophone hours at a time, driving everyone else in the house bonkers."

Tom laughed. "Why is that easy for me to imagine? You, engrossed in your own passions, oblivious to the ordinary household chores. Were you always musical?"

"Yes, classical and liturgical music. Growing up, I sang in choirs in church and choruses at school, and at university. Also, I played the piano. Had a crush on a piano teacher. That was in my Caucasian phase before I discovered the charms of the Asian boys and men. Also had something of a crush on a football coach in school, but of course, I didn't act on it. One didn't know what one was in those prehistoric days. But I loved the piano."

"Can you still play?"

"A little. Classical music has always been a passion of mine."

Philip went to the radio and adjusted the dial so the radio signal came in more clearly. He glanced out the window at the shop

houses across the way, which were busy with people unloading
merchandise from lorries. The street was alive with the bustle of
shoppers. Tom's voice carried him back into the room.

"Philip, you're very traditional, aren't you?"

"Oh yes, very staid and proper. And I'm very much Church
of England. I love the ritual, the mass, the music, and I'm a
believer. I make no excuses for it—whether it puts me out of
style or not, I don't care."

"You are so conventional."

"Don't mock me."

"Oh, I don't mean to mock you. I admire you. I envy you,
your traditional set of values, your ability to believe in your
God. Your British sensibilities. But you are quite exciting in
bed when we are making love because you act like you don't
get it very often. You are so needy and so responsive."

"How true. I wish I could get it more often."

"I think you feel entirely at ease being in the nude in front
of me. We're both at ease with our own bodies. But do you
have such a hard time meeting bed companions?"

"Yes, it's very difficult for me. I seldom meet anyone, and
my brief trysts are very infrequent. I have never met anyone
like you."

"We make a good couple."

"And now, my dear Thomas, how about that Singapore
sling and some lunch or as they call it here, tiffin?"

They kissed and embraced again. Then their kissing
became more charged, more intense. Both men were getting
aroused. Tom lowered Philip's shorts revealing an erection.
Tom slipped from his shorts. He, too, was erect. He led Philip
over to the bed. The two nude bodies coiled and intertwined
as their kissing became more and more urgent.

Philip tried to tighten his eyes more, to close out the outside world. He must will his mind even harder back to those
halcyon days, but it was not to be. He could hear Sir
Charles's voice above him.

"Sit up, Philip. Listen to me. Heed my advice. Give them
names."

Philip sat up, a dazed look on his face.

"I must go now. Please give them what they want. Make it easy for yourself."

"For a few moments, I thought I had escaped from this horror."

"Goodbye, Philip."

Philip didn't answer. Sir Charles left the room, closing the door quietly.

5

Hours later, in a different room of the Terminal, Philip was face down on what looked like an operating table. He was nude, strapped down. A big light over the table shone brightly. His right buttock had an inflamed, swollen area, extremely red. It seemed to glow. A doctor, a woman in her late thirties, in white scrubs with a white surgical mask hanging below her chin came into the room. Sergeant Whaley entered, also in white. His surgical mask was also hanging down around his neck.

Trimmer rolled in a shiny metal cart of surgical paraphernalia, several kidney-shaped stainless steel pans of gleaming instruments. A great metallic din commenced as Whaley and Trimmer orchestrated these instruments to clang and clatter. It sounded as if they were being transferred from pan to pan.

Then rubber gloves were removed by each person from a box. A great ritual began of putting on these gloves, snapping rubber, of rubber stretching, as if each person put on and removed the gloves several times. Rubber squeaking. The sounds of gloves snapping and metal surgical instruments banging drove Philip round the bend. This noisy show went on for quite some time. Finally, the three positioned themselves around Philip, who was by now panicky.

The doctor touched Philip on his shoulder. He flinched.

"Mr. Croft, I am Doctor Dorothy Lessman, and I am here to examine you."

"Doctor, please, the pain . . ."

"I see from your chart that while you were in boarding school, you had an attack of boils. Nasty things, boils. Especially when you get them on your backside. Can be the worst place for them. Sometimes they erupt on the testicles or in the anus. Very painful, dreadfully uncomfortable."

The doctor touched Croft's tender backside. The pain shot through his body.

"No, please. Doctor, please, no."

"This abscess is particularly virulent. Quite nasty. It is in its penultimate stage. It has not begun to drain yet. Very large."

Whaley, like a Dickensian villain, as if he were doing a co-diagnosis or serving as a consultant, leaned over and exuded, "Very nasty, indeed. Hmmm."

The doctor calmly, professionally, continued, "A series of furuncles, boils, a huge carbuncle. There may be a network of channels or canals where these boils interconnect. They can be dangerous."

Philip cried out. "Doctor, please. I'm in great pain . . ."

"The venom can work its way into the blood stream and affect the whole body. I can imagine how much pain your are in. Orderly Whaley, see here, they have honeycombed and spread out from what looks like the nucleus."

Whaley sniggered. "Looks wicked, doctor."

"Now this one here, this purplish mass here; this may be the primary. It's hard to tell where the pus is centered. Philip, I am going to apply pressure and see if we can't get this one to come to a head for draining."

"Oh, God, No, please. Don't . . ."

Philip let out a piercing scream of pain. It could be heard throughout the building. Sir Charles down the hall could hear his screams, and he gasped. These parts of the performance were not for the queasy or faint of heart.

The doctor leaned closer. "Just a little more. It's very hard here, this spot. Nothing will drain. I'm going to make a tiny incision."

"Please, Doctor, oh, no, . . ."

"This is going to have to be lanced. Orderly, scalpel. Give me those pincers too. Now, the bigger blade, over there."

Trimmer's voice croaked. "Oh, I'm going to be sick." He turned away from the table, rushed toward the corner of the room, gagging. Whaley laughed uproariously. This was better than watching a football match.

The doctor, ever the cool professional, mused, "We won't be able to use a local on this because it might cause infection. Orderly Whaley, Orderly Trimmer, please hold the patient down, if necessary."

"Yes, doctor."

Philip cried out, "Please, doctor, oh, please, don't, I beg you."

"Mr. Croft, this has to be done. Often the anticipation of the pain is greater than the pain itself. I've never seen a system of boils that looked so intractable, so unyielding. I'm going to try squeezing here."

Philip cried out in extreme pain. "No! Oh, God, please no."

Trimmer returned to the surgical table, looked at the mess, gagged, and turned his head away.

The doctor appeared calm, analytical. "Often with this type of eruption you get a small bloody discharge, and the big pus sacs remain deeply buried in the honeycomb of secondary abscesses. How did you ever get this horrible thing?"

"They gave it me. ARGH!."

"Terribly messy. Very disreputable looking, eh?"

Philip twisted in pain and howled.

"Oh, my God, stop."

The doctor persisted. "It won't give up its pus as yet. Orderly, squeeze this spot while I try to put pressure here."

"Argh, Stop." Philip cried out in pain, in agony.

The doctor said, "Orderly, scalpel. No, not that one, the narrower, longer one. Give me that number four needle. We have to be able to penetrate. Here, now this will only smart for a minute, Mr. Croft."

"No, dear God, no!" A piercing scream of sheer pain could be heard through the halls of the old building. The screams were getting worse. Philip was sobbing.

A discouraged tone to the doctor's voice. "I didn't get anything at all out of that. No discharge. It seems dry there, yet this swollen part has to be full of gook. I'll have to open up some of these secondary canals."

Whaley's voice clucked, "An awful mess, doctor."

"I count eight canals, all radiating around this central hardened hub. I hate it when they are so clandestine, compartmentalized, such canals of contagion with hidden pockets of pus."

Whaley punctuated his comments. "Channels that deceive. Yes. Indeed."

The doctor commented, "Give me one big liquidy boil any time over these dispersed fistulas. Here, Orderly Whaley. Help me. Squeeze here, apply pressure here."

"This spot?"

"No, not there. Here. See if you can get some pus, some excretion."

Philip cried out, writhed in unbelievable pain. "Ahhhhrrrr. No!"

Orderly Whaley used both hands. His mouth tightened as he exerted pressure. His eyes betrayed his pleasure. Philip's shrieks were penetrating, shrill, horrifying.

The doctor said, "Now I am going to squeeze this."

When she squeezed, she hit raw nerves. Pus, blood, and ooze spurted out. One boil being lanced, and Philip's will gave out altogether.

Philip screamed, "Alan Tomlinson."

Whaley took over. He was now in charge. He edged the doctor aside. "What was that again, Mr. Croft?"

Philip's voice could barely be heard. Tears coursed down his face. "Alan Tomlinson Archives. I believe he is a homosexual."

Whaley persisted, "Believe?"

Philip reaffirmed, louder, "He *is* a homosexual."

Whaley turned back to the doctor. "Continue, please, madam."

The doctor, returning to Philip's buttock, said, "All right now. We're going to try to open this up and see if we can drain sections of this honeycomb."

Philip anticipated them. "Troy McCall. That's all I know. I swear. By almighty God, I swear I know no others."

The doctor said in a flat, even voice, "Orderly, swab this

with alcohol and let's see if we can clean and dress this. It's going to leave a big scar on his bottom. I'm going to have to take a culture and a biopsy. The carbuncle was made up of tunnels and passages, a labyrinth of deception, a labyrinth of infection, a maze of corruption, infection, and contagion. Ugly mess, this."

Whaley agreed, "Thank you, Doctor. We may have opened up new channels of contagion, new mazes of deception. Yes indeed."

Whaley laughed, cackled like the stage villain who had just compromised the heroine.

Philip could hear much snapping of rubber, the banging of metal surgical instruments being tossed in pans. And then abruptly, thankfully, he lost consciousness.

Sir Charles left the room where he had waited. He was exhausted, dispirited. When he got outside, it was dark, very chilly. His driver opened the limousine door. As he walked to the car, he shivered, drew his coat and collar around him. He turned and glanced up at the shuttered windows. *Was any of this worth it?*

6

They said they were through with him. They had apparently gotten as much as they thought they could literally squeeze out of him. Philip was an entirely changed man. His private, comfortable world had been shattered. His buttocks bared to them, his intimate life penetrated, violated, gone.

He knew he'd have to build a life for himself, something different from the one before. Life for him would never be the same. One thing he knew was that he wasn't going to deny his sexuality anymore, not when push came to shove.

Had he really been so closeted after all? He had friends in London who knew he was gay. And he certainly had numerous friends in Asia who knew his proclivities. Now that he had been outed, couldn't he be freer?

Philip stood by the window, looking out at the bleak winterscape, the naked black trees, the dark sky, those forbidding clouds. God, it would be good to be in some warm Asian country again.

He was in a room in the back of the building. An old Land Rover was parked behind the building. It was better for him to stand, because his backside still throbbed and was very sore when he sat down. He'd have to get one of those rubber doughnuts to sit on. Tentatively, he touched his right buttock, feeling the heavy dressings.

Atherton came into the room with his worn brown briefcase, the leather rubbed soft and supple by the years of train rides in from his semi-detached in Reading. Philip knew him slightly from the headquarters building; he was a thin, mousy little chap with thick glasses, annoyingly officious. He dealt with office personnel matters.

You saw Atherton if you needed a typist or if your room was too warm, or because the tea caddie had come around too late. He was a nothing, but probably now in Philip's new world he was going to be an everything. They nodded to one another. Atherton looked at Philip as if he were the naughty boy caught wetting the bed.

After rummaging in the antique case, he turned to Philip, looking at him above his glasses. It was a disapproving, schoolmarmish, disdainful perusal of a miscreant. Atherton's voice was difficult to hear in the best of times. Now he seemed to be whispering. "You know, Mr. Croft, that you shan't expect any honors other than those you already have."

"Honors I already have *deservedly earned* you mean," Philip corrected.

"Yes, you received your M.B.E. and C.M.G."

"Yes, I did. Thank you for acknowledging it."

"You shan't expect anything further though. There shan't be any upgrading of those honors. It's not going to happen. Not now, not ever. Any chance you might have had for a knighthood or other distinctions when you left the service has been conclusively foreclosed. Your top secret clearance and your blue status under the official secrets acts—these have been revoked."

Philip wanted to make some retorts, but he deemed it wise not to rile this little mouse, because his future depended on this petty tyrant. Better to cater to him for now. Atherton only followed the orders of others anyway.

Atherton cleared his throat. "When you feel sufficiently well enough to resume duties with the service, you are to notify me a few days ahead of time. Please ring me. I shall be arranging for your placement. You will be assigned light office duties. Your future work with us will be of a more cler-ical nature. Of course, you will have no contact with field work, operations, files of a sensitive nature, information gathering."

"Shall I do the tea trolley then?"

"Mr. Croft, you may use as much levity as you wish, but I cannot alter what I have to impart to you. Your salary shall remain the same. If you should decide, we would hope, at some time in the not too distant future to sever your relationship with the Service, you shall be granted early retirement with the full normal pension to which you are entitled. All pension rights shall remain intact and have not been forfeited."

"Which I earned by my years of loyal service."

"Good day, Mr. Croft. I shall be expecting to hear from you in the future."

The mouse scurried from the room back to his London office chores. A dull man back to his dull life. Philip thought *You never can tell; the mouse might be gayer than I am. God knows I'm a pretty inactive gay. All that is going to have to change now.*

Soon Philip was led to the Land Rover parked in back of the building. A minder drove him back into London, where they had picked him up in the dead of night, how many days ago Philip could not remember. When they got to London, it was evening. He was deposited outside the Sagnes Close archway on Albion Street without any words being exchanged.

Exhausted, depressed, and pain-wracked, Philip headed through the archway. In his pocket, he fingered the three pill bottles, one with a strong antibiotic, one with pain killers, and the other filled with a strong sedative. Perhaps they had given him such a large supply of sedatives in the hope he'd use it all at once to tidy up another of their embarrassing security lapses.

7

Sagnes Close was off Albion Street in the Bayswater section north of Hyde Park. It was a cul-de-sac mews that had once served as the stables and servants' quarters for the grand town houses on Albion Square. Local legend held that Sagnes was a corruption of St. Agnes. At the archway entrance to the close on Albion Street stood a newsagent's store to the left and a wine merchant's establishment to the right.

A series of small attached houses ran down both sides of the rough cobbled street and along the dead end of the close. The houses, two or three stories high, were painted in different muted colors. There were ten of the small houses on each side of the street, with three at the dead end. The whole compound bore the look of a set on a Hollywood back lot that had been built to resemble a street in a British village—or a Disneyland creation. Cars were able to enter and leave the close, and some were parked for a time, though none were allowed to remain parked there overnight in the street dividing the two rows of houses.

In those years, the close was not greatly in demand. It still had its bohemian cachet, but the real estate boom had not yet begun. The houses were small, modest places; after all, these had once been stables and servants' quarters. Around the corner the gravitas was still lodged in those beautiful old Georgian glories on Albion Square.

After he had been dropped off, a beaten-down, dazed Philip stood outside the archway leading into Sagnes Close. He walked, almost staggered, through the passageway into the close, along the narrow sidewalk to his house at Number Thirty-One. He turned the latchkey, entered, and pushed the door shut behind him. He leaned against the back of the door and sobbed. Tears rolled down his face, but he soon straightened his body and knew he had to get on with it. Whatever *it* was going to be.

Philip's house was eighteen feet wide. One entered the ground floor through his bright green outer door on the right into a narrow hall, barely wide enough for two people standing abreast. At the end of the hall was a small chest, which Philip used as a bar. Behind the chest was a door opening into a tiny half bath. Stairways from the hall ran down to the basement and up to the second floor.

To the left, off the hall, was the lounge, a very homey and cluttered room with well-worn furniture, walls covered with oil paintings and gilt-framed mirrors, and a big desk shoved in a corner, atop which sat an ancient typewriter and piles of papers and correspondence. On the street wall, two worn club chairs faced a sagging sofa that, though homily comfortable, had seen better days. Ensconced between the chairs and sofa was a large cocktail table laden on top and on a packed shelf underneath with stacks of big picture books, histories, photo albums, and magazines. The table seemed to sag under the weight of all the stuff piled on it. Small spaces on the tabletop had been left for cups of tea and cocktails. The Oriental rug that covered most of the floor was of good quality, but it was threadbare and scuffed.

On the further wall opposite the hallway was a marble-mantled fireplace. Much of the back wall was taken up with big picture windows looking out on a mass of evergreens. Occasionally, some very plump pigeons would appear on the hedges. Behind the shrubbery, a brick wall and then lawn, and at some distance, a tall apartment building of recent vintage.

In the basement were a small breakfast nook with a wooden booth and an antiquated kitchen. In the old days, there had been a coal chute from the street and a coal bin where the dingy nook now stood.

On the second floor were two small bedrooms and a full bathroom with an ancient tub sitting on claw feet. On the top floor was a low-ceilinged attic. It had a small skylight so that it could serve as an artist's studio, if need be.

Philip turned on the hall light. His mail was on the table; it had been picked up from the floor where it fell when the postman dropped it through the brass mail slot.

They've been in here. Probably Whaley and Trimmer, when they weren't harassing me. Searched the house. What have they found? Photographs? The letters? What is left of my private life?

Philip started looking around. The house had been carefully searched. Some things were not where they had been. The lounge had so much clutter, so many books, magazines, and papers, that it would have been difficult to put them back where they had been, but it was possible for Philip to tell what was out of place. He did notice that two framed photographs on the fireplace mantle had been reversed. His mother's photograph was now at the end and Rupert's picture was to the right. Rupert had been his university chum, a man with whom he had had a platonic love affair. The good-looking blond Rupert stood in his lederhosen, beaming out from the picture, the snow-covered Alps in the background.

Philip went through the whole house looking for signs of the search. After all, he had often done the same thing himself—searched houses and apartments. He found that the whole house had been scoured, not too neatly—ransacked, really. Looking carefully, he discovered spots where the boffins, or whoever, had lifted floorboards, drilled holes in moldings. The house had always been untidy; now it was a real mess.

He found his letters had been rearranged and probably read, and he sensed his large collection of photographs had been gone through. Everything had been checked, but as far as he could see, was still there. Now he knew what it felt like to have one's personal things touched, pawed over by strangers. The tables had been turned on him. He who had been the nosy, thorough investigator, and who had had no second thoughts about turning over houses, had to now face this desecration himself. Strangers knew more about him than they had a right to know. The worm had turned.

This added another layer of despair, finding his own home violated after the dehumanizing experience of having his body violated in the Terminal. The humiliation of it all, being demeaned and degraded, being made to feel less than human. He felt like crawling into a corner of the attic and hiding like a frightened child looking for safety in his own home.

He had been told it was over, had ended. They meant the interrogation, the inquisition, but they also meant his career. He had been notified that he would be someone of no worth in the service, persona non grata. But they said he would not be bothered again, ever. Atherton had made it clear that if he stayed in the Service he would be paid as usual, still get his pension.

He should shut himself up in a closet for safety, but hadn't he in effect just crawled out of one closet? What—give up one closet for another? They might be perfectly happy to be rid of him completely, see him commit suicide, get out of their hair.

He had never had illusions about the people in the Service; cruelty was a given, built into its culture, especially when it was being attacked from without. Heads would roll at appropriate times. Politicians were quick to blame the intelligence services.

"It was a failure of intelligence," they would say after the country lost some skirmish in the Cold War. "Our intelligence requires beefing up." They needed new blood, so old blood was offered as penance.

Philip was that month's offering to the gods of eternal security, vigilance, and internal housekeeping. When he gingerly touched his buttock, he could feel the oozing out of the corruption they had lodged within his body.

8

In the weeks following his fall from grace, Philip did a great deal of thinking. He visited his own doctor several times. His wound was examined, dressings were changed, and the skin gradually healed over the incisions. He would always have a scar on his buttocks, but in time that might become a badge of honor. The doctor had said, "Whoever this doctor is you went to in Scotland, he was closer to being a butcher than a surgeon. He should really be reported."

Philip had said nothing, just that it had been an emergency treatment while he was in Scotland. His doctor was understanding. "Oh, well, the Scots. Sorry you're one of them, but they've always been one tiny step away from barbarism and savagery. A bunch of tribes, clans, still less than civilized."

Weeks later on a Friday when Philip felt he was sufficiently able to go back on active service, he telephoned Atherton, who told him to report to his office on the following Tuesday.

That Tuesday morning, Philip arose early, took a little more care with his dress, and started out for the office at eight-fifteen. He shut and locked the door and started toward the mouth of the close.

Philip left Sagnes Close and walked down Albion Street to Bayswater Road. He crossed over into the park and onto one of the walkways that headed south. His walk was brisk. Large swaths of flat lawn stretched out in all directions. People were out walking their dogs; others were marching purposefully for serious exercise. Like him, a considerable number were cutting through the park on their way to work. It felt good to be going to work, even if it was only to shuffle papers.

When he reached Hyde Park Corner, he went down steps through a series of subways and came up in the road called

Constitution Hill. He followed this until he reached the circle with the Queen Victoria Memorial in front of the Buckingham Palace gates. People had already begun assembling for the daily Changing of the Guard. This route was a well-traveled one for Philip. Many times when posted back to London, he had strolled to work over the same paths and walkways on pleasant days or even on drizzly days. His mind was working over the day that lay ahead.

He headed through St. James Park and then to a building on King Charles Street, which housed his section of MI6 operations. He entered the front door and headed for Atherton's office on the ground floor. Atherton looked up from his work, hardly acknowledging Philip's presence. "Croft, we'll be assigning you to the library."

Philip's spirits rose. *It isn't going to be so bad after all. They've relented. They aren't going to send me off to Coventry.* The library on the sixth floor was where all of the sensitive material was kept. Almost all of the agents and staff went in and out of there during the course of the day.

Atherton saw Philip's elated expression and puzzled over it, then came to a realization. "Perhaps I've misled you. I mean our general reference library on this floor."

Philip's spirits plummeted. This was the dogsbody library where almost everyone was free to go. It was just an ordinary reference library with the standard texts. It had all sorts of dictionaries, encyclopedias, travel books, even fiction, including a selection of silly romance novels for the secretarial staff. Philip said nothing. He knew that he mustn't rile this officious ass.

He began work in the library that morning under the supervision of Miss Hornsby, a tall, imposing woman in her fifties with short hair. She and Philip had always gotten along well, so he knew she'd be easy to work with. She had been with the Service for too many years to question why Philip was assigned there. She thought he had been ill (perhaps one of those nervous breakdowns), and that he was doing this work during his convalescence.

In the days following his reintroduction into the headquarters building, things went along satisfactorily enough.
No one questioned him; everyone was quite supportive, but
Philip knew from the Service's practices that very few would
be made aware of the true situation. Because of compart-
mentalization and a culture of secrecy, the Service's right
hand never knew what the left hand was doing. Philip was
being treated like someone who was getting over an illness
and needed light work during the healing process.

Philip realized he could survive for a time in this menial
job, but he knew he had to plan for the long haul, a life apart
from government service. His days as a spy were finished.
This saddened him greatly, but life had to go on. There had
been a time many years ago when he hadn't been an intelligence operative; the time had come again. *Look at it as an
opportunity for a new life, not as the end of your life, you
ninny.*

9

One of Philip's closest friends was Frederick Binkstone, known by his intimates as Binky. He had been a friend since Philip's days at Cambridge. They had gotten to know each other rather well. Philip possessed one quality that Binky appreciated; he was a good listener and therefore a good audience for Binky's weak jokes.

At university, Binky had made no bones about the fact that he preferred the male gender. Philip, of course, was deeply closeted. He and Philip had never had it on, and that was perhaps why they had remained good friends. In those early years, Binky had never become aware of Philip's preferences, and indeed Philip himself wasn't completely aware of what was going on in his mind and body. He dated the occasional girl, and it seemed to Binky that Philip was an ordinary heterosexual.

Binky had a large hawk-like beak, bulging eyes, an aristocratic overbite, and a weak chin. He could never have been considered good-looking or even passably average in looks. His was a caricature of a face, a visage that required him to try to be somewhat of a comic. He had learned to compensate for his lack of clothed visual sex appeal, but from the tennis changing room, Philip knew the larger than average size of Binky's sexual member could easily have been entered in the record books.

Binky's family had financial resources, land holdings, and a provenance with connections to the Royal Family. After university, Binky had wangled a job as an equerry to the royals. The position required very little of him other than the unonerous task of escorting visiting deposed or ensconced royals from insignificant countries.

He was allowed, or the royals were happy to grant him, winter-long leaves of absence. On these extended leaves, he traveled the world in search of sex partners. His tastes in men ran the gamut; he was only marginally a rice queen. He'd go wherever the pickings were best. He quite salivated over good-looking Americans. His reasoning: "They're almost universally cut, my dear boy."

He and Philip had continued their friendship over the years. Because he served the Royal Family, Binky had known that Philip was in MI6, but each perpetuated the myth that Philip worked for the foreign office. Philip was out of the country for very long periods so they saw each other infrequently in England.

Years after Cambridge Binky happened to be in a sedate gay bar in Hong Kong where rice queens were wont to meet young Asian men who favored older foreigners. He was astounded to meet Philip there. He approached him and said, "Aha, what have we here, Watson? Do I spy Philip Croft, my fellow Cambridge drudge, slumming here in a queer bar. Now please don't tell me you are here in your official role as one of Her Majesty's far-flung civil servants. Apparently you are ready to drop the beads at long last, eh?"

Philip laughed and told him in Asia he occasionally took his leave of the closet. It was then and at later occasions that Philip and Binky started exchanging intelligence about the sexual activities in the Far East. Binky was conversant with London and European gay life, but Philip was not overly interested. Binky's knowledge of and experiences in the Far East gay life were far more extensive than Philip's because of Philip's need for discretion. Binky flaunted his gayness and profited from his flair and flamboyance whereas Philip had to rely on luck.

In the first weeks in Hong Kong that followed their meeting and Binky's discovery, he introduced Philip to some rice queens of his acquaintance; they were invited to house parties where young Asians and Caucasians mingled, and Philip began meeting the large network of fellow ricers that he would become friends with in the years to come. Philip's network of gay friends widened considerably. He became acquainted with the Mad Hatter and the March Hare, features of the Asian rice scene.

Binky called those Westerners who were looking for very young Asian partners the seekers, and the name stuck. As the years went on, the term became more generic, since it included non-gay pedophiles, as well as the more traditional gay rice queens.

The weekend after Philip had returned to his innocuous work as a librarian in the MI6 headquarters, he phoned Binky. They met on a Tuesday night in Binky's club, the Nelsonian, one of the numerous private men's clubs that dotted London's cityscape and which perpetuated the country's undeniable class delineations.

The two old friends had drinks in the bar, a dreadful dinner in the dining room, and coffee and cognac in the lounge. Philip told Binky what had happened, the details of his outing, his interrogation and torture. He wasn't giving away any state secrets; it was necessary for him to unburden himself to someone, and, at any rate, Binky had a high-level security clearance because of his equerry status.

Binky was outraged. "Philip, they're nothing but outright bastards. After all the years of outstanding, really heroic service, that you gave them. The swine. Those shites will regret treating you in such a fashion. And I am distressed that Sir Charles was a party to it."

Philip appreciated Binky's sympathies and his indignation, but he also wanted his advice. "What am I to do now? I'm eligible for retirement and pension in the fall. Should I retire then, or do you think I should soldier on for a few more years?"

"No, get out this fall, while the getting is good. Spend your retirement in long trips to your beloved Orient. It's time you lived an open, free life. You've been a meek church mouse for too long. Do what I do. Do whatever you damn well please. Forget propriety and devotion to duty. Have your fling. They've accused you of being a queer. Prove it to them now. Thumb your nose at them. Stick it to them, by God. The pricks."

Philip had an extra cognac and started feeling better about himself. Good old Binky.

But Binky couldn't quit when he was ahead. He gloated,

"Don't say I didn't warn you years ago. The Service canni-
balizes its agents eventually, and being gay, you always ran
the risk of discovery and being eaten alive. The Service
knows how to eat its own. In this case, they went for your
rear end first, the way a hyena would."

Philip twisted in his chair. His buttock gave him a quick
twinge of pain. He drank a quick gulp of cognac and the pain
eased. Binky started reminiscing about some trick in
Amsterdam, so Philip sat back and listened without being
reminded of his own less than finest hours at the Terminal.

Philip's nights and weekends were spent reestablishing
contacts with friends and building a life that had nothing to
do with spying, undercover operations, and intelligence
gathering. One night a week, Philip went to his own club.
Weekends, he drove out to the country houses of either
Anthony St. Wills or Binky.

There were meetings and get-togethers of the Long Yang
Club where he could make contacts with young Asians. The
club held various events: picnics, outings, and a bi-monthly
club night at one of Soho's nightclubs. It was held in the
middle of the week when club business was slow. The do's
were usually in dive bars or basement clubs. They were
sedate all-male affairs. Everyone was quite genteel with no
serious drinking; only a few couples danced together.

While the Caucasian men who favored Asians were called
rice queens, Asians who liked Caucasians were labeled
potato queens. All of these terms were generally shunned by
those with such proclivities, because they were felt to be
derogatory and degrading. People outside the circle used the
terms in dismissive, derisive, bitchy tones. Insiders only
used the terms in jest.

Philip no longer had to be discreet. One night, he brought
home for sex a young man recently arrived from Canton.
Another time, he had met a Malaysian lad who was eager to
go home with him. These were great liberating events for
Philip. Perhaps the Service had done him a favor by sidelin-
ing him.

10

Philip had always been an inveterate traveler. He had been almost everywhere in his professional capacity as one of His or Her Majesty's secret agents. Apart from his overseas assignments and postings, he felt the need and desire to travel in his blood. After a week or two back in London from a trip, infected by wanderlust, he'd be turning over a future trip in his mind even though he loved London.

He had taken many auto trips throughout England and had often driven up to his own home turf in Scotland. He'd taken car ferries to Ireland and motored around most of the island. He liked to travel to the Continent in his car if possible; he often went, bringing back cases of French wine in the car boot. He didn't like the idea of taking cruises on ocean liners. They were too confining; one was too much at the whim of amateur minders.

With his newfound liberation, he began planning a longer winter Asian trip. Wherever he went, everyone in his gay circle seemed to be talking about the Philippines. Sex with young men there was plentiful, enjoyable, and cheap. The Philippine economy was not thriving, and it seemed as if the Marcos regime was promoting sex travel to the islands. He decided to include the Philippines on his itinerary and agreed to meet Binky on his Asian trip.

Philip thought Binky had a rather crude slant on things and tended to be too indiscreet at times. Binky had said, "We're the predators looking for our prey. You and the other rice queens go after those cute, silken, hairless bodies. We all go where the pickings are good. Someone hears there is a good crop in the Philippines. So we gradually all show up there to sample the merchandise. Or someone says he had a great time in Sri Lanka. Then on to Sri Lanka. We descend like lemmings en masse on the new capital of easy, cheap, and plentiful sex."

Philip did not say such things. Surrogates such as Binky spoke for him, and he was allowed to keep his cloak of respectability and conventionality. He smiled when *they* said it though. Philip was more the incurable romantic. Sex to him had to have a romantic quality to it or at least the trappings of romance. It shouldn't be crass or commercial.

He did not like the idea of paying hustlers. Of course, if one were in a Third World Asian country where a young man was struggling to eke out a living, it didn't hurt to help the person out with a small contribution.

Binky had said, "Oh, the way we salve our consciences. I calls 'em as I sees 'em, and I pay them without a qualm. I'm not in love with them, and God knows, with this visage of mine, they are certainly not in love with me."

Philip's friend Anthony St. Wills spent six months a year in an apartment in Thailand where he had a stable of young Thais available. He wouldn't consider traveling to any other Asian country.

Philip was not anxious to compete with Anthony in sexual matters. Anthony and Binky differed in the matter of sexual conquests. If Binky saw that one of his friends was serious about a young man, he would never attempt to "make" that person. Anthony was the opposite; what was yours was also his. What was yours was his by dint of his deeply competitive nature. As soon as someone showed interest in a number, then Anthony was ready to pounce. Several times, Philip's friends had had to warn Anthony off from their companions.

Philip had to consider where he would go on his Asian trip. He would visit Anthony in Bangkok. He wanted to make other stops, but decided he had to suss out the Philippines. He had decided on a fairly long stay of a few months there to get to know the territory.

For three years, Philip had been stationed in Japan where he had built up friendships with those men who preferred Asian boyfriends. Sex among the old and young in Japan had practically dried up years ago. After the war, many young men venerated older men, actually liked older Caucasian gentlemen. Then the economy took off. Everything became fearfully expensive; the youth culture hit Japan like a cyclone, and the number of younger men desiring older men was severely decimated. He would probably leave Japan for a later trip.

He loved Malaysia, Hong Kong, Sri Lanka, Singapore, and Thailand. When he was making plans for his future trip, it was a matter of which places to leave out, which to include. He had gay friends in many countries; some were as discreet as he had been. Most were ex-pats who had given up England years ago.

Philip decided he wanted to earn his salary as long as he could. He thought of taking a leave of absence for a long six-month Asian trip, but he determined it might not be a good idea. He was going to be more active and open sexually, not a wild man, but still pursuing more sex than he had been getting in the past. If he took a leave of absence, he would still be an employee of the Service and could be severely disciplined for some infraction. He'd still be living by the Service's rules. No, not a good thing at all. He had been dramatically punished once. The next time might result in a trumped-up criminal charge. Better to cut the cord completely and sow one's oats as a retiree.

He'd put in for retirement in October and spend November through May in Asia. The initial trip would be on his own, and he would hook up with friends at spots along the way. He had money in the bank, had inherited money from old aunts and uncles who had died off, and had built up other assets over the years.

When October came, his friends in the Service, and he had made many, held a big retirement dinner for him in the Ivy restaurant. His friends were sincerely sorry to see him leave. At the bar, out of Philip's presence, complimentary adjectives about him were flying: *avuncular, even-tempered, kind, humorous, soft-hearted, unassuming, unselfish, courageous, bright, loyal,* and on and on.

Miss Hornsby, the librarian, said he looked and acted like Alec Guinness when the actor was playing one of his shy, unassuming roles. The assumption was that Philip could be sly and playful as well. The fact that he had been compared to the actor who could submerge himself in a part made a few think that perhaps Philip, too, had been playing a role, quite skillfully, quite adeptly, and that the man was greater than the sum of his parts.

Sir Charles gave a wonderful, rousing, going-out speech that recounted many of Philip's triumphs in the Service. Most had become public knowledge by then. He told of Philip's brave work in maintaining tunnels under the Berlin Wall, tunnels which compromised the Russians and East Germans. He highlighted Philip's actions sabotaging German interests in neutral countries like Switzerland during the Second World War, his liaison work with the OSS and the CIA, his work in post-war Japan.

He said with great emotion and earnestness, "I am deeply, personally sorry that this honest, magnanimous, courageous man is leaving us. We shall not see his like again, and the Service and we shall be all the poorer for his going. I am proud to have known him, and I hope that I'll be able to retain his trust and friendship in the future. I greatly value this man who has helped define our mission in the world. Philip, you have our thanks, our gratitude, and our good will. Godspeed to you."

Sir Charles's eyes were clouded with tears. Many knew these two went back a long way, to boarding school days.

Philip's reactions to Sir Charles's kind words were tinged with skepticism. Either the man was a cynic, a hypocrite, or else he was trying to make amends of a sort.

Philip was driven back to Sagnes Close in a ministerial limousine. He had his retirement gifts, a considerable buzz from the congratulatory drinks, and a strange new feeling of liberation. He was now truly free to live his life the way he chose.

11

Philip was on his way to Asia for his first holiday since his retirement. His first stop was Bangkok, where he would visit his friend, Anthony St. Wills. As he was riding in from the airport, Philip found the Thai capital as he had in the past: smoky, smoggy, traffic-clogged, overcrowded, unbearably noisy, and intimidating.

He was looking forward to again seeing the glorious temples, the vibrant river life, but he wasn't apt to dip his toes in the sexual waters. When Philip traveled, he did a great deal of sightseeing. His trips included sexual encounters, but his weren't sex trips in his eyes. Binky took sex trips with a small bit of sightseeing thrown in. Binky went deliberately looking for sex; Philip waited for it to fall into his lap by happenstance.

To him, the modern Bangkok sex scene was too commercial, too blatantly crass. Years ago, he'd been in the district known as Patpong where there were scores of gay bars. In such bars, the young men wore numbers. One would approach the host or hostess and say, "I like Number Eighteen." Or conversely, Number Eighteen would give you the eye, strike up a conversation, and suggest an assignation.

Number Eighteen would join you for a drink, you would decide on the nasties together, you'd make a financial arrangement with the host, and you and Eighteen would go to your hotel or a convenience hotel and have sex. Eighteen was paid for his services, the host got his take, and to Philip you were left with disappointment bordering on self-loathing. To Philip, the experience was too much like buying a toaster.

Ever the romantic, Philip found it far too commercial and too degrading. Many Thai boys had been so used to being paid for their services, were so mechanical as sex partners,

that he found them unappealing. They were bored, and they
bored him. It was different helping a poor young man out
with a little cash for necessities, but going out with a whore
who did it for a living was too demeaning for the purchaser.

The cab trip to Anthony's apartment was a nightmare and
took hours. Anthony lived in a pleasant apartment. He jug-
gled three Thai boyfriends who were perfectly willing to
share him because they also had other fish to fry.

Anthony met him in his foyer. He was tall, imposing, aristocratic, good-looking, and broad-shouldered with thick
white wiry hair. He was a congenial man who genuinely liked
Philip, and a man Philip found to be a gracious host.

Anthony didn't care much for Binky, because he thought
he held too much sway over Philip and tended to be vulgar
and impolitic.

For his six-month winter break from Britain, Anthony
stayed only in Bangkok where the sex was easy and where
he had a circle of other Brits and foreigners to help him while
away the time.

He had invited Philip to spend a few months with him, but
Philip had said a week would suffice. He had a spare bedroom. Philip acknowledged that the apartment was spacious, that Anthony had a wonderful cook and a handsome
houseboy, but Bangkok was not his idea of paradise.
Perhaps the Thais had been spoiled since those early years
when he had had that wonderful experience with the Thai
boy in Chiang Mai.

Anthony had never really done a day's work in his life. It
seemed as if some rich old grandparent, aunt, or dotty uncle
was always dropping dead and leaving him another pile of
pounds. He had several life estates and trusts. His so-called
cottage in the countryside outside of London was imposing
and more of a demi-mansion.

Philip stayed with Anthony for a week enjoying the good
food, the wines, and the company of Anthony's circle of Thai
boyfriends. One of the short-time Bangkok visitors while
Philip was there was the man they called the March Hare, a

Brit in his fifties, an academic, who had an insatiable desire for sex, and who was an inveterate rice queen. He seemed to always be on the move, and was a frequent companion of the Mad Hatter in Hong Kong. People years ago had christened him the March Hare because of his association with the Mad Hatter. The two could often be seen together straight out of Lewis Carroll flitting through the Asian sex scenes. Both were hyper individuals, frenetic and harried.

When Philip left Thailand, he was quite satisfied with his visit, even though he hadn't found a suitable sex partner. He flew to Colombo, the capital of Sri Lanka. Philip had formed an affinity for the island when he was posted in the Orient years ago. The island, a pearl drop off the subcontinent of India, could be a delightful place, tropical, off the beaten track, and it was known as a sexual port of call for some rice queens. Many of the local men were dusky (not, by any means his favorite skin tone), but Philip had had some very satisfying sexual encounters with some quite handsome men.

A friend of Philip's, Colonel Niles Eckers, lived near Kandy, the former island capital where the Famous Temple of the Tooth was located with one of Buddha's teeth enshrined there.

On arrival in Sri Lanka, Philip took a bus to the city of Kandy. It was a fascinating trip through the Sri Lankan countryside where Philip saw elephants at work in the timber industry. Niles, gap-toothed, frizzy-haired, and pop-eyed, met him and drove him to his small villa. Niles was another of those Brits who spent half the year in a country where he could get available native sex.

For ten days, he and Niles toured the island, bathed in the Indian Ocean, stayed at a Mount Lavinia lodge, visited the elephant orphanage, and dined on coconut curry dishes. Philip had two brief but pleasant flings with a laughing hotel room boy of eighteen who said Philip was the spitting image of Cary Grant. The five-foot nine Philip was thrilled.

Philip's next stop was Hong Kong where he could again save on hotel rent. He stayed with the Mad Hatter, an ex-pat Brit who was a professor of linguistics at a Hong Kong

university. The man had wild gray hair that was ungovern-
able. Hair grew in great bunches from his ears, nose, and in
his clumpy eyebrows. The man was frenetic and hectic, and
Philip swore he was as mad as the sobriquet implied. He
never stayed still. A perfect match for the March Hare.

On his university recesses, the Hatter traveled constantly
all over Asia looking for teenage boys. Out of doors and
sometimes indoors as well he always wore a pork pie hat,
hence the hatter part of his name. Usually, he sported a
khaki campaign vest that had eight pockets. All of the pockets were stuffed with notebooks, pens, pencils, penlights,
airline tickets, gum and lollipops in all flavors, which he dis-
pensed to his boys. "Better candies and gum than those horrible fags," was his constant refrain. Americans blanched
until they realized he meant cigarettes.

He gave Philip the run of his cluttered apartment drowning in books and lollipop cartons. The day after Philip
arrived, he had the apartment to himself. The Hatter had
gone off to Bali. He and the March Hare were due to see
Philip later in Manila. Philip laughed to himself. All of his
friends were in constant Asian orbits, continually looking for
that sexual paradise. Seeing these seekers flitting through
Asia and assembling in one spot to cruise reminded Philip of
the confluence of the planets and moons.

In Hong Kong, Philip had time to take a breather and
think about his new life. That first winter of his retirement,
he had left a cold dreary British winter behind for the
warmer weather of Southeast Asia. The people in Asia he
thought were warmer too, more receptive, easier to bed,
more pliant, and handsomer than most Caucasians.

The Asians he liked could almost be called beautiful. Not
feminine, but with features more delicate, as if their bodies
were in equilibrium, in equal and balanced contact with their
masculine and feminine natures. To him, they had a happy
conjoining of male and female traits. Most young male Brits
it seemed to him were always trying to assert their manliness,
their masculinity. When they went overboard, they became

pub hooligans, football rowdies, and gay bashers.

Philip hated the dark, damp, chilling days of London winters. He became depressed and dour when he had to endure a British winter. London was his beloved city, but even in good weather, he often felt the need to get away from it for a change of scene.

Binky had agreed to meet with him in Hong Kong a few days after Philip's arrival. Binky was coming in from Taiwan where he was having a fling with a hunky Olympic water polo player. Binky called Philip at the Hatter's apartment, and the two met in a Mongolian barbecue restaurant on Hong Kong Island.

After dinner, they decided to go to the Dateline Club where young Eastern gays met older Western gays. Philip was good at meeting people; he was a quiet, unassuming, pleasant man, not loud or boisterous. He and Binky made a good combination.

They were soon chatting up a couple of attractive young Chinese men who had impeccable manners and who spoke English with a public school precision. Binky concentrated on one, a handsome twenty-year-old Chinese lad whose father owned a junk anchored in Aberdeen Harbor where a number of junks formed a floating village.

Soon the two lads agreed to go to the Mad Hatter's for drinks. One thing led to another, and Philip was having it on with one of the lads in the Hatter's bedroom, while Binky was going at it on the couch in the study.

The next morning, Binky and Philip had coffee in the Hatter's kitchen, their two guests having left in the early hours. After discussing their pleasant interludes, they talked about the future weeks.

Binky asked, "What about the love of your life, Tom, your Raffles partner?"

"This trip I shan't be able to connect with Tom. He is working in South Africa, Capetown actually, and I'm afraid that's a little too far off the track for this go-round."

"Pity. You two are quite compatible."

"Tom never wanted a long-term relationship. He's another one like you who prefers to play the field."

Later that day, Philip and Binky were sitting around with a group of their fellow seekers in the Waltzing Matilda, a mixed pub in Kowloon, talking about the Philippines. Philip had been in the Philippines for very short stays before. He had never really gotten to know the people or the country. This time, because he had heard so many favorable reports, he was going to stay for a few months. He arranged to meet up with Binky and others in Manila in the coming weeks. Binky said he had other fish to fry before his Philippines interlude.

12

When Philip stepped out of the airport terminal doors in Manila, it was a mad house, and the air was hellishly hot. A score of taxi drivers and cab touts descended upon him. He guarded his suitcase and his carry-on as the horde tried to wrest it from him. He had buried his wallet and passport inside a secure pocket in the lining of his coat. The yelling and screaming were fierce, each of the cabbies imploring him to take his taxi.

Out of desperation, Philip chose the biggest man in the bunch who insisted on carrying Philip's luggage. The behemoth muscled the others out of the way as he escorted Philip to his cab. The others drifted away with unkind remarks about his parenthood.

The small cab headed into the city. Traffic in the city was wild and rambunctious. Dilapidated rickety old buses spewed fumes. Trucks cut in and out of traffic. Every vehicle was spitting noxious exhaust fumes.

The most exotic vehicles, signatory of the country, were the garishly colored jeepneys, elongated jeep-based vehicles that carried ten or twelve in their covered rear sections. Two rows of benches faced each other in the back. The jeepneys were decorated with vivid designs, and each had a sign proclaiming its route. These jeepneys were the heart of the Philippines transportation system.

Passengers mounted a few steps into the rear seats. They were open at the sides to let in some of the fetid air. If overcrowded, two passengers would ride in the front with the driver. Several companies in the country had factories where these vehicles were made. A visit to a jeepney factory was on the list of tourist attractions.

Philip had booked a flat in the San Pedro Apartment Hotel where flats were let for long-term rentals. It was a place recommended by his friends, where one might, without problems, bring one's pick-ups or live with long-term partners. It was across from the large Rizal Park and a short distance from the streets where the sex joints were located.

When the cab pulled up to the hotel, he noticed three young men, late teens, lingering outside. They gave him broad smiles and said hello. In the small lobby, two teenagers sat on a small sofa. After he had registered, he was on his way up the stairs to his second-floor apartment when he heard the sound of childish voices. A stream of laughing, very young boys, locals, seven in number, who looked to be about ages five to eight were rushing down the stairs.

They were followed by a six-foot tall beaming Caucasian in his late thirties. He was a handsome man with movie star looks, a man many women would be attracted to. The man was in seventh heaven judging by his huge smile. As he passed Philip, he gave him a loud "G'day" and Philip knew him to be Australian. Unbidden, he introduced himself as Larry and told Philip he was from Melbourne. Seeing these very young boys with this man made Philip uneasy; it disturbed him, but not as viscerally as it should have.

More irritating to him was the idea of these boisterous young kids having the run of the hotel, making noise, being in the same building with them disturbing his sleep and threatening his need for quiet time.

His apartment was spacious enough: a living room facing the park, an airy bedroom, and a small pullman kitchen where he could prepare meals if he was so inclined.

That afternoon, he took a walk over to United Nations Avenue where a high-rise Hilton Hotel dominated the area. On the corner of United Nations Avenue and Pilar Street was The Lifebuoy, an open air café where one could sit and watch the passing parade. Philip had been told it was a cruisy spot. He went in and took a table and ordered a Coke.

On the sidewalks passing by The Lifebuoy, there wasn't a great deal of intriguing male pedestrian traffic. Philip watched the young men who passed by. He didn't see anyone who looked vaguely attractive to him. They seemed so dark, and he had to admit that some were positively homely. He knew from his experience in other Asian countries that it took time to get used to the type in each country. Tanned and brown was fine, but dusky was less inviting to him. And good looks counted for a great deal, trumping skin color.

Two Brits near him acted like two clowns trying to top each. It didn't take long for them to establish the fact that they were after males. They were from Manchester, and liked threesomes with hunky young men eighteen up to about thirty. The tall one with the red hair was nicknamed Sandy, while his short pot-bellied companion was named Clifton.

Sandy and Clifton told him they were going to a folk club on Pilar called El Sutro that night where young men of the type they liked hung out. They asked Philip to join them there later, but he demurred, saying he had just arrived in town and needed to wander around and get the geography of the area firmly in his mind.

They also mentioned they planned a long weekend trip to Pagsanjan Falls where hundreds of hunky, well-muscled boatmen were available. Philip realized he had a lot to see and do, because he also planned to visit some of the other islands in the archipelago. He was the inveterate sightseer as well as being a man in search of sex partners. His sex drive was never as all-consuming as Binky's. He reminded himself that Binky was due to arrive in a few days.

The two from Manchester also told him about the male strip clubs that were springing up all over Manila. Philip wondered how much President Ferdinand Marcos knew of this sex business in his country. Perhaps he even encouraged it; the gays brought a great deal of money to the islands. The Japanese who had been conquerors of the islands in World War II came in by the planeloads, either on straight or gay sex junkets.

That evening, Philip was doing his reconnoitering alone. He started at the Lifebuoy, where he had spent the afternoon with his two fellow Brits. He had studied his gay guidebook and the notes gathered from friends. The minute he turned the corner and started down Pilar Street, he was surrounded by female whores from the various clip joints. It was a blatant sex area where the women were aggressive and obnoxious.

They tried to lure him, herd him into the sleazy girlie joints while they were patting him down, grabbing his arms, feeling his rear end, rubbing his crotch. They were relentless and luckily Philip had hidden his wallet because while a whore was pawing all over him, a young boy bumped into him and tried to find his money.

It was decidedly distasteful to the fastidious Philip. Thank God after a few blocks, this gauntlet of tarts thinned out, and the street became much less threatening and more manageable. Prostitutes still stood in doorways, but they did not approach him. He had to be careful because begging children would jostle him, try to frisk him, and feel his pockets. The women working near the corner of United Nations must have been the most desperate of the lot. Pilar Street had a number of bars, cheap restaurants, sex stores, as well as ordinary businesses.

Burly, beefy and beery Australian males, American servicemen in civies, and various other Westerners were on the prowl. Some were drunk and boisterous.

Further down the street, he passed El Sutro, the gay bar where folk music was played, the bar recommended to him by Clifton and Sandy, but he decided he would try it another night, perhaps with Binky. Philip wasn't, by nature, a bar person. He never went out of his way to frequent bars. He was more into private homes and parties and assignations arranged through friends. Though Philip was no barfly, Binky was perfectly at home in bars and pubs. Philip also shunned any sexual encounters with other males in restrooms, and found the practice deplorable. No cottaging for him no matter what a brute like Whaley might imply.

He walked seven blocks down Pilar, then walked one long block until he came to Remedios, a main cross avenue with several popular restaurants. He walked up one block and then started down Mabini, a street that paralleled Pilar. He was heading back in the direction from which he had just come toward United Nations. Mabini had several well-known gay friendly apartment hotels and was nominally less over the top with wild joints than Pilar.

About three blocks down the street, he reached a lot that had some tiki huts and stands. At one corner of the lot was the Happy Talk, a bar with a group of tables next to the sidewalk with a small service shed where waiters got drinks. This place was on Philip's list. He sat down at a small table, ordered a San Miguel beer, and observed the action.

Several tables had older men sitting with young Filipino men. As he was sitting there, a small white-haired man with an entourage of kids stopped at a table. The man, like the Pied Piper, was trailed by four young kids who looked to be about ages five through nine. The white-haired patron stopped to talk to two of his fellow seekers seated at a table next to the street. Both men were in their late fifties or early sixties, and both were wearing baseball caps. Two of the boys stuck straws in the seated men's Coca Cola bottles and sipped drinks. The capped men were indulgent and laughed. All four kids were having a good time; the older men basked in the glow of being with the kids.

Again Philip was uneasy. These men were flaunting their extremely young conquests. They were not discreet. Probably only gays would latch on to what was going on. Why were the kids allowed out so late by their families? Where were their families? Were these pedophiles serving as surrogate fathers or uncles?

More of the young boys paraded by in a convoy of five escorted by a big six foot man of forty. This seemed to be a beauty contest of sorts. This place was where the brazen pedophiles showed off their child-conquests.

For all Philip knew, this was even a place where bartering of the kids went on. He looked around at the other tables. There were no young men of the type Philip liked. He decided in future he would avoid this place. On succeeding nights as he walked by, he noticed less and less activity with the young children and their hosts at the place.

By the time Philip reached United Nations, he was tired. He decided to return to the San Pedro and get some sleep. That night, the hotel was quiet. Perhaps the children were all asleep.

In later days, as Philip made the rounds in Manila, he heard the gay tourists of his set again making frequent mention of Pagsanjan, a village about three hours south of the capital. To some it was a paradise, to some the promised land. Everyone spoke highly of it. Most said that though they loved to visit this Eden for gays, most preferred not to live there for extended periods, but rather visit for weekends or short stays. Manila was livelier and offered more choices. One could get lost more easily in Manila; it was a city after all, and one didn't stand out quite as much as one did in a village.

Binky arrived and took up residence in the San Pedro in a flat next to Philip's. Philip quizzed him about Pagsanjan.

Binky gushed. "Ah, Pagsanjan. Heaven on earth. It is close to Pagsanjan Falls, which is a great tourist location. People travel there on day trips to take a ride up the rapids to the falls, and, of course, the wild and thrilling ride back down the rapids. Two or three visitors sit in the center of a long, narrow wooden boat while two muscular, hunky boatmen, one in the front, one in the rear, paddle the boat, haul it, carry it over a series of rocks until they get you to the foot of a quite impressive waterfall. Over the years, gays found that of these two or three thousand or so boatmen, a considerable number of them could be enticed into the boudoir for sex. Some pesos do, of course, inevitably change hands."

Philip and Binky explored the Manila make-out scene. Many gays lived there year round; others visited for extended periods. They met some new friends and also reconnected with gay friends who were part of the Asian sex circuit. Few could pretend they were only tourists interested in sightseeing since Manila offered little for sightseers. These were sex travelers seeking young sexual partners.

The city sex circuit included visits to the parks, the big stores, especially the sixth floor of the Good Earth department store, a few shopping malls, the streets, some swimming pools, and some notorious movie theaters where sexual encounters took place.

As they listened to their fellow seekers, they became aware of the larger sex circuits throughout the archipelago, the big concentric circles that the seekers traveled around the country, the orbits with Manila as the hub—with trips to Bacalod, Pagsanjan, the Hundred Islands, Baguio, Iloilo, and Cebu. A few went to Banaue to see the astounding rice terraces, but the sex pickings were not good there.

The seekers were restless, haunted, relentless, always on the move looking for the greener pastures. A rumor started that two sixteen-year-old American boys were living on the streets near the Subic U.S. Navy base, and seekers were soon on their way there.

In Manila there was the inevitable trip to the indoor Harrison Plaza shopping plaza. The focal point was to sit out in front of the Vips café and watch the school kids as they came in after school or walked around in the early evening. The prey could be under ten to the low thirties.

Vips at Harrison Plaza, with its murky gallery lights and minimal air conditioning, was at least out of the heat, pollution and humidity of the streets. Schools would let out and the beauty parade pageant would commence. The male contestants would parade up and down, and then would come the contest; the prize would go to the cutest boy who would then be pursued by the seekers. The students would come pouring in, all in their neat white tee shirts, the official school uniform of the Philippines.

The movies were across from the corral of tables and chairs set outside the restaurant. The little ones paraded by, sometimes with their patrons; the teenagers wandered by knowingly, cockily. One afternoon, Binky was sitting there with Philip when a young man drifted by and glanced knowingly at them. When the young man made his next pass, Binky leered. On the third go-by, Binky waved him over.

The young man was a very macho and handsome merchant marine cadet of twenty named Jamie. Soon Binky decamped with Jamie, and Philip was alone for a time until he was joined by Sandy and Clifton from the Lifebuoy. If you were outgoing and made friends, you would always have companions among the other seekers because almost all of them wanted to compare notes with one another.

On the Manila circuit, Philip reconnected with the Welshman with a beard that he had dubbed Monty Woolley, an entomologist in a Singapore university. Monty Woolley was traveling in a trio consisting of himself, the Mad Hatter, and the March Hare. They hardly ever stayed still, always scurrying from place to place in a feeding frenzy looking for "keeds." He would see them everywhere from the San Pedro, to the Luneta, to the Good Earth department store, to Vips. The March Hare and the Mad Hatter would sometimes scuttle across the shopping mall promenading teens and sub-teens.

The foreign colony often met at the Vips tables. While they waited for contacts, Philip would listen as they swapped sexual encounter anecdotes, penis sizes, body types, degree of partner participation, penetrations, proclivities, fetishes, what the conquest did or didn't do. Philip listened, but he didn't participate. Certain things to him were beyond the pale. You had to maintain some level of decorum and conventional behavior. Philip was not a prude, but he did not believe in being crude and a sexual tell-all narrator.

With Binky, Philip visited three male stripper bars. A number of them had sprung up. Most of the dancers were straight. They almost all undulated their stomachs in what was supposed to be a sensual, suggestive gesture, but Philip found the whole undulating belly bit dull. He and Binky went to 950 Retiro, one of the most famous, actually notorious, of the bars, which had rooms upstairs. You could arrange with the owner to take the boys up there for a short tryst. Binky knew that Philip was not really a bar person and was not a lavish spender; after all, he was a Scot.

Binky took a boy upstairs while Philip waited downstairs and fended off a posse of boys who wanted him to accompany one of them upstairs.

On their return from the Retiro, a sudden rain pelted the taxi windows; the vehicle was a disaster, falling apart with a hole in the floorboards of the rear seat. Binky accidentally dropped a twenty peso note on the floor, and it was sucked out into the street.

They reached the San Pedro Apartments in one piece. Philip was glad to get back into his apartment. He locked his door and wedged a chair against the knob. He just wanted sanctuary from the travails of the night.

13

Philip and Binky were on their way to Pagsanjan Falls one morning. Binky had been there once before; it was Philip's first trip. They took a cab to the B.L.T. Bus Company terminal in Manila. A packed red bus with three seats across on the left and two across on the right departed at eight in the morning. It was a three hour trip to Santa Cruz, the provincial town near the village of Pagsanjan.

Philip, always inquisitive, and a veteran traveler, was eager to learn about new places. He enjoyed the bus trip. The other passengers were farmers, families, students going home, and people who had been in the capital on some kind of business. The net bins above the seats were loaded with packages wrapped in string, plastic bags, and beaten-up suitcases. Philip and Binky had only small carry-on bags. One woman had two live geese with their feet tied together crammed under her seat. The birds were strangely passive.

Other passengers were friendly, smiling, welcoming. Philip thought they probably felt there was something worthwhile here in the province if foreigners wanted to come. The locals liked the idea of tourists and outsiders coming in. It helped validate their lives.

When Philip laughed at one of Binky's jokes, people around them smiled and looked upbeat even though they had no idea what they were saying. Philip and Binky were never deprecating and did not make bitchy remarks about the locals they saw, the ordinary, salt-of-the-earth people. It took a petty person to demean the ordinary man or woman going about his or her business, and Binky and Philip were not mean or petty people. That was not their style. Binky could be very bitchy about people of his own ilk, but even then it was done in jest and in his faux-queenish manner.

Once outside the smoggy city, the countryside opened up

before them with rice fields, hamlets, and small farms. Along the road, Coca Cola signs perched atop small sari sari convenience stores where people gathered. They rode through dusty hamlets where motorized bicycles with side cars transported passengers around the village roads, their engines putt-putting loudly and spewing smoke. Sometimes these tricycles would be loaded with freight or overloaded with four or five people.

Along the road were the spavined, mongrel dogs, those Third World icons, just barely being swept off the road by the rushing bus. Some Filipinos were known to eat dogs for birthdays, Binky told Philip. Then came pigs with piglets, chickens with chicks, and goats with kids. Everywhere, hundreds of school children in white shirts were on their way to school. Some waved when they saw the two middle-aged male Caucasians gawking out the bus window.

The bus skirted the left side of the huge lake known as Laguna De Bay, but the waterway was seldom visible on the trip. At Los Banos, hawkers with white pastry boxes held on high got onto the bus shouting, "Buka pie, buka pie." A few people bought it as a treat to take home. Binky bought one, and he broke off two pieces for Philip and himself. It tasted faintly of coconuts and was a dry, bland custardy concoction.

Finally, the bus ended up in Santa Cruz, the provincial capital of Laguna. Outside the terminal, they found a jeepney that had Pagsanjan placards. They climbed into the back of one headed for the village. Two fellow passengers, a well set-up young man and his buddy immediately asked them if they wanted to take a boat ride up to the falls with them. Binky told them they could not make any commitments. They persisted, but Binky was adamant. The boatmen took it politely and changed the subject by giving them an overview of the area.

The jeepney drove over level ground dotted with rice fields where water buffalo, prodded by their handlers, were at work in the paddies. They passed a batik shop-factory and the ever-present sari sari stores. The jeepney came to the end of its run where the Santa Cruz road intersected the Pagsanjan river road. The two Brits alighted at the village plaza.

There was very little to the village center itself: a main street running adjacent to the river, four or five stores, a bar called the Sawali, and across the street on the river side a small coconut husk processing plant. A tricycle driver shouted to them. "Joe, where are you going?" Every Caucasian was called Joe.

Binky answered, "The Lodge."

The driver said, "Hop in," and they were soon in the tricycle's side car putt-putting up a hill to the right of the village plaza. The road ran parallel to the river. They passed clusters of villagers' houses, many built on stilts. Roosters, hens, and mongrel dogs had the run of the yards and street. Boatmen shouted to them, asking them to engage them for boat rides. Philip saw that the men there were definitely more muscular and better set up than the men in Manila. Binky said they were all "hunks." It was a short ride.

The tricycle drove through a spacious parking lot on the river side and left them off in front of a building with a large sign proclaiming, "Welcome to Pagsanjan Lodge." The parking lot was loaded with tour buses that had brought many day trippers for the ride up to the falls. To the right of the Lodge's main entrance was a row of six motel units. Binky pointed to them and said, "Those are the air con units. No one in the know stays there. None of the seekers. They're for straight overnighters."

Up a few stairs and they were in a large open air terrace restaurant with a wide expanse of tables and a stunning view of the river a considerable distance down below. Beyond was the opposite shore with its forest of coconut palms. Below the entrance level was another lower terrace level with other restaurant tables. A number of Chinese tourists were at the tables talking in loud voices. It seemed as if their normal conversational level was the equivalent of shouting.

Binky led Philip to a small reception desk next to the

entrance. Behind the desk, they could see a large gaping kitchen. The reception clerk, a hefty man, confirmed their reservations. Philip had Coconut Room One, and Binky had Coconut Room Two, the rooms Binky had stipulated when he called for reservations. They left their valuables in a small case that the receptionist deposited in a locked cabinet behind the counter.

A genial, good-looking, hunky, nineteen-year-old who was certainly built like a muscled boatman introduced himself as Wendell, the pool lifeguard. He threw a bag on each shoulder and led them through the two levels of the restaurant.

As Wendell walked ahead, Binky whispered, "That lad is definitely movie star material." Philip nodded in agreement. He knew it wouldn't take long before Binky added this piece of eye candy to his long list of conquests.

At a few tables, Philip could see some of his fellow seekers talking together in animated conversations, probably discussing conquests.

A few steps down and they had entered what was called the Coconut Grove, a tropical park with palm trees, brilliantly colored bushes, flowers, and paths that led in various direction. To the left out over the river bank was a high round lookout terrace that Binky called the promontory. Their guide led them to the right of a large serpentine swimming pool that snaked through the property foliage. The pool was a busy place with more than a score of very brown bodies splashing around amidst some anemically white middle-aged bodies.

They walked over a metal footbridge that arched over the pool and led to another path through coconut palms and a stand of hibiscus. In the jungly grounds of the Lodge itself, Philip could see various kinds of housing, some one-story and a big two-story unit that was built out over the river. Before them by itself was a one-story building with three units, Coco Groves One through Three.

At the left end next to Coco One was a public shower and toilet in an attached section. Each unit had a screened porch with comfortable chairs. A good place for reading, Philip decided.

On the porch of Coco Grove Three, a gawky, Ichabod Crane look-alike was reading a book. He gave them a hearty greeting in a loud voice. "Glad to have you aboard. Gentlemen, where are you from?"

"Britain."

"Good show. Cheers. Welcome."

Their guide put Philip into Coco One next to the shower, and Binky into Coco Two, the middle unit.

After they had unpacked their essentials and changed into bathing suits, the two ghostly white figures with unremarkable bodies in unflattering ballooning trunks stood outside the units. Ichabod from his cage inquired, "Going to the pool, gentlemen? Good hunting. I'll be joining you shortly for my afternoon dip."

On the path to the pool, Binky said, "Bit presumptuous and forward, isn't he? American, I'm sure."

Philip answered, "Be grateful. We may need friends and experienced guides here before we're through."

Binky said, "Onward to battle, Philip, my dear."

14

The center of activity, the courting arena, was the serpentine swimming pool encircled by palm trees and flowering bushes that snaked its way through part of the jungly interior of the sprawling Lodge grounds. It looked like an Eden. The pool was long; it could have six or seven centers of action going on at once.

A family could be picnicking at the far end while early teens could be practicing dives off the bridge. A group of older Caucasians could be paddling around talking about their conquests. Meanwhile a dozen or so of the "midgets," the kids from five to eight, could be practicing their social skills by trying to entice the white-skinned men to show some interest. The nine to twelves contingent could be making lots of assertive noise as the thirteen to seventeens (actually the most in demand) could be trying to find their niche. All this activity while the eighteen to thirty-year-old boatmen might be striking athletic poses or swimming laps in hopes of being noticed by some patron.

The pool had been constructed with small boulders and rocks cemented together to form the sides and bottom. The water originated from a spring source; the water was clear and fresh. It was drained every two weeks and severely scrubbed. Above the pool along its perimeter were cement walks. One reached the poolside ledge walk by a short flight of four steps.

Around the poolside was lush growth, a variety of flowers and bushes, carefully tended. In this tropical climate, exotic flowers flourished and bloomed riotously. Orange puffs of flowers with tiny petals overhung the pool at one point. It was a haven for brightly colored butterflies and for hundreds of circling scarlet dragonflies that buzzed the pool and maneuvered throughout the area.

An informal parade wandered past above the busy pool. It included seekers staying in the Lodge looking on as they made their way to and from their rooms, or straight Falls day-trippers meandering through the Coconut Grove. Some of the admirers of the young had their cameras and video recorders at the ready or in use.

Around the pool was a set ballet each day with the choreography set in motion by older men who wanted to exercise their libidos and young men and boys looking for some kind of a stake. The performance continued throughout the day with various scenes and new characters. On rainy days or days when the pool was being drained, much of the courting action was suspended or carried out along the Lodge paths or in the park ground's gazebos and open-air huts.

The choreography was quite intricate. The midgets, "the keeds," engaged in a great deal of splashing and squirting to attract attention. They were also thought to pee in the pool. Their particular and peculiar admirers were delighted by their vitality and playfulness. Others in search of more mature bodies merely tolerated them or occasionally pushed them out of the way. The midgets, or midges as some people called them took no offense; they knew the routine. They had to search out those men who were driven and obsessed about the very young. Even a five-year-old could detect the craving and lust in the eyes of those driven ones. The interested seekers fawned over and indulged the very young boys.

For pedophiles, this was a paradise. Reviled, persecuted, despised, and imprisoned in their home countries, here they had unlimited freedom or license to seek what they desired. The most glaring and socially irresponsible conduct could be conducted with no fear of disapproval. Gayness was a meaningless concept to most of these seekers.

Who was directing this dance? Who was stationing the native principals at their various points? Who costumed the late teenagers in those basketball uniforms to make them look sexy? Had a director shown one lithe young man in a Speedo where to stand on the bridge, where his calves and thighs could be shown to the greatest advantage? Who had decided upon the chiaroscuro: the patches of shade, the pool in bright sunlight, the shady spots ideal for a certain type, the brightly lit areas favoring another? It was an idyllic setting; a gay felt as if he were in some kind of paradise, a new Eden for those who had dreamed of an abundance of available male sexual partners.

Along the cement walls of the ledge around the pool, concrete benches had been carved out. As the sun filtered through the leaves, a young, beautifully sculpted young man was shaking off the water, sending drops shooting off in all directions, his head rotating, his hair spinning off water. He was a cock of the walk. To some of the gaping seekers in the pool he was a living, walking cock, the embodiment of sex and desire.

Some young men went strutting by, stripped toreadors showing off their supple bodies, their maleness in all its splendor. Over time, as they had evolved from one of the "keeds" into these preening, yet subtle cocks of the walk, they had quickly realized they had a commodity to barter; the commodity was their bodies and their sexual essence.

At the pool, an assignation was arranged. The seeker and the boatman didn't leave together; a room number was exchanged. The seeker hurried back to his lair. Minutes later, the cock knocked lightly on the door, was admitted, often wordlessly; he came in, stripped, took a shower.

The European, Australian or American john, pale as a ghost, watched greedily, hungrily, as the young man soaped up, showered, rinsed off. The stud stood in the doorway of the bathroom, approached the older man on the bed and sex commenced. Forbidden fetishes might be practiced and fantasies fulfilled.

The white, cruelly pale, muscleless Western males with bodies like sexless crones were deeply repressed from their years of sublimation and desperation and quiet masturbation. They would survive at home thinking of these moments of renewal at the Falls, thinking of affirmation and validation for their eccentric desires. At home, they would relive these stolen forbidden moments, imagining the quick thrusts, kisses, hugs, the clinging and twining—like the bamboo clinging to the palm trunks around the pool, the bamboo stalks integrating into the palm trunks. In the rooms, two bodies were twining; or even three or four bodies were sometimes twining together.

Quick warmth, the clinging, the coupling, the binding, human bodies bonding together, blessed human contact at last. Life wasn't so desperate after all for either one. For the donee: "I have some pesos to give to the family." For the donor: "It feels so good being with a younger male." It was a symbiotic relationship as old as human life itself.

Philip and Binky stood on the bridge for a few minutes, taking in the whole scene. Each was delighted by what he saw. Soon they walked down the few steps, stood briefly on the pool ledge walk and then climbed down the metal ladder into the delightfully cool pool water. An armada of splashing midgets soon descended upon them, little brown bodies laughing, diving around them, testing them out.

The "keeds" surrounded them in the water, water beading and rolling off their tan skin. The Lilliputians were diving and swimming like porpoises all around them. They played tag between the two Westerners, using them as pylons. A little one came floating up to Philip and whispered, "Shower? Massage?" Another one descended upon Binky. "Move my bowels in your room, please." Any excuse to gain access into a room.

Another came up to Philip, "Hot water in your room, please, sir?" Every few moments: "What is your name? Where are you from? What is your room number?" The three basic questions that Philip and Binky soon found were asked by everyone.

Philip and Binky swam away from the "keeds." They both emphatically shouted, "Go away." To Binky, they were irrelevant and a distinct nuisance. He was soon shooing them out of the way like annoying flies. Philip tried to be more tactful, but he soon learned he had to gesture them away, otherwise they swarmed around him.

Binky made it clear they weren't into the elementary school crowd, and the midgets moved away. Binky and Philip paddled over near the area where three teenagers of seventeen or so were preening. The teens studiously avoided looking at the two Caucasians, but managed to make themselves look very provocative and erotic.

Because of dense foliage, Philip was unaware of the relationships of the paths to the views he had from the pool. While floating, lazing in the pool, he caught a glimpse of a boatman sneaking out of a cottage, coming down a path from one of the rooms. Then the boatman was momentarily lost in the foliage, then brief views of muscled brown flesh, more shade and foliage, and then he reappeared on the footbridge, nonchalant.

Binky and Philip were lazing in the pool, paddling around, taking in the sights when their neighbor, gangly Ichabod from Coco Three, entered the pool, dipping in a long ivory leg to test the temperature. He was bald, had an elongated head, long sharp nose, was six feet tall with a thin frame. All in all, not the least bit handsome, not a comely body. He introduced himself and started a conversation in a voice that carried, resonated a little too well.

"My name is Craig Wallace. I'm in Three, next to you all."

Philip's even-featured good looks, his pleasant visage qualified him as a movie star when seen in company with the oddities of his two ugly duckling companions.

Binky and Philip introduced themselves. Soft-spoken Philip's voice was at a level that required listeners to be next to him in order to hear him. Binky's voice was slightly louder, but Craig sounded like he had a megaphone built into his throat. He had been a colonel in the U.S. Army, probably used to giving orders in his loud commanding voice.

Teenage boys, thirteen through seventeen, were acting coy, walking by the poolside, occasionally diving near them.

Rather than be annoyed by all this water ballet and maneuvering, the three middle-aged men loved it. They loved being the center of any kind of male attention. In a British or American pool they would have been ignored and would have been invisible. All three had chalky skin that stood out in vivid contrast to the deeply tanned bodies of the locals around them.

Craig was telling Binky and Philip, "I've retired from the U.S. Army and live in Manila. I come here to the Falls about every other month. I try to come up when there's a full moon so I can look at the ripe moon from the Japanese hill above the village. That's where Japanese soldiers from World War II are buried."

Binky, always bold, laughed and said, "Yes, and, of course, while you're here gazing at the moon, it doesn't hurt that you get your pipes cleaned out and your ashes hauled."

Craig looked shocked and nonplussed for a brief moment, and then all of them laughed, most of all Craig. That had been the ice breaker. Now they knew they could enjoy each other's company and be frank about sexual matters. Craig clued them in on which of the boys he knew, which ones secretly gave oral sex, which ones were two-way. His own scene was that he wanted a boy-man to give him oral sex or he wasn't interested. He said, "I like the guys who give head. One seventeen-year-old named Marcello is very adept at oral sex, but when he's finished, he always warns me, 'Don't tell your friends.'"

Philip was naturally more reticent than Binky about sharing his sexual preferences (Philip favored participatory sex by both participants), but he found Craig held nothing back. He enjoyed listening to Binky and Craig get down and dirty— as long as he didn't have to participate. He learned a great deal about the scene without having to sacrifice his dignity or reticence, his aura of the decorous Philip persona.

Craig talked about the aspirations of the boatmen or teens. "Everyone has the idea of making it on his own, driving a tricycle, having a boat, operating a beer and soda boat on the river, running a sari sari store, owning a jeepney, any sort of cottage industry, any independent source of income to break out of the mold. For a couple of years, I had a boyfriend in Manila, who has long since decamped with a wealthy woman. I bought him a car, and he wisely turned it into a taxi. He made good money and was able to beat the system. But hundreds don't. Most don't. An awful lot of them end up going to Saudi Arabia or elsewhere to work at jobs for low paying jobs the Saudis or others won't do themselves. Contract jobs that last a couple of years. You'll hear many of them talking about going to work in the merchant marine or cruise industry like Two-Time George up there."

Craig pointed out Two-Time George, a tall, handsome, sexy boatman in his early twenties who was standing on the bridge. He was smiling, welcoming. Craig told them George, when he went to a seeker's room, always came twice. The first time he would be deeply involved, and would be two-way and engage in sixty-nine.

Craig said, "After he gets his rocks off the first time, he waits a few minutes, rests. Then gets back his energy, gets a hard-on and the second time it's more of a one-way proposition where he becomes a lay-back. He never varies his routine. Never."

Binky was interested, aroused. "He's definitely my type." He and George made eye contact. With considerable, quite emphatic nodding and gesturing, something was arranged between George and Binky.

With an "I'll be back in a while," Binky climbed out of the pool, approached George on the bridge, said a few words, and scurried away to his cottage. Two-Time George stood looking vaguely at the pool; after a minute, he turned, and strolled in the direction of the Coco units.

Philip was left conversing with Craig in the pool.

Craig said, "Boy, he's a fast worker."

Philip replied, "Where sex is concerned, Binky does not believe in letting the grass grow under his feet or stifling his urges. You said some magic words, implying reciprocation.

That was all he needed to hear. He may be gone for the next
few hours."

"Oh, no," Craig assured him. "George is also very fast.
Your friend should be back in about forty-five minutes. That
includes a shower for George. He's studying to get in the
merchant marine, and he probably has to get home to do his
homework. Never fear though. If you're interested, he'll be
here tomorrow, hot to trot again."

While they paddled around, Craig gave Philip a run down
on Manila cruising. As they floated near the quiet area
beyond the bridge, a soft voice could be heard above them,
which came from a seventeen-year-old, half hidden behind a
bush. "Pssst. Craig."

"Oh, that'll be Marcello. He gives me a massage every
afternoon. For massage, you can read blow job. Would you
excuse me? He doesn't spend too much time in the Lodge. I'll
be back shortly."

Craig climbed out of the pool and headed for his cottage.
Through the underbrush, Philip could see Marcello heading
after him.

He was left in the pool, deserted by Binky and abandoned
by his new acquaintance, the American Craig. Such was gay
life. Dates, flings, tricking took precedence over friendly conversation in a place like this. Not to worry. Philip liked being
alone in the pool. It gave him a chance to suss out some
things on his own. Seeing him alone, a solitary target, a
flotilla of four of the midgets bore down upon him, splashing
and playfully diving under him lightly brushing his body as
they did so.

Philip swam away; they followed. He gestured for them to
get away. "Please go. Go away." He was about to get out of
the pool to escape them, when they got the message and
swam toward a new target, a smiling Caucasian with snow-
white hair who was obviously mesmerized by them. Philip
again had an area of the pool to himself.

A very good looking boatman wearing a baseball cap was
eyeing him from the bridge. Philip shot looks at him, and

they continued playing eye games. Then a teenager of about sixteen or seventeen swam up to him. The lad had a winning smile. "What's your name?" he asked.

"Philip"

"Philip, my name is Carlitos."

Philip noted that many Filipinos had Spanish names left over from the Spanish colonial period, though they neither spoke Spanish nor had any knowledge of Spanish culture.

"Where are you from, Philip?"

"England."

"Did you ever meet Princess Di?"

"Yes, I did, once actually."

Carlitos was thrilled. Philip had met her at the Queen's Chapel one Sunday. He had been one of a score of people who had shaken the hand of the recently wed Princess of Wales. Carlitos seemed more interested in information about England than he did in talking Philip into tricking. They continued a pleasant conversation for quite some time until a grinning, contented Binky returned to the pool.

Philip introduced Carlitos and Binky seemed uninterested. Ten minutes more went by, and a spent Craig was back in the pool. Carlitos said goodbye and floated away; he seemed content with just the conversation and friendship. Both Binky and Craig were willing to loll and laze in the pool for a time. Finally, the three agreed to get dressed and go over to the Lodge restaurant for lunch.

15

Binky, Craig and Philip were having a late lunch at the Lodge restaurant. Philip had a passable omelet, Binky a toasted ham and cheese sandwich, and Craig a thick noodle soup. They were seated by the balcony railing where they had a panoramic view of the activity out on the wide river. Long lines of the canoe-like wooden dugouts were being towed back by a motorized barca. The last of the day-trippers were coming back from the visit to the Falls. In each barca would be a boatman in the bow and another in the stern with one to three usually soaked passengers huddled in the middle. Some day-trippers were having lunch at the tables around them.

Craig said, "After four o'clock in the afternoon, or earlier, we have the Lodge to ourselves. The tourists leave. The pool becomes less active. Most of the boatmen disappear. It's really a beautiful, quiet time of day. Occasional tricks show up in the grove, but usually people have set up dates ahead of time."

Philip still hadn't chosen a partner, but that didn't bother him. Better to be cautious than sorry. He wanted to observe the workings of the Pagsanjan assignations before or if he had sex. Binky reminded Philip of his tardiness. He said to Craig, "Philip always wants to get the lay of the land before he gets laid. Funny expression that, 'getting laid.' It often doesn't involve any laying at all, but can be quite generic, indicating strictly oral rather than anal contact. I think you Yanks are defiling our common tongue."

Philip was somewhat put off because the place was so active. Where was the romance, the courting, the dating, the growth of a relationship? Craig was right when he called it a meat market.

Philip was cast in his role of the typical spy doing his

reconnaissance before acting. Philip would really prefer a relationship more than a fling. Craig already had a relationship with a boyfriend in Manila, while Binky was eternally on the prowl looking for quickies, one-night stands, always seeking eternal variety. He had never been known to settle down with anyone and never would. It was kiss and run with him.

Following lunch, Craig and Binky went back to their rooms to take needed naps. Philip decided to take a look around the grounds. He stood on the terrace promontory, the highest spot, and looked out again over the river. To his left he could see the thick tropical tangle that swallowed the river on its way up to the Falls. Like Conrad's "Heart of Darkness," he thought. He could spend hours looking out over this sea of palms, the murky river, the occasional fish that jumped free of the river. A very serene, peaceful spot. He thought back to his ordeal in the Terminal, his torture. While he was undergoing that ordeal, he could never imagine he would ever find peace and quiet again.

That was partly why the sexual fulfillment was not so pressing for him. After enduring the intense shame and excruciating pain, the sexual coupling seemed less pressing a need, less necessary; it was just good to be alive and be placid, serene, and safe. Sometimes when one single-mindedly pursued sex, it led to trouble of one sort or another, and the last thing he wanted in life was trouble, disequilibrium. Not that there was anything wrong with sex; he just didn't want hassles along with it.

One time he had picked out a young local in Hong Kong, gone to the fellow's dumpy apartment for a fling, and discovered that while they were hugging and having a mutual feel, the man was so adept with his feet and toes that he was able to extract Philip's wallet from his pants pocket and actually take bills from its interior with his toes. Talk about hustler ingenuity. Philip had rescued his money and wallet, pushed the man down, dressed and fled the scene. Sex often came with hassles. Some participants got crabs, others got scabies. Philip cringed when he heard stories of gays who contracted crabs, scabies, gonorrhea, syphilis, hepatitis, herpes or some other horror from sex partners.

After his time on the promontory, Philip wandered over to a gazebo that overlooked the river but which seemed to blend in with the foliage. The hut had crude wooden benches built into its sides and a wooden table fixed between the rows of benches. Four late teens about sixteen through nineteen were spread around the hut. Two were smoking. Carlitos, Philip's companion from the pool, was there; he called out to Philip. He had a chess set arranged in front of him.

"Philip, will you play a game of chess with me?"

It seemed funny to Philip that a boy a third his age would be addressing him so familiarly, but what was wrong with it? After all, many of these boys were used to sharing beds with men many years older than themselves. Sex was a great leveler.

"Not right now, Carlitos."

Philip entered the gazebo and smiled a greeting to its inhabitants. One teenager was sullen and hardly spoke. Was that a hint of pot he detected? The other two boys were friendly enough and asked his name, country of origin, and room number. Philip had gotten into the habit of saying, "I'm in one of the air con units," which everyone knew to be false. By jungle telegraph, everyone in Laguna province probably knew his room number by now.

As late afternoon verged into a murkier dusk, the sullen boy left. Two more came on stage in the gazebo. These two were distinctly effeminate and said they were from Santa Cruz. Carlitos sat staring at his chessboard. Philip heard a boatman whistle to another out on the river.

Who had directed tonight's drama? The setting: a hut overlooking the river, below the promontory. The lighting: dusk, oncoming darkness. One new arrival looked dusky and sinister. Two boatmen had come and were on the stairs leading to the path to the restaurant dining rooms. One Adonis seated himself on the stairs leading to the cottages.

They were all relaxed, talking among themselves; Philip

was largely ignored except for occasional questions from Carlitos. One teenager entered the hut and lay face down on the table, his head facing the chessboard.

As darkness came on, all was silent for a time, no talking, just staring, eyes unsparing, gazes that never let up; not eyes of desperation but eyes determined and steady, not at all threatening. There were only the tiniest moments of epiphany—a light was struck by a match and all the eyes for a moment turned toward the aura of light.

The light grew dimmer in the corners of the pool area nearby. Philip focused on the boy lying on a table in the hut. He remained lifeless for a time, but then it was his turn to exit the stage.

As Philip walked back to Coco Two, he crossed the bridge over the pool where a smoldering seventeen year old was posing on the bridge. Philip smiled to himself. This place was full of temptation. When he got back to the three units, Craig and Binky were seated in Binky's screened area enjoying cans of beer.

16

That first night, Philip and Binky decided to have pre-dinner drinks with Craig in the Lodge restaurant. Then they would go downtown to dinner. At seven-thirty, the three sat at a table on the upper terrace of the Lodge. Each had a gin and tonic. They looked out over the river. This time of night was beautiful. It was cool with a persistent, refreshing breeze; the river was peaceful and tranquil.

Philip looked over at the opposite shore. He saw a series of lean-tos at the river's bank where upwards of six barcas were stored on shelves, sometimes two or three shelves high. Many of the boatmen lived on the other side of the water where there were coconut plantations, as well as small subsistence farms.

Philip observed a scene across the river that would become familiar to him while he was at the Lodge. Two boys with sticks showed up at the top of the hill overlooking the river. They had a water buffalo tied to a rope. They coaxed the buffalo down a steep path to the river's edge. The animal and the boys entered the river. The animal was soon in the murky water up to his back. The two boys played and dove around him. The waiter came over to their table. "Those keeds have a lot of fun with their carabao."

"Carabao?" Philip inquired.

"That's what we call our water buffalo."

The boys scrubbed the carabao's skin, washed him and ladled water over his back. One boy climbed on the animal's back and dove in the water. The animal would probably have stayed in the cooling water for hours.

When the three middle-aged men had finished their drinks and risen, Philip saw the boys trying to pull the huge animal back up the hill. It was much harder getting him back up than it was getting him down. They were working against gravity now.

Just as the three stepped out into the Lodge parking lot, a tricycle pulled up. Craig yelled, "Dura Fe." The three squeezed uncomfortably into the side car, and the loud vehicle sputtered and stammered down the hill. It passed the plaza, putt-putted a few blocks, did a quick U turn and stopped in front of a low building a few steps down from the main road, the Dura Fe restaurant.

The Dura Fe public area consisted of a large room, plain and utilitarian with ten tables. Some of them were round tables where a dozen could be accommodated. Near the door was a refrigerated case with glass doors that contained sodas and beer. In one corner was a jukebox playing a Beatles song. The record had been played so many times the sound wasn't quite right and skipped at times.

Only three tables were unoccupied. Philip, Binky, and Craig were shown to one of the vacant ones by a friendly and helpful owner-hostess.

In one corner, a round table was presided over by two beaming men in their early fifties. Around them were eight midgets, small brown kids ages five to eight. Philip recognized some of them from the pool. The two men, obviously Scots from their burr, were playing Mommy and Daddy to this noisy brood. Three of the young boys were given coins. They ran to the juke box where they noisily quarreled over their music choices.

At another table, Otto, a German was with his gang of five. Four boys were from ten to thirteen, but one handsome boy of fifteen named Miguel seemed to be odd boy out. Craig told Binky and Philip that Otto had given Miguel his walking papers, but he lingered on. Miguel had outgrown Otto's age preference. Otto had been coming to Pagsanjan for years, and a number of boatmen had once been in his clan.

The boys grew to know when it was time to leave one john, one clan, and move on to some other john who liked older types. Miguel knew his days were numbered. He was trying to put off the final day by being Otto's second in command, acting like a foreman and a gofer. He was looking over the other johns to see if he might attract a new sponsor.

Craig said, "Otto looks after his graduates. He will often help them when problems come up with their present johns. Miguel once told me one of my tricks was going to be late for a date. The trick had asked Otto to smooth the way for him, and he had Miguel seek me out. It's a case of a dean taking care of his alumni. Otto will also clue you in on the older boys, too—if he knows them, and he's known a quite a few in the Biblical sense."

One table had two Belgians who were seated with three hunky boatmen in their early twenties. One very overmuscled specimen was nicknamed the Incredible Hulk because of his bulk and his exceptional musculature.

Two Americans were with four teens ages fourteen to seventeen. They were the logical inheritors of Miguel, so he passed their table several times doing a little networking.

One table was unique. It had a husband and wife, a grandmother, and three daughters. The parents did not seem to like what was going on around them, but they weren't belligerent. They minded their own business. The three daughters admired some of the boys around them, but were uninvolved. This was a small village after all, and probably most people knew each other and had intertwined familial relationships. It was perfectly possible for three of their brothers or cousins to be in the room, one with the Scots, one with Otto, and one with the Americans.

Miguel passed the table several times, giving Binky a suggestive look. Binky said, "Do you notice? We're the only ones here without dates. We really are outcasts. Tomorrow night we'll have to get ourselves some presentable escorts."

Philip said, "I find the caste system here very interesting and immutable. The foreigners have very strict age guidelines."

Craig, the Philippines veteran, offered, "Some of the foreigners prefer uncut boys. Since boys in this country are routinely circumcised at ten or eleven by an older male family member, this transition might cause a boy being put in a different category."

Philip said, "If I were a young boy in the circuit past ten growing up here, I would always be worried that I was going to sprout genital hair or that my voice was going to change, forcing me to be thrown out into the street."

Craig answered, "Never fear. All of these kids have families and places to live. In some cases, a teen will move in with his buddy and live with the buddy's family during the formative years. They'll sleep in the same bed together, perhaps with another brother or buddy or two. These kids can develop friendships that are more like close brother situations."

The owner helped them make their food choices. It was a short menu of Filipino and Chinese dishes. She suggested they order various dishes and share them. The dishes, she said, were all large. They ordered lumpia, which were like egg rolls, bowls of chicken vegetable soup, fried chicken, a vegetable dish like chow mein, and pla pla, a whole fish similar to a carp broiled in a sweet and sour sauce.

When the food came, the fish was very tender. They carved out hunks, skin and all, with their soup spoons. At other tables, locals were eating head and all. The three had San Miguel beer to go with their dinners.

Craig said, "If you're here in Pagsanjan very long, you'll tire of the small list of selections in this restaurant. This is really the only restaurant in town except for the Rapids Hotel up the street where local dates are not particularly welcome. The food at the Lodge for dinner is the same as the lunch menu and is mediocre at best."

It was a feast for the little "keeds" and boatmen dates who traditionally brought leftovers home to their families. Craig said, "God knows how many of these boatmen have wives and children. It's something that we outsiders are not usually privy to."

Philip said, "When you look at these tables of johns and dates, these are essentially families that these patrons have formed. Probably never had children of their own."

Philip felt sorry for Miguel. He was very good-looking, well set-up, obviously bright. He drifted from one table to another

looking for a new base. He knew he was being eased out of
the family, Otto's brood, one he had been with for four or five
years. The teen group thought of him as a potential rival.
Miguel knew the Scots with their babies quite well so perhaps he had been in their group, or a group like that, and
had graduated into Otto's group years ago.

The jukebox with an unfaithful tone was still blaring,
playing mostly Beatles songs. Later, it played a song in
Tagalog, which the owner told them was called "Boat on the
River." She sang along with some boatmen the lyric in
English, "Take me down to my boat on the river." Later that
night at the beer hall, Philip would see burly boatmen get all
teary-eyed over the song.

After their dinner, Craig asked them to join him at D'Plaza
for dessert. D'Plaza was like a small ice cream parlor located
at the corner where the Santa Cruz highway ended at the
Pagsanjan river road. At Craig's suggestion, Philip had ripe
split mango halves served with ice cream while Binky
selected a mocha banana split. A table of four boatmen
ignored them. Many of the village boatmen did not participate in the foreign gay sex scene.

Craig was a good guide; he knew the ins and outs of the
Philippines scene. Philip had already decided to meet up
with him in Manila so that Craig could show him that scene
in more detail. Craig described his favorite French restaurant in Manila run by nuns where prayers were said and a
hymn was sung before the evening meal.

Binky suggested that they make a night of it. On his previous trip, he had gone to the Sawali beer hall. It was diago-
nally across the street from D'Plaza. It was a very small bar
with an arched ceiling, looking almost like a catacomb with
about six crude tables on each side of the room. Low wooden
chairs were lined up along the tables. All but one table was
occupied with boatmen.

A forest of San Miguel brown beer bottles were lined up on
the tables. The boatmen were boisterous. They smiled at the
visitors; some drifted over later, trying to mooch drinks.

Beside each table was a wooden crate where the empties were stored. Sometimes several crates would rise next to the table. The empties would be tallied, and the bill collected at the end of the night. Most tables had bowls of Spanish peanuts. A juke box was playing the inevitable Beatles songs, and some tipsy banqueros were singing. Some had a small buzz on, some were feeling very mellow, and some were absolutely drunk. It was a smoky room. The three Westerners were non-smokers, so were unable to supply their fellow drinkers with cigarettes. Other foreigners drifted in and out, some with male dates, some seeking.

Two handsome boatmen, early twenties, asked if they could sit with them. One was startlingly handsome with a Chinese tinge to his look, high cheekbones, even features, and a well-muscled body. He sat next to Binky and introduced himself as Joe. Philip could tell when Binky was in his cruising mode. He bought beers for the two. Joe's taller partner, Perry, was more talkative. Joe was quieter, taking his lead from Perry, who offered, "All his friends call Joe here Coconut Joe."

Binky asked, "And why are you called Coconut Joe?"

Perry laughed. "When we paddle up to the falls, we go through high gorges. Monkeys sit up there on cliffs and in trees. Sometimes when they see us go by, they get pissed and throw coconuts down on us. One of them beaned Joe here; he got knocked unconscious, got a concussion, and hasn't been the same since."

Joe gave a derisive look to his partner. If looks could kill. But Perry, wound up now, wouldn't quit. "The monkeys have never forgotten Joe, so they still aim for him special and try to bean him again."

Joe said, "Shut up, Perry, we're here to relax, not talk about those little fuckers."

As the night progressed, everyone had more beer, Philip could see the unmistakable signs. Binky was going to issue an invitation for Joe to accompany him to his boudoir. Philip would soon lose count of Binky's Pagsanjan conquests. Perry was not Philip's type, nor did Craig seem to warm to him, though he was a pleasant enough chap. Craig had ordered coconut wine and seemed to be more intent on tying one on. Abruptly, Binky rose and said good night, and he and Joe went outside to take a tricycle back to the Lodge. Perry drifted away.

Craig and Philip stayed on talking for a time. Finally, Philip had had enough beer and second-hand smoke for one night. He and Craig took a tricycle back to the Lodge. It had been a long day beginning in Manila, and he would be grateful to finally lie down and get a night's sleep. He hadn't yet had a sexual partner, but there was plenty of time yet. Like a professional spy, he'd have to investigate the territory further before making his move.

17

Philip was an early riser. That morning he had a slight hangover. Cocks were crowing in the neighborhood beyond the high walls that enclosed the Lodge. How appropriate, cocks crowing here where the cocks are so dominant, Philip thought. Cocks were the dominant theme, the Wagnerian leitmotif of the place.

Binky and Craig were not yet up. Probably too much sex for Binky, too much beer and coconut wine for Craig. Philip, wearing shorts, a tee shirt, and flip flops, decided to take a walk around the grounds. Two men were sweeping the walks and raking along the bushes. A young man in a bathing suit of about nineteen or so with a well developed body was skimming the pool. When he got closer, he found him to be Wendell, the lad that Binky had described as movie star material. He saluted Philip as Philip continued up the path.

At one end of the pool was a stand pipe that came out of a hillock. From it came spring water that fed into the pool. Four women were getting water from the pump. Two women had yokes over their shoulders with large rectangular cans suspended from each yoke end. Philip could see from the worn labels that the cans had started out holding vegetable cooking oil. One woman balanced the yoke skillfully as she went up the steps to the street. Philip noticed that the women studiously avoided any eye contact; not everyone in Pagsanjan was quite so welcoming to the foreign intruders.

The gazebo was vacant. From the promontory terrace, Philip looked down at a houseboat which was one of the Lodge's rental units. He had heard that it had been rented by three young Australian men. The Australians, in their twenties, wearing Speedos with bodies rivaling any of the boatmen, were on the boat's deck talking with two boatmen who had tethered their barcas alongside.

From the promontory, Philip stepped down a few steps to the restaurant. He sat at a table by the railing where he could watch the river coming to life. Some boatmen were working on their boats, boys were coaxing a carabao down for his morning wash, and women were washing clothes on the opposite river bank. One older man was giving himself a good scrubbing in the river.

The waiter gave Philip the small breakfast menu. He ordered a plate of fruit, ham and two eggs over-easy, tea and toast. When the large fruit plate came, it had sliced banana, pineapple, mango, papaya, and orange. On the table was a large jar of Crosse and Blackwell strawberry preserves. Philip sat there quite contentedly, savoring his toast with jam, and his tea while he continued surveying the river.

This was much better than being in dank, damp, chilly old Britain. He made a promise to himself that from now on his winters would be spent in Asia. Christmas, Boxing Day, and New Year's always brought bad weather and the loneliness that Philip couldn't stand. When you were single without close family, the holidays in Britain always provoked in him fits of depression.

Philip was there at the table for over an hour and a half; he lost all track of time. Binky and Craig approached him. Craig looked positively ridiculous. He was wearing a lime-colored one-piece playsuit of short pants, a bib with shoulder straps, the kind you would dress a five-year-old in.

"I had a tailor in Manila make three of these for me in different colors. Seven dollars apiece. In the States, they'd cost me hundreds. I wear them here in Pagsanjan. I do it as a lark, but hardly anyone sees it as a joke. They think it is the latest fashion in the States."

Philip laughed; here was a man that was willing to make a fool of himself, compounding his weird physical appearance by his outfit. Binky said, "Yes, they do look incredibly cheap to make and quite garish to boot." They all laughed at this.

This was the day Binky and Philip had decided to shoot

the rapids, take their trip up to the Falls. Binky asked Craig if he was going to make the trip.

"No thank you, Sir Binky, I have no intention of going up there again. I did it years ago, got badly sunburned, ruined my camera, got soaking wet, and was charged an exorbitant fee by two grasping boat persons. Besides I don't want to get my playsuit wet."

Craig continued, "You two go. It really is a worthwhile experience. Just make sure you choose the right boatmen and fix the price and tips ahead of time. Incidentally the best time to make the trip is in August or September, the rainy season when the river is higher, the falls more dramatic, but it's still exciting any time of year."

Binky interjected, "I've retained Coconut Joe and Perry as our boatmen for today."

Philip asked, "Is that wise, given Joe's track record. We may get beaned if a monkey throws a coconut at Joe, and it goes astray."

"No, it'll be fine. I trust those two. I've fixed the total rate with trip fee, cushions, and tips, so we won't end up haggling with boatmen which I've heard can be a hassle. And Joe is divine in bed. Quite a lover. All of my bedfellows should get the coconut treatment if that's the effect it has."

Craig asked, "Not a lay-back then?"

"Oh, no, far from it. Quite responsive. Loves to kiss and cuddle. Quite interested in seeing his sex partner equally satisfied. I think that coconut bash turned him gay."

After a time, Philip excused himself and left the two sexual athletes to their breakfast. They would be describing their conquests. He'd been at the table long enough. He needed to walk off the ham and eggs. He didn't want to venture out of the Lodge for a walk downtown just yet. He still wasn't too sure of the locals' attitudes, particularly the women in the barong who seemed to have a secondary role in this male-oriented society, in a place where the local males were the sexual targets of horny foreign males.

Day-trippers were pouring into the lodge. The buses had

arrived with the people who had been driven down from Manila for the trip up to see the Falls and to ride the rapids back. Philip and Binky had had an option of going early before the mob of tourists descended, but they had decided to go at the height of the action when there were a lot of other tourists around.

Philip went back to the promontory. In the background he could hear Craig's loud voice recounting an adventure he had had in Baguio, the summer capital of the Philippines way up north. God, the man had a voice that carried for miles. And he said some very indiscreet things. But Philip still liked his company.

18

Standing on the promontory Philip looked down at the morning preparations for the trips. About seventy feet below him was the staging platform out over the water. Boats were assembling there, coming from all over the river. They were beginning to tie up their boats. Sometimes a lone boatman would be in the stern effortlessly oaring the long boat into position. His partner would join him later.

Some banqueros were walking around the platform. They were lithe and graceful as they moved. Almost like dancers. They were decidedly masculine, but there was often a very slight, almost gay swing of the hips and buns. They were real athletes, for their jobs were grueling and required considerable skill, agility, and strength. Their boatman, jock swagger was deserved.

Some daytrippers were going down the long stone steps to the staging platform. They had gone to lockers, changed for the trip, and wrapped their cameras and photographic equipment in plastic. All put on the mandatory life jackets. They had to rent cushions if they were to be comfortable. Banqueros would steady the boat and one, two, or three persons would sit in the middle of the canoe-dugout. Then the Lodge photographer would take the obligatory shot. On their return the daytrippers would find the pictures displayed on a big board in the restaurant.

As seen from above, the boats, with their brightly colored interiors, were tied up around the pier forming a flower blossom, twenty or thirty boats radiating out from the center like enormous petals, the flower undulating with the actions of aphids, the people far below moving in and around the boats.

The brightly colored barcas were long, thin boats hollowed out of a single log. Philip watched as one canoe-like boat

swung away from the pier; a sturdy, supple, muscled boatman at either end with a short paddle, shouting back and
forth in Tagalog.

As Philip continued to monitor the embarkation proce-
dures below, Binky came walking up the path with Coconut
Joe who was wearing one of the small helmets that bicycle
racers wear.

They descended to the loading platform where Perry had
their barca ready. Wearing their life jackets and seated on
thin cushions, they took their spots in the center of the
dugout. "That helmet is not a propitious sign," Philip whispered to Binky.

Soon they were off in the barca with Perry paddling in the
rear behind them and Joe paddling at the bow, paddling
smoothly, effortlessly. About twenty boats had formed themselves into a daisy chain and the line of boats was being
towed up river by a motorized, sputtering barca. Joe tied up
his boat to the end of the chain. The boatmen would husband their energies until they came to the first of the series
of rapids.

When they approached the first of the shallow rapids, a
rocky area of the river, the boats separated. At times it was
necessary for Perry to get out and push the boat over the
shallows. A process that would be repeated at most of the
rocky rapids.

Philip and Binky were pleased by the sight of the rich
tropical jungle foliage that covered both shores of the river.
Palms grew in profusion up the sides of the ravines. Vines
hung down from tree tops, and they could see orchids hanging from vines among the foliage when they got close to the
shore. At some river clearings they saw thatched napa huts.
Sometimes a few children would wave at them from these
lonely spots along the river.

At some of the rapids both banqueros had to dismount to
ease the boat upriver. Philip could see Joe's taut, well-
defined thigh and bulging calf muscles as he struggled.

As they got to each of the fourteen rapids, Binky and

Philip could see what grueling work it was to get the boat over the rapids, especially at this time of year when the water level was low. The two banqueros had to get out of the boat, pull it, drag it, cajole it over the shallows. The river was working against them. They were gleaming with sweat from their exertions.

Already Philip and Binky were beginning to see some returning boats with early morning passengers rushing past, shooting the rapids. On the return the rear man had to serve as helmsman and guide the dugout with his paddle so it would hit the rapids just right and avoid the moiling whirlpools and rocks.

They started going through steep green gorges a hundred or more feet above them. From the topmost cliffs, coconut palms reached up an additional hundred feet or more. Joe pointed out what they called the Japanese Falls. The Filipinos still bore a great deal of hatred for the Japanese who had been cruel occupiers of the islands during World War II. If some Japanese daytrippers were in the boat, and they didn't like them, or simply felt perverse, they would say that the lesser falls were the famous Pagsanjan Falls and return to the starting point, charging the hapless Japanese for the full trip. The trick didn't always work so they had to go on when the passengers insisted, but a good dunking might lie in store for the protestors.

They were going through the Great Gorge. Perry was singing behind them. Every once in a while Joe would look up to the cliff tops, an apprehensive look on his face. It seemed like he was paddling faster to get through this area. Then suddenly, a loud plop, a splash. A coconut bobbed to the surface. Joe looked up and shouted, "Bastards. I'll get you, you little fuckers."

Binky and Philip covered their heads and ducked down in the boat. Perry reassured them, "You don't have to worry. They don't ever waste more than one coconut on Joe. Although sometimes they'll take a shot at him on our return trip."

Binky inquired, "With hundreds of banqueros, and from hundreds of feet up, how could they recognize Joe?"

"They'd know him anywhere. Now it's the helmet, but they would still be able to pick him out because he's so good-looking."

"Shut up, Perry, and just paddle. These gentlemen don't want to hear your bullshit."

Binky, sitting behind Philip, tickled him and kiddingly said, "This is more fun that a barrel of monkeys, providing we don't get conked."

Binky added, "Yes, Perry, on with it. Let's stop the monkeying around."

Joe looked around at Binky with murder in his eyes. He rocked the boat dangerously letting him know that he was in position to give them a dunking if need be.

Later, Joe calmed down and became the genial guide. "These Falls are also called the Magdapio Falls. There are thousands of licensed banqueros, too damn many for all of us to earn a living."

The sights were worth the ride: the towering cliffs, the jungle vegetation, the dramatic gorges. The boats were dwarfed by the sheer enormity of the natural world.

After about an hour and a half of going against the current, going upstream, the giant falls rose ahead of them. From three hundred feet above, a stream of water cascaded down the cliff face. It was a single broad stream of water whose fall was broken by an overhanging rock awning that sent a wide water wall gushing over into a pool before a grotto under the rocks.

All of the boats pulled onto a spit opposite the Falls. Scores of spent boatmen sprawled over the rocks. Other boatmen offered the tourists a chance to go under the falls on a bamboo raft that had pull ropes tied to two fixed locations. The raft was pulled back and forth under the falls. The tourists paid an additional amount for this added ride.

Philip and Binky paid the fee, and the raft slowly traversed under the waterfall into the pool behind it. As soon as they got under the waterfall, Philip felt overwhelmed by the water and the thick mist. He found himself gasping for air. He had to place himself face down on the raft to get any air at all. He felt like he was drowning. It was his claustrophobia, and the terror of the water smothering him that made him react in that way. When they got under the falls into the pool, he could catch a few gasps of air, but the experience completely unnerved him.

When they were back on dry land, he was very grateful. Binky reported that he did not have any difficulty, but Philip realized that he'd have to avoid situations that approximated what he had just gone through. One Chinese woman, who had had a similar experience, was on the ground gasping for air while her family ministered to her. *Ah, the pleasures of touristing*, Philip thought.

The downstream trip was exhilarating as they were shooting the rapids. Both boatmen were carefully guiding the boat around rocks that poked above the water as well as treacherous underwater shale. The boatmen had made the trip so many times they knew the river's hazards. Binky roared with pleasure as they shot over one high spot and splashed into the downspout.

Soon they were going through the monkey gorge. Joe was looking up at the steep walls. He couldn't hear the shrieking of the monkeys. Perry reported all clear when they were out of danger. Binky said, "They are probably up to some monkey business elsewhere. Perhaps they've shot their load, their coconut load, for the day."

Philip complained, "Your American trips, and your gay friends there, have filled you too full of Americanisms."

When they had shot the last of the rapids, their boat joined other boats at a river clearing which had a few napa huts and some locals tending a barbecue fire. Under Joe's directions, Binky bought four orders of barbecue chicken and four bottles of San Miguel beer. They sat at rough picnic benches and enjoyed the meat and beer. To Philip and Binky, it was a delicious treat.

A group of brown, scrawny, spavined dogs were working

the picnic tables. People were throwing them chicken, bones and all. Philip had been taught that feeding sharp, brittle chicken bones to dogs was a no-no. But apparently these dogs had been eating them all their lives. "I would hate to see their intestines," he said. These dogs were mongrels; dogs were eaten here; it was just one more hint to Philip that this country had other priorities than did Britain.

Binky downed a second beer and said, "Actually, it makes quite a delightful day." Philip thought that outsiders would never know from looking at them that Binky and Joe had been sex partners the previous night. And what difference did it make anyway? Philip's emergence from his English closet was progressing apace.

After the chicken and beer stop, their boat again became part of a daisy chain and was towed back to the Lodge by a motorized barca. Other boat chains were returning to other resorts, to a government staging point, and to the pier at the Rapids Hotel past the plaza of the downtown. It was a busy river because, after all, the Falls were one of the Philippines' leading tourist attractions.

19

Philip and Binky were exhausted after their trip to the Falls. As Philip started up the path to the Coco rooms, Binky amazed him by confronting Wendell and inviting him back to his room. On his deathbed he would be reaching out for a sex partner. As they approached the row of the three screened porches of the Coco cottages, they caught a quick glimpse of Craig in his lime playsuit ushering Two-Time George into his room.

Binky laughed, "Horny blighter, I'd reckon." Philip looked in wonder at his companion who was bringing back Wendell. *It takes one to know one,* he thought.

While Binky was entertaining Wendell in his room and adding to Wendell's earnings as a lifeguard cum porter, Philip went to the pool to cool off and relax. A beaming Carlitos was there by the poolside to greet him. He had made a lei of the delicate ilong-ilong flowers that grew near the poolside. They had a wonderfully buoyant perfume. Carlitos presented the lei to Philip. Philip bowed and thanked him.

"Princess Di would love this, Carlitos. Thank you, kind sir."

He entered the pool wearing the lei. It would not get too wet because Philip was planning on just lazing and lolling in the cool water. A gang of the midgets were playing tag and squirting water by the ladder. The boys dove and made loud bubbling noises like seals as they broke the surface.

He propelled himself away from the crowd, floated gently under the bridge, and ended up near the picnic shed end of the pool where he could just relax by himself. He noticed that the plant known as the wandering Jew grew in profusion along the bank at this part of the pool. Orange bougainvillea vines dipped in the pool near him.

The pervasive fragrance of the ilong-ilong flowers was very pleasant. Carlitos at least played the romantic, but he wasn't quite his type. For some reason Carlitos was never forward about sex.

Near the pool, two men were gathering Santol fruit. Inside it was white and grape-like, similar to lichee.

Huge fronds, fan-like, jutted over the pool while big coconut palms rose above, with ball root structures growing out over the edge of the pool into an enormous mass.

A teenager on the bridge, probably sixteen or seventeen, was showing off his new pair of silky, shiny basketball shorts. He half sat, half leaned on the bridge railing. When he was eighteen, he'd probably join the ranks of boatmen. He had the legs for it. A cat, crossing the bridge slowly, quite regally, paid no heed to the teen, to the water below, or to the pygmies thrashing around; he had his own rounds to make and was not to be deterred by mere human beings. His prey was probably the army of geckos that swarmed around the grounds.

Philip was getting used to the rhythm of the Lodge. It was pleasant to bathe in the pool, to laze around; it was a tranquil life; one fraught with sexual innuendo and sexual opportunity.

There were innumerable intrigues, assignations, encounters, rendezvous and meetings. To many, this was paradise. Unlimited sex, easy, willing companions, young men who would sleep with you, cuddle with you.

It was pleasant, but yet it wasn't quite his scene—not for any extended period of time anyway. Many of the seekers lived here for months. To Philip, it was too much, and penny pincher that he was, it seemed expensive, even though it wasn't. Did Philip need the pretensions of culture, the pretense of purposeful living? Was he hypocritical about his sexual desires? He had a donnish desire to look and act as if he were out learning things, an academic's curiosity, but wasn't all that just pretense and a phony, face-saving stance? *Hey, Philip, old boy, why don't you kick up your heels and get with it. Look at Binky and Craig. They know why they are here and don't make any bones about it. Who are you trying to kid?*

Coconut Joe appeared on the bridge. The teenager had gone. Joe smiled down on him. He was shirtless and wore a Speedo, not the shorts worn during their trip up to the Falls. The helmet had disappeared. He smiled down at Philip. *God, he had a beautiful body. His upper body was well muscled, but not in any way overdone. His legs were magnificent. Those beautifully formed calves and thighs. That crotch bulge through the Speedo! Those classic, handsome Chinese features.*

Joe seemed to raise his eyebrows, widen his eyes, and tilt his head. Then a big smile. A big nod. *Could he mean? After all that toil, could he be up for it? Could he be meaning . . .?*

Joe nodded again. Then looked questioningly at Philip. He perhaps thought, *Am I dealing with a eunuch here or what?* Then Philip nodded, very emphatically. Joe smiled and gestured with his head in the direction of Philip's room. Philip practically shot out of the water exiting by the picnic table end of the pool closer to his room. His lei fell off as he hurried toward the room. When he got there, Joe was leaning against the screen door. Philip pulled his key from his bathing shorts pocket, unlocked the door, and the two entered. There was no life visible in Cocos Two and Three, thank God.

Inside, Joe quickly stripped off his Speedo. He was even more magnificent in the nude. Apparently, the river trip had invigorated him, as he had an erection. Joe tugged Philip's bathing trunks down as they kissed. They went into the shower together where they spent considerable time lathering each other up. At one point, Joe knelt and enveloped Philip's hard dick in his mouth.

Later, they dried each other off and were soon on the bed in a deep embrace. Philip felt as if he'd died and gone to heaven. *This beautiful man with this splendid body making love to me.*

It was late afternoon when Philip and Joe left the room. From Binky's porch came his friend's voice, "Cheers, Philip, good show. Hello, Joe. Thank you for that boat ride. It was an experience I shall never forget. Wouldn't you agree, Philip, that Joe has on this day provided us with an unforgettable experience?"

Philip said, "Yes, thank you, for all you have done."

From Coco Three came the resonating voice of Craig, "Yes, Philip, sometimes ice-breakers can be quite exciting." Philip looked over and saw that Craig had changed into a pink playsuit identical to his lime one.

Philip went back into the room for a well-needed nap. Hours later, when he weaved his way, still tired, over to the top restaurant level, he joined Binky and Craig, who was still in his pink playsuit. Philip wondered whether he was a fool, a joker, or both. Craig announced that before they went to dinner, he would change into something more conventional. That night, they had decided to eat in the Rapids Hotel. Binky and Philip had bad sunburns on their heads. They hadn't realized how much they would come in contact with the sun's rays on their trip to the Falls. Philip felt quite marvelous after his lovemaking episode with Joe and sipped his g-and-t while the other two babbled on.

Craig told about his adventures in the Eros movie theater in Manila. The place was notorious. He would go there in the afternoon, leaving his wallet and other valuables at home, carrying only a few peso notes with him. He would take a seat by himself in a isolated section of the balcony, and would soon be joined by a young man. Craig said these young men were always attractive, but it was difficult to make out their exact ages or features in the movie darkness.

The young man would help him remove all his clothing. The man, like a valet, would fold and pile these neatly on an empty seat. Then he would begin by sucking Craig's toes and feet, and gradually work up his body until he had licked, sucked, and lapped every part of him, until he ended with his penis and testicles. He would suck these to a fare thee well. The sex act would be consummated. The stranger would redress Craig, Craig would give him a few pesos, and leave the theater fully satisfied.

Philip thought parts of the story to be apocryphal, but

laughed heartily and said nothing to indicate that he thought it to be fanciful. How all this could be managed in the tight confines of theater seating, and why a grown man would take off all of his clothing in a public place was beyond his comprehension. Philip found the whole thing silly, and it certainly wasn't something he would engage in or enjoy. Craig also recounted the story of the heavenly blow job he had received years before from an eighty-year-old man in a Wall Street sauna.

They were in the middle of rather boozy remembrances when the March Hare, the Mad Hatter, and Monty Woolley showed up. They were at the Lodge for a two-night stay. Woolley had a net for collecting butterfly specimens for his research. Around the pool, there were scores of different types of butterflies. The Hatter was wearing his trademark hat and a cardigan, which Philip couldn't imagine in such a warm climate. All three seemed dressed more for a European city in spring or autumn than for a tropical resort. They talked with them for a few minutes, then the trio flitted away toward the pool. Craig knew the Hatter and Hare slightly from their frequent Manila forays and called them Frick and Frack.

That night, Philip, Binky, and Craig took a tricycle downtown past the Dura Fe Restaurant to the Rapids Hotel on the river side of the main village street. The Rapids had one large building set in the middle of a large sumptuous garden with walks and hammocks for relaxing. It was a much smaller property than the Lodge. The management did not allow locals upstairs in the rooms, and it wasn't a whorehouse as the Lodge essentially was. Seekers did not frequent it except for an occasional meal or drink. The hotel had a staging area on the riverbank from which a number of barcas left with daytrippers, but boatmen were not allowed above this river staging area.

The hotel did accommodate some straight overnight visitors. It had a bar and restaurant with a somewhat Westernized menu. The Rapids was the best there was in

Pagsanjan, but the food was still only passable. It had mainly Filipino dishes, but it did offer some variety from the Dura Fe's simple, unchanging menu. The three had a clam soup that contained the smallest clam shells Philip had ever seen. In fact, he had never been served chowder with shells in it, either big or small. They ordered steaks which were edible but not in the least noteworthy.

After dinner the three walked to the plaza. Binky was hot for the Sawali beer hall, but Craig and Philip, essentially not bar people, opted out and returned to the Lodge in a tricycle. They decided to sit in the Upper restaurant terrace near the railing. As they drank their San Miguels, they looked out on the river.

Bugs flew into and around the fluorescent lights on the ceiling but were not that bothersome. Philip counted nineteen lizards on the ceiling, geckos and bigger ones. They'd make quick dashes in one direction, then reverse course and head off somewhere else. A few bats detached themselves from the ceiling and flew out over the river hunting mosquitoes. Out on the river, they could see flashlights. Some people were out there fishing in the darkness. Whistle signals could be heard in the darkness. The moon shone brightly behind the palm trees.

Philip was relaxed, ruminative. "It really is an idyllic place in many ways. Such a relief from London." Philip explained to Craig his MI6 torture and outing. Of course he would never divulge any intelligence secrets with his friends.

Craig was an Anglophile and pressed Philip about British titles and the decorations he had been awarded. He would be thrilled to have a series of initials after his name.

After a few more beers, they headed back to the Coco units. The paths at night were barely lit. A few dim lights were around the pool, and then a brighter light shone over the three Cocos. They said good night. Philip decided to sit outside on his screened porch for a while before retiring. If he still smoked a pipe, this would have been the time he'd light up and relax.

After his exhausting day, Philip had almost nodded off when he heard a light scratching on the screening. He looked up and saw no one. Then he looked down. It was one of the babies, a kid of around five or six, he thought. Behind him in the semi-darkness, two others of the same age hovered. A tiny voice implored, "Sir, please, move my bowels?" Another in a tiny whisper, "Can I take a shower?"

Philip said, "No, no, go away. Go home. Go!"

Another little one from the darkness said plaintively, "Philip." He was appalled one of these babies knew his name.

"Go home. Now. Go away."

The lead boy looked very sorrowful. His face pouted as if he were about to cry. "Please, shower." From the darkness a small voice, "Shower, please."

"Go away. Now!"

The boys backed off, but only as far as a bush where he could see them eyeing him in the darkness, testing his resolve.

Philip was shivering, whether from the sunburn or the shock of this dark encounter, he didn't know. Should he give them some pesos? No, definitely not. He rose, trying to avoid their eyes, and sought refuge inside the cottage. He stood with his back against the door shaking. Even though he had not yet changed for bed, he turned out his room light.

This was how easy it could be, he thought, *if one slipped . . .*

The walls of his room were over ten feet high. At the top of the left wall was a narrow opening. From it he could hear the noise from the shower in the alcove next door. He heard the water running. Childish talking, whispering. Very faintly he heard a call, "Pirrip?"

He lay down on his bed holding his hands to his ears. He remained that way for several minutes. When he removed his hands, he could not hear any noise from next door. Soon he fell asleep with his clothes still on. He had an uneasy sleep with disconcerting dreams that exhausted him further. He was sweating as he slept on top of the bed coverings.

20

The next morning, Philip was up before the others. He took his customary table in the restaurant and looked out at the river coming to life. A short-lived but fierce tropical rain exploded, and Philip watched as water gushed down from the roof. He watched the river surface roiling under the downpour. The rain fit his mental state. Last night had scared him, appalled him. Some things were too blatant here for him. He sensed a danger and a menace that was too much for him to handle. Was it a dangerous temptation?

Yes, he decided, in the future he would come to Pagsanjan for short stays, but he did not want to be here for long blocks of time. One could fall into a trap here, an abyss. Abundant, pleasurable sex was wonderful, but also people here were toying with . . . no, toying with was too weak a phrase, too non-judgmental. People here were sinning and desecrating. But he also knew he would return to Manila in future years.

Binky and Craig were approaching the table. Craig was festooned in a baby blue playsuit, the last of his three bespoke creations.

Philip asked Binky, "What do you have planned for today?"

Binky said, "Diddling in the pool and doing a few auditions. The lad I brought home from the Sawali last night may even do a repeat performance."

Craig was content to laze in the pool and bring the occasional boatman or teen to his room.

Later when Philip, his eyes closed, was floating around in the pool on his own, his mind raced back to the night before. Tiny plaintive voices in the darkness. "Philip." "Move my bowels." "Shower." Pleading, anxious faces. Little babies. Children. In bed, holding his hands over his ears. Fear. Temptations. The closeness of danger. What might be done out of pity could turn into a horrible legacy. He opened his eyes to stop the flood of scathing memories. Better not to think about the horrors of last night.

Before dinner, Philip was sitting in his screened-in porch. Binky emerged from his cottage. Philip asked, "How did your afternoon and last evening go?"

"Same as always. One reciprocal in the morning, a perfectly gorgeous one for siesta time, and last night that unusually fine specimen that I brought home from the Sawali."

Within minutes, Craig was out his door, this time in the lime playsuit. He greeted them with, "Tonight I'm going up on the Japanese hill to see the full moon. Do you gentlemen care to accompany me?"

Philip considered it a typical Craigian affectational foray.

Both very quickly said they were not interested. Craig went on, "I'll be leaving tomorrow. My sojourn here in the Garden of Eden has gone on long enough, but I do hope you'll be able to join me for dinner in Manila. I would like to see you two again."

Philip did want to continue the friendship, as did Binky, so they agreed Craig would call them at their hotel, and they would join him at his apartment for dinner.

Craig inquired, "When are you two returning to Manila?"

Philip looked over at Binky, who spoke for both of them. "A day or two longer. We're going to play it by ear, but I should think it wouldn't be more than a few days." Philip readily agreed.

Curious, Philip asked Craig about pedophilia in the Philippines.

Craig began, "As in all human activities, refinements are made over time. Those foreign individuals who preferred teenage males found there was a ready supply in the Philippines. And then unfortunately the pedophiles showed up, and they preferred ones as young as five up to the early teens. The economic conditions being what they are, a supply of these kids became available often with the parents' complicity.

I fear economic need and necessity drive the situation."

Binky interjected, "Here, living in this village and among a group of johns or seekers the abnormal can seem to be the norm"

Craig continued, "We have to face it. Pedophilia is a horrible crime. A sin, perhaps the most pernicious crime of them all. Many of these men have no conscience left if they ever had one.

"They are living in the Philippines in a vacuum, a cocoon, where the norms, the rules of a moral society don't apply or have been set aside because of economic necessity. The morality of their home countries was left at home. These men have their own codes.

"Listen to their rationalizations: 'These kids would starve, have nothing without us.' 'Many of these kids get no love because of their big families. We give them love, comfort, security, sustenance.' They are fools of their own making. They lie to themselves and, unfortunately, they reinforce each other. Many of them come here, meet other pedophiles, and pedophilia becomes the norm.

"It is of little use to talk to these men; they have all sorts of justifications for their behavior. They are in a world of their own, have erected defense mechanisms. I would say they are in a state of perpetual denial. They sincerely think love is involved. 'They love me. I'm like a father to them. They care about me.' That can be true of younger ones, but those kids would care for anyone who cared about them, paid attention to them.

"Does it scar these kids for life? Probably not in the least. But would they survive without these patrons? Yes. The motto should be 'Do no harm.' Aberrant behavior toward young children can't be condoned.

"In fact, in this country, there is little finger pointing. It is not stopped by government, the police, the families, or the Church. There is no real serious social pressure to end such practices. The forbidden fruit is plucked here so far with impunity.

"Parents don't realize or don't want to know what is going

on. Some of the fathers and brothers were brought up with older patrons when they were very young, and to them it is a natural world. Some claim they have benefited from it. They received attention, which was absent at home because of the big families. Some have no objections. Need and want wipe away a lot of moral niceties and scruples.

"Well, that's enough lecturing on my part. Now I'm going up to the Japanese hill to view the moon. Since you gentlemen don't want to go, I'm going on my own."

Craig left. After a short time, Binky and Philip walked over to the restaurant and ordered beers, which they sipped while watching the life on the river and on the opposite shore.

21

The next day, after a second breakfast in the Lodge restaurant with Binky, Philip watched as a day at the Lodge unfolded. In the morning between ten and eleven, a large number of tour buses arrived. Bus loads of people from Taiwan, Hong Kong, Japan, Singapore, Australia, and occasional stray Americans and Europeans descended on the Lodge. A few tourists had hired a cab in Manila for the long trek to the Falls.

As Binky and Philip sat at the table, Philip looked at the river. It was often a lime color, but it could be brown depending upon how much rain had fallen, how much sediment had been stirred up. A sudden torrent of rain exploded. The strings of rain drops, like beads on a necklace, came down from the roof of the terrace. The water lapped further up the riverbank, and some of the barcas on racks were soon under water.

The river surface was completely dotted with the huge drops that roiled the surface. Boats went by, the boatmen paddling fast, their heads bent over to shun the rain. The leaves near the balcony were sodden and drooped heavily. On the restaurant terrace, some Chinese women tourists continued their mahjong game, loudly clashing the tiles and shouting and laughing. The radio blared, and the tables were full of tourists eating lunches or breakfasts.

Occasionally, one or two tourists would go to the balcony terrace railing and take a picture of the deluge on the river. One trough over the roof gushed water, sending a solid stream of water falling down the bank below. A motorboat chugged by, towing a string of boats with soaked passengers and boatmen.

Binky took a walk over by the railing to watch the rain and cruise a young male Chinese tourist. While Philip was sitting at the table, enjoying another cup of tea, Carlitos, the chess player and Princess Di devotee, came over and asked if he could sit with him. Philip assented readily and ordered a Coca Cola for the boy.

Carlitos said, "We've been studying haiku in school. I wrote two for you. Would you please read them and tell me what you think of them?"

He opened his composition book with the marbled cover. Philip read the poems which were meticulously printed.

The coconut palm
Stately trunk piercing the sky
High fronds; a star burst.

The gray carabao
Body deep in the river
Only his head gleams.

He turned to Carlitos. "These are really quite wonderful. You are writing about what you know and what you have seen and experienced. Would you make me a copy of them and sign your name and the date? I have a feeling some day you will be famous. Thank you for showing them to me."

A thrilled Carlitos laboriously made the copies and presented them to Philip. Binky returned, and Carlitos excused himself. Binky shook his head and said, "I think that lad is wary of me. Afraid I might try to bed him."

Craig arrived with his bag and said his goodbyes. After a time, Philip left Binky so he could take a dip in the pool. He changed into his bathing suit and went in the pool. As he floated listlessly, Philip knew he would talk Binky into leaving for Manila in a few days. They had never planned on staying too long.

Sunlight flitted through the branches. He caught quick views of brown bare skin passing through the property. The room boys' feet in their flip flops were slapping the walkways as they scurried back and forth doing their chores, cleaning the rooms. In the neighborhood, cocks were crowing, and it was the time of day when cats explored the grounds without too much interference. Two brown mongrel dogs walked around the pool perimeter to check out the area, being sure to avoid the cats as they did so.

Philip could hear a local boy talking to a foreigner on one of the paths. The boy said, "I go now." The foreigner said something, and in typical Filipino fashion, the boy said, "It's up to you." It seemed as if they were always agreeable, acquiescent and compliant—a Filipino trait, Philip thought.

Later, when Philip was sitting on one of the cement benches on the walkway above the pool, he was joined by a small, sturdy looking man in his early sixties who was chaperoning a half-dozen or so of the very young kids who were cavorting in the pool. The man introduced himself as Mac, a fellow Scot with a heavy burr to his speech.

He had worked for UNICEF, which Philip found ironic and disturbing at the same time, though he said nothing to Mac, who seemed anxious to tell his story. Mac liked boys from five to eight, children who came in clusters. Sometimes when he was in Pagsanjan, he'd have as many as eight of them sleeping in his room, cuddling together with him and each other in his bed, in chairs, on the floor, and on the porch. He cooked food for them, dribbled out tiny amounts for spending money. They helped support their families with his small handouts.

He pointed out Otto, the German from Hamburg, who had his group of kids from ten to thirteen or so. Mac said that when Otto's kids started to grow pubic hair and hair under the arms, he would gently ease them out of his family. Miguel was still teetering at the edges of Otto's family. Mac offered, "He'll probably have to get himself some regular johns in his progression up the sex ladder to that of the handsome boatman. These are essentially family units."

Mac said, "The Swiss gent named Peter likes them from thirteen through seventeen. The American Craig likes them from seventeen up through their twenties. There's two Italian restaurant owners who like the bigger, muscular types."

Philip was discovering the strata in the gay life there.

Later, Philip and Binky spent the day lazing in and around the pool. Binky found a new boatman to his liking and took him back to Coco Two for an interlude. Philip looked for Coconut Joe but in vain.

Philip stood alone on the promontory thinking. He preferred his own apartment and the routine of Manila where he could at least pretend to be more of a sightseer, enjoying the occasional fairly good restaurant. In Manila, he could participate in some semi-cultural events.

Pagsanjan was too commercial for his tastes; there was too much doling out of pesos directly for sex. He preferred the young men who wanted to be treated to dinner; who didn't ask for or seem to be in it for the cash. He didn't like to dispense money. That was too crass, too demeaning. He wanted young men who went with him because they liked *him*.

Besides, the amount of sex in Pagsanjan was beyond his capacity. He was not as sex-driven as all that. Horny sometimes, yes, but not sex-addicted like Binky. Basically he wanted a steady, a boyfriend, a companion, not a partner for an hour. One you could control—no *control* was too strong a word—one that you could direct, a young man who was your constant companion. Perhaps motivate the young man to seek more education, and you could through your knowledge impart some enlightenment to the young man. He was in essence sentimental, but there are some that would say he was only deceiving himself. Binky thought all that separated Philip and himself was some reticence on Philip's part and an ability to mask his natural impulses.

Philip, therefore, decided his future trips to Pagsanjan would be infrequent; this would separate him from some of the lechers that abided there. Deep down, too, the Scotsman in him found Pagsanjan a little expensive if one doled out too much largesse.

Then, too, Philip had noticed the Lodge had very lax security. It was so full of young men, strangers, almost anyone could wander in. They could just walk in the entrance, come up from the shore of the river, by boat, or come over the wall. One flirted with a certain amount of danger here, but the same could be said about Manila. Jeepney muggings often took place in the capital.

That night, Philip and Binky took a walk downtown to the plaza. The road and hill leading down from the Lodge reminded them of Bali's eerie black roads at night, with virtually no lights. A number of people walked along the road; some guys gathered in small groups, lit by the flickering light of matches or lighters, the glow of cigarettes in the dark, tiny patches of light as they went by. Creepy. Up the hill came the occasional jeepney or tricycle, shouts asking them if they wanted a ride.

They passed the coconut mill where charcoal was made, the tiny stores, the open air butcher shop, the streets leading down into the barongs where the life they were not privy to went on, where children played, and where some women gave them unfriendly and sullen stares.

They had dinner at the Dura Fe where the scene was much the same as before. Big tables of little ones with some Westerner or two serving as mother hen, and all of the other age groups represented. They looked around. Again they were the only older men without dates. From there they went to the Sawali.

Later that night, as Philip sat alone sipping a beer at the Lodge restaurant, he saw bursts of lightning streak above the river shore in the tropical sky. Across the river, torchlight erupted from the darkness as two men brought a carabao down the steep bank to the shore. Philip had experienced the Pagsanjan passage; it was now time to move on.

22

Philip and Binky left Pagsanjan two days after Craig had departed. They had been back in Manila only a day when Philip received a call from Craig inviting him and Binky to lunch at his apartment. A date was set for the next day since Binky would soon be leaving for sexual exploits elsewhere. Craig gave Philip directions. The apartment was off Adriatico Avenue within walking distance.

The next day, they started out with a walk down Mabini. A block away from Craig's street, they passed one street that had an enormous mountain of garbage and rubbish, about ten feet high and a block long. It had been piled there very neatly. It was quite pungent and must have been a feast for rats, maggots and other vermin.

Binky said, "Let us hope this is only a temporary measure. It wouldn't be par for London unless there was some awful binmen's strike."

Philip shook his head. "I could never see that sight every day. Of late, I've been complaining about how dirty London has become, but nothing as ugly and devastating as this."

Craig's apartment was in the first floor of a three-story building surrounded by a wrought iron fence. It looked like a big house that had been converted into a series of apartments. Craig met them at the door and ushered them into a tiny foyer. He was soon joined by a Filipino in his late twenties, a sturdy, rather good-looking young man wearing glasses. He was polite and welcoming, more down to earth, a good contrast to Craig's occasional pomposity. Craig was full of himself and self-satisfied; this guy was unassuming and nice.

Craig introduced him. "This is Oliver, my roommate."

He led them into the small living room where two men were seated on the couch. They both stood when the newcomers arrived. Craig said, "These are two of my American friends. I met them at the Lodge last year. They come here almost every year and spend six weeks or so in the Philippines, much of the time in Pagsanjan."

The taller man, Paul Rowan, six-foot two, weighed about two-hundred pounds, but carried his weight well. He was bald on top. Paul was a handsome man with a loud, carrying, assertive voice and manner like Craig's.

The other man was Hal Turner, five foot-nine and good-looking with a full head of hair. He wore glasses and seemed to be in good shape, though he did get out of breath at times. Both men were deeply tanned. Both were in their mid-forties.

Craig filled in more details about them. "These guys have been lovers since 1956. It's 1974, so do the math. They've been together for eighteen years, but since they've been partners, they've had more sex with strangers than any two guys I know. Paul is a playwright and university teacher, and Hal teaches high school and does real estate.

"I'm warning you in advance. Be careful what you say in front of these two. Some of it is apt to turn up in print. Paul has had several plays produced, and over the years Hal has published two novels. If you see them taking notes, you may turn up in a novel or a play."

Philip and Binky took seats while Craig prepared drinks. Oliver served as a gracious waiter. He seemed to take an instant liking to Philip and treated him very attentively.

When they were given a tour of the apartment, the visitors found it consisted of the small living room, a small dining room, a tiny kitchen, and another small room that was Craig's bedroom with an uncomfortable-looking narrow bed. The bedroom seemed Spartan, monkish. Craig said Oliver slept on a cot in the living room, a cot he set up each night and put away in the morning. He said he and Oliver were sex partners, but this sleeping arrangement was Craig's choice. Craig lived his nighttime ascetic's life and didn't want anyone sleeping with him.

After the six men had been conversing for an hour or so,

Philip found that Paul would sometimes interrupt someone while that person was talking, at times in mid-sentence with that voice that carried just like Craig's. In a room with the two of them broadcasting, having a normal conversation was strange. Their loud voices were like those of lecturers, actors, or radio announcers.

Paul, though, was very interested in Philip's past; he listened intently, and asked searching questions. He seemed mesmerized by Philip's spy history and his cruel outing. Both he and Hal were Anglophiles and had spent considerable time in England.

Hal was quieter, seemed nice. He was a good listener; he had to be living with Paul. He was easy to get along with, polite, but took his lead from Paul.

They were on the way to Pagsanjan. They would spend up to six weeks there. This trip was unusual for them; they usually came in July and August. They didn't mind the heat or the rainy season. Some vague time in the future they intended to retire to Florida because they preferred heat to cold. Both admitted they kept extensive journals of their travels, and said that sometimes they took notes on conversations they had with people.

Binky was talking about rice queens. Neither Hal nor Paul was really a dedicated rice queen; they traveled where the sex was bountiful and reasonable. Binky said, "Rice queens have an informal but very effective network. In Asia, the available boys and young men are plentiful; they are basically 'nice guys;' prices aren't steep; and the governments and police aren't intrusive or engaged in crack-downs. The word among the ex-pats, the sex travelers, and the rice queens through their network is that Thailand is becoming increasingly commercial, becoming too overrun with sex tourists of every persuasion and nationality."

Picking up on Binky, Craig turned to Hal and Paul and said, "Especially Americans. Legend has it that when the Americans started showing up in great numbers, the place was near the end of its run. They seem to always be the last to arrive in large numbers. The prices for boys skyrocket when they are in a place in force. The Americans are too competitive and too willing to be overly generous. They spoil the boys."

Paul countered, "My dear Craig, I seem to remember that you were an American before you became entrenched over here."

Hal said, "Here in Philippines it's a problem: A boy can be anywhere from five to thirty and he is still a boy, fair game; it just depends upon which age bracket you feature. Paul and I like the hunks, anywhere from seventeen to thirty."

Oliver quipped, "Oh, so I'm still in the running. Not completely off the charts yet." Everyone laughed.

Binky bitched, "But why can't the Yanks stay within the price guidelines established by the others. They want to be overly generous, and they spoil the whole scene. Some Brits on a limited income have settled in Thailand to be near the boys; now they are being priced out of the market by the rapacious Americans."

Craig offered, "In countries overrun by sex tourists, the tricks are no longer unsophisticated about assignations. They are no longer lovable and loving. They become shrewd, grasping, greedy, and sometimes venal. Often they become dangerous. And you hear of tricks trying to roll a queer."

When Craig had finished his comments, he and Oliver excused themselves and went into the small kitchen where they readied the lunch for serving.

Binky noted, "Certain countries where the Yanks have not descended in large numbers are still viable, like Sri Lanka, Malaysia, and Indonesia."

Paul said defensively, "Don't blame Hal and me. We pay the going rate and often try to go below it if we can get away with it."

Philip, ever the peacemaker, changed the subject. "The hub Asian cities like Hong Kong and Singapore were never ripe for the sexual travelers because of their firm anti-gay stances and anti-gay laws, also because of their burgeoning economies. When the economies are good, boys go into other lines of work."

Craig announced lunch was ready, and everyone crowded into the tiny dining room. They were seated around a table with a bouquet of hibiscus blooms in the center. Craig served a white wine, a salad, and crisp baguettes. Oliver helped him and then all six sat around the table.

Craig had made a beef bourguignon and served it with goblets of red wine. It was delicious. Philip complimented Craig, "This is a great wine, and these are the most delicious carrots I have ever tasted. They are so large and yet very tender; sweet, with a rich flavor."

Craig said, "The secret is they are grown with manure, and it makes a great fertilizer full of nutrients."

The visitors complimented Craig on the lunch. He served a flan and coffee and placed a glass of cognac before each person.

After lunch, Oliver selected Philip especially and invited him to a garage behind the building to see the motorcycle Craig had bought him. He had traveled all around many of the islands on a tour with other cycle enthusiasts. They left and went outside to the garage.

Craig was finishing in the kitchen. Paul asked Binky about Philip. He was fascinated by Philip's career. Binky gave him some background information and described his terrible outing. "You've heard me with all my vulgar sex talk. That was never Philip's style. He seldom swears or uses crass expressions."

Paul said, "He has class, is a class act. I can see that."

Binky continued, "He is a polite, genteel person, a true gentleman. He'll listen and laugh at those of us who use the gay argot. He doesn't disapprove of it; he just doesn't deign to use it himself. He was never craven, bawdy, queeny, bitchy. He hadn't grown up in gay life and his predilection for Asians has thrust him further from that world. He really doesn't have street smarts even though he was in a dangerous profession. He is naïve in many ways. He has life smarts, but not the down and dirty street variety of smarts that tarnishes me at times."

Paul asked, "How did Philip happen to choose the intelligence service?"

Binky replied, "Where did the United Kingdom get its spies in the thirties and forties? From its educated classes, from the brightest at Oxford and Cambridge, especially the latter. These were the young men who could be trusted, the cream of the cream. Men who in most cases didn't know squat about the working man, who puffed their pipes, exchanged cricket esoterica, could punt on the Cam, and who looked the part of intelligence officers. But they knew languages, had traveled widely during holidays, had social contacts. It was like a movie casting agent looking for people who could look the part and play the role. To the Service recruiters, if their novices had flirted with Marxism, it was considered a petty affectation, like showing an interest in badminton."

"So Philip was an ideal recruit?" asked Paul.

"Philip had been approached for intelligence work in the late thirties. He was from an upper-middle class family, but showed great promise. He hadn't disported with Marxism. He was interested in music, history, and architecture. It was a limited choice for a university graduate; either you became a university don or you went into the government, the military or became a financier in the City.

"Philip had gone to public school. Then to University. In his case, it was Cambridge where all of the notorious moles and turncoats came from. Fags as well. That's why Philip seems donnish, professorial. Because he could have easily gone into the academic world, been a fussy old don perhaps. Philip seems like a slightly absent-minded academic.

"It is hard imagining Philip as a man of action or a man of deceit, yet he was. He was clever and never really gave away what was going on inside his mind.

"Philip was destined to become a gentleman; he would belong to a private men's club in London, not the best but a respectable one. He never made the top tier socially, but he fit in well to the middle tier; he was a devout Church of England member, a definite plus. He had made friends at public school and university with some of the country's future M.P.'s, ministerial class, and business leaders.

"He was from the right class, a good family. He could be trusted; he was discreet and intelligent. He was a minor cog in the old boy network. Had he married well, he probably would have gone very far and reached a higher status in life. Since he remained a bachelor, he dwelt in that netherworld where a wife's social position was not a step-up available to him. Some gay men of his class courted young men, which tainted their status and made them unacceptable. Since he was not openly gay, he was not hindered in that way."

Later while the others were busy, Paul jotted down some notes in his little notebook.

Philip and Oliver came back in the apartment and talk of Philip ceased. When Philip and Binky left Craig's, they had by that time had a little too much to drink so they hailed a cab to take them back to the hotel. That way, they would also avoid close contact with the mountain of garbage in the nearby street.

23

A few days later, Binky left for Australia where he had a boyfriend; in reality, a trick in Melbourne whom he saw every few years. Philip spent his time with Craig. One night, they went to Craig's favorite restaurant, a place with French cuisine run by an order of nuns. Philip was delighted when they said prayers and sang a hymn before the meal. The food and wine were excellent.

After Binky had gone, Craig often made cracks about him, disparaging remarks that annoyed Philip. He tried to ignore them, but it seemed as if Craig had launched into a campaign to drive a wedge between Philip and his long-time friend. One time when Craig had belittled Binky, Philip said, "Many people are envious of Binky because of his family lineage and his royal connections. I have never found a truer friend."

One Wednesday night, Philip and Craig had finished dinner at a noodle shop on Mabini. Though neither spent much time in bars, they decided to go to the El Sutro, the folk music club frequented by gays. It was often a pick-up place for young men, and several of Philip's friends had had good luck there.

They went in, found a vacant table and ordered beers. On stage under the floodlights, a young folksinger was rambling on with an endless monotonous off-key chant about the horrors of pollution. Craig began one of his incessant stories. Philip was paying minimal attention to him while at the same time his eyes did the gay creep well-known to gays the world over. It's the traditional way gays cruise and talk to one another simultaneously.

Philip's eyes were beginning to lock onto the figure of a young man, about nineteen years old, seated at the end of the bar. He was talking to a similarly aged friend. Every once in a while, he would glance over at Philip and smile. Philip liked the look of him: clean-cut, handsome, and lithe. His sleeveless shirt showed well-muscled arms, not overly developed, but giving the suggestion that this young man played sports, exercised, or had a job that made his arms and shoulders well-turned out.

When the singer took a short break, the eye contact intensified. Philip smiled; the boy smiled. Then the young man approached the table. He addressed Philip. Craig turned to see who was speaking.

"Hello, sirs. Are you here on vacation?"

Philip smiled warmly. "Yes, I'm here on holiday, and I live in England. What is your name?"

"Reynaldo, and yours?"

"Philip Croft. Would you care to join us?"

Closeup, Philip liked the cut of the young man even better. He was very good-looking. Quite a bit of sex appeal.

"This is my American friend, Craig."

Craig grunted acknowledgement. Reynaldo soon joined them with his half finished bottle of San Miguel beer. He sat close to Philip.

He told them about himself. "I'm from the island of Cebu to the south. I am a student at the university. I play football and I do gymnastics."

Craig thought, *They all say they go to the university or some school. They all play football.*

While he saw how handsome and sexy the lad was, Philip, who had been trained to be guarded and skeptical, forgot all the professional training when his libido entered the equation.

Reynaldo soon became Rey. One thing led to another, and Philip invited the young lad back to his quarters. He left Craig sitting there. People just didn't abandon Craig in that manner; he was not pleased.

Later, Philip was in his room with Reynaldo, who had removed his shirt and trainers. He soon stripped to his bikini briefs. He did a graceful cartwheel, executed a perfectly balanced handstand, and did a back flip from which he landed lightly on his soles. Philip admired the boy's physique, his graceful movements, the way Rey put him at ease.

Philip removed all of his own clothes except his drawers. Reynaldo slowly slipped his own briefs down exposing the white untanned portion of his body, his clump of black pubic hair and his well-formed penis and testicles. Philip was entranced, besotted, and his own penis became richly engorged and erect. He pulled off his drawers. Reynaldo smiled, leaned over and kissed him on the lips, lightly, tenderly. Philip was ga-ga with delight.

They were soon rolling around on the bed. Reynaldo kissed Philip and then started a tongue trip down the older man's body, giving sensation to the neck, both nipples, the chest, the stomach, the loins, the balls. He lightly slipped Philip's penis into his mouth. It was not a wholehearted acceptance of the penis. His mouth had a very light touch with as few parts of Reynaldo's mouth making contact with the penis as possible.

An overcritical Craig might say these moves were the clever moves of an experienced straight man who had learned the techniques that brought pleasure to his sex partners while maintaining as much "straightness" as possible. A crass Craig would even say he was merely servicing clients or customers. An uncritical Philip was over the moon however. *This boy was magnificent. So giving. So loving.*

Philip was soon providing the boy with oral sex. Reynaldo did some oohing and ahhing, and occasionally his belly would undulate in a suggestive fashion. After the boy ejaculated forcefully and satisfactorily, he stood and let Philip admire his body.

Philip was thrilled when the boy did a handstand using only one hand. From time to time he would manipulate Philip's penis with his hand. He kissed Philip and gave Philip's mouth an incredible long tongue job, while his right hand jerked Philip off. Philip shot his load onto the bed spread.

Reynaldo agreed to stay the night. He slept soundly; Philip rested his own head on his raised forearm and watched the boy for a long time. This was heaven—to be with a lad that was so giving, so sexy, so limber, such a beauty.

The next morning, Philip brought his new conquest to breakfast at the corner coffee shop. The boy ate heartily. He told Philip he was a good cook, and that he'd like to cook for him. Sports City in the Makati section was having a giant sale on Nike trainers. Could they go over there and could he get a new pair? "Of course. And I'll buy them for you as a gift," said Philip, for which he received a sexy little squeeze on the thigh from Rey.

After shopping for the trainers, which Philip thought carried a rather steep tariff, they went grocery shopping. Rey, as Philip now called him, bought plenty of fresh ingredients. That night, Rey prepared a meal of meat, vegetables, and rice that Philip found very tasty and nourishing. And it was a lot cheaper than bringing the chap to a restaurant. *By God, he's saving me money.* Again, Rey stayed for the night, and Philip was delighted.

Rey could form the widest halo with his mouth, position it above Philip's erect penis, and then lower his head so that the mouth engulfed the male organ, and do all this barely touching any of the penis. Rey's lips would close lightly, chastely. Philip could feel Rey's breath and was agog.

Craig would have called it the straight man's faux blow job, a feat in itself, how to give a blow job without any suction being applied. Craig was a man who demanded the real thing, a vacuum cleaner, lots of suction, lots of slurping noises. Craig was a skeptic, a nitpicker. Philip was a Don Quixote to Craig's Sancho Panza.

Soon Rey was spending most of his days and nights with Philip. They ate together, slept together, lived together. Philip could enjoy his scotch or beer at home without having to go out for company. Rey did back flips, cartwheels, handstands, headstands, even could undulate his belly like the male strippers in Manila's bars.

Philip and Rey would take strolls through Rizal Park. Usually, Rey wore brief shorts and an athletic shirt. On the grass, he did his handstands, cartwheels, gymnastic stunts. He liked to show off. He would balance and twirl a soccer ball on his finger, anything to impress Philip, who was delighted by his physical prowess.

Rey always seemed to have errands to run, and he needed money for things. He had to pay this month's tuition. He needed new textbooks. He had to send money home to his ailing mother. The amounts weren't that large, and after all he was Philip's constant companion. Sometimes his errands would take him to the other part of town, and his trips would take hours. Philip was grateful because this gave him time to read and write letters to his growing circle of friends throughout the world.

One night, he and Rey were in the Lifebuoy sidewalk café together. An artist with a large portfolio of drawings and paintings introduced himself. He was from Baguio, the summer capital. Philip looked over his work. The man had real talent. There was a nude drawing of a boy that was naturalistic, detailed, and lifelike. Philip asked Rey if he would be willing to pose in the nude for this man. He readily agreed. Philip told him he wanted a portrait of him that he could bring back to London. Philip agreed on a price, and the artist was commissioned to do an oil of Rey.

Rey said, "Will I be paid to model and pose?"

Philip hesitated for a moment, but Eros won out over the Scot in him.

"Yes, of course, silly," he muttered.

The portrait took three long afternoons. Philip sat on the couch while the artist worked at his easel. Rey stood by the window in the nude. He was patient and liked the idea, wondering if he could be a model for other artists. Philip was proud of Rey, the model, and he admired the way Rey stood and posed. It made him horny seeing Rey nude with another person in the room.

When the painting was finished, Philip was delighted with

the results. This would go into his bedroom in Sagnes Close. He thought the artist had drawn the penis larger than life, but that delighted Philip even more.

When Binky showed up in Manila for a short stay on his way back to Britain, Philip showed him the painting and described Rey glowingly. "Reynaldo has become my steady while I've been in Manila. I call him Rey. He is a genuine athlete. Does cartwheels with ease. He's a gymnast, football player. He has a beautiful body."

Binky realized his friend was besotted. Philip later introduced Binky to Rey, and made it clear that he was special, not someone to be shared. "Not at all a communal feast, thank you." Binky and Rey hit it off. Rey would listen and laugh while Binky would talk dirty and describe the coarser details of gay life.

Philip offered to take Rey for a weekend to Pagsanjan, but Rey made it clear that he did not like it there. Craig thought, though he didn't say it to Philip, that Rey wouldn't like the competition there. Rey had little to fear. Philip was in love with the Filipino and would not have strayed from the reservation.

From Rey, he learned a few words of Tagalog. He also discerned a Filipino habit. When he asked Rey if he wanted to do something, Rey would answer, "How about you?" or "It's up to you." He had a tendency to defer to Philip in most things except when Sports City had just received new Reeboks, Nikes or Pumas.

24

Six weeks after his meeting with Rey, it was time for Philip to return to Britain. There were sad goodbyes between Philip and Rey. Philip promised he would stay in touch, that he would return in the fall. Philip said his goodbyes to Craig, who was talking about returning to the States for good. He said he had tired of the Philippines and had been away from the States too long.

When Philip left for England, he had the rolled-up canvas portrait of Reynaldo with him as carry-on. No one in customs bothered to look at it. When he got back to Sagnes Close, he had it framed and hung it up opposite his bed in his small bedroom.

Philip had been back from his Asian sojourn for two weeks. He was just getting used to London as a man of leisure. On Wednesday night of the second week back, he decided to go to the bi-monthly meeting of the Long Yang Club. The dive bar club Chaps was packed. Two young Asian men beamed and gave him the eye as he came down the steps. The social had the usual blend of two Asian men for every Caucasian.

Some of the Asian men were rejected out of hand by Philip; they were too long in the tooth for his tastes. He had found that some of them, particularly the Japanese, tried to use to their advantage the fact that it was difficult to figure out the age of many Asians. They could be anywhere from the mid-twenties to the forties. But Philip was always excited by that bloom of youth he could always discern. When he saw a man for whom he couldn't assign an age, it invariably meant he was older than he looked.

Through the haze of smoke in the club, Philip heard a voice calling out to him. It belonged to Archie Westerfield, a chubby man about five-foot seven, just turned fifty. He was wearing a very loud, checkered sport coat. Philip always thought he looked like the movie star Bob Hoskins.

"Phil, Phil, for God's sake, I've been looking for you for months. What the hell have you been up to? I heard you were off chasing wogs in paradise. Come over here with me, and I'll get you a gin and tonic."

Archie ushered him to a small table wedged into a corner. He pulled up a chair for Philip, hailed a waiter, and ordered a drink for his guest. Philip sat opposite him, looking at his friend, a man with a big head framed with gray hair, big scraggly eyebrows and hair creeping out of his ears.

Philip told him about the high spots of his trip and mentioned a few of his conquests, dwelling in more detail on the Philippines and his affair with Rey.

"You rascal you. You certainly know how to make full use of your retirement. Making up for lost time, eh?"

They continued talking about their mutual interest, the cultivation of Asian friends. Years ago they had met in Bangkok. They had sometimes swapped casual Asian chums. Each liked the other as a friend because one or the other would meet a young man and then put the other onto the lad. Then Archie began a fateful conversation that was to change the course of Philip's genteel London life and alter his reputation.

"I thought of you a few months ago and knew you were the man for me."

Archie had been for many years a car salesman selling Morris Minors. He went on. "I have a plan that you might be interested in. A small gay sauna in Soho has gone belly up. It's for sale. It's quite reasonable. A five-year lease at good terms. On Wardour Street right in the heart of the action."

Philip laughed and said, "Surely you're not suggesting that you and I go into business together running a gay sauna. It's laughable really. I've been to saunas on the rare occasion, but what I know about their operation would fit in the tiniest of thimbles."

"Phil, this one would be different."

No one ever called him Phil, and he wasn't pleased by the shortened, unbidden form of his name, *but, after all, Archie was a former car salesman. What could you expect from that sort?*

Westerfield explained, "Listen, all of those beautiful young Asian chaps who work in restaurants in Soho. The Asian students. The young tourists from the Far East. Parading around with or without towels. Those beautiful lithe bodies with skin like marble. Those tiny nipple beads. Think of it."

"You're laying it on a bit thick, aren't you?"

"No, I'm just stating facts."

"Why would young Asian men choose your sauna?"

"In *our* sauna, we'd give them discounts. Word of mouth advertising. We'd advertise in the Long Yang newsletter. We'd pass the word to all our friends and acquaintances. Certain nights would be free to the young lads."

"It doesn't sound like a recipe for great financial success. What about the profit motive?"

"Philip, it would make money. I promise you."

"I don't see how, when most of the customers are there free or on discount."

"But think of all the beautiful friendships we could make. Many of these lads don't mind going to a private sauna, but they are afraid to come to a club like this one."

"What about the police?"

"We'd make sure that everything was discreet. Phil, I've spent half my life in saunas. I know how they operate. If we shared the initial outlay, you'd be in the background. Wouldn't have to do the heavy lifting. I'd do all that."

"But, Archie, I was a public servant, had some degree of respectability. If my straight friends found out, I'd be a laughingstock."

"Do you really care what your straight friend think? Only the ones you wanted to would know about it. Most of your real friends are gay now anyway. Potential customers. And your government service? Don't make me laugh. After what they did to you, what you and others have told me, what do you care what they say? It would be a way of thumbing your nose at them. Really declaring where you stand sexually. You're often saying you're not going to hide it any longer. Well this would be your chance."

Philip was beginning to like the idea. But he had serious doubts. "Why did the sauna go belly up?"

"It was making a bit of a profit, but the owner played the ponies."

"Was it a completely gay sauna?"

"Yes."

"The Mercury?"

"Yes, that's the one. I can guarantee you we'd make more than a wee bit of profit from it. We wouldn't lose money, and we'd have a great deal of fun in the process. Think of it. We'd cater to Asian lads, offer them a stiff discount, ha ha, on certain days of the week. Pass around cards. Let in Asian men at half price. Sure there'd be the occasional nob who'd bring in a hustler, but we'd make sure it was well-managed and well-supervised. Not leather or rubber or any of that trash."

He and Archie talked for two hours. Archie went through all of the financial details. They were so intent on their conversation that they ignored the mating rituals going on around them.

Archie was persuasive, and in some ways, Philip was gullible and quixotic. His naïveté and unworldliness about some things was amazing in a man who had been a top spy. He was not greatly credited with street smarts by his friends. Someone had once said that he was far too trusting for his own good.

The idea of having a sauna intrigued Philip; access to young Asian men, but what he also liked best, it would be thumbing his nose at the Service and those who had crucified him—he did think of it as his crucifixion. This would be a resurrection. He'd been a stick in the mud too long.

He'd always been adventurous, always willing to take chances. That's why being a spy had appealed to him. When traveling, he often did the daring, the challenging things.

After what the Service had done to him, he wanted to break out and show his colors. He was sick of appearing to be the dull, clandestine, closeted Philip Croft. It was time to be himself. Now if asked if he was gay, he'd admit to it, no matter who it was, family or friends.

In the next few days, Archie and Philip visited the sauna with an estate agent. It was in fairly good shape. The place had recently had a facelift and was in almost move-in condition. Philip and Archie conferred for hours about the enterprise. Archie carefully went over the books with him. It was never going to be a gold mine, but what they were both hoping for was that it would be a honey pot to attract willing, able, and fetching Asian lads. Their thinking was more glandularly than economically grounded. Both were canny enough to realize they couldn't lose their shirts, but both realized there were more sure-fire ways of making a pound.

So it was that they signed the papers, and Philip became a partner in a Soho sauna. When one is ruled by the libido, red ink often follows. If one is a careful Scotsman as Philip was, the amount of red ink is carefully calculated into the equation and, therefore, any serious losses could be avoided. But for Philip, it was a good way to tweak the intelligence service that had outed him; here he was running a gay sauna a few scant miles from their citadel of power.

When they did take possession, they found that there was work to be done. Plumbers had to fix rusted-out pipes, new tile floor had to be laid in one section. Two young Malaysian friends of Archie whose feet barely touched the ground turned out be perfect for the task of scrubbing and disinfecting the cubicles. They took pride in applying elbow grease to the task of making the whole place clean and spotless.

One auspicious day, Kwan showed up, a sexy, handsome, well-muscled Chinese masseur in his early twenties. Masculine, charming, without attitude and with a good business sense. Archie was anxious to hire him as masseur and as the person who would operate the sauna on the inside. Archie was bowled over by him and easily convinced Philip to give him a trial.

The sauna opened, and the first few weeks were a triumph. It seemed as if every rice queen and gay young Asian man wanted to try out the sauna's facilities. Kwan proved to be a great asset. He also turned out to have a shrewder business sense than either Philip or Archie.

Philip developed an infatuation for Kwan, and he and Kwan came to the realization they might need an assignation to sort out things. So it came to pass that the employee and the employer had a date.

25

It was an afternoon in Sagnes Close. Philip and Kwan were walking along the narrow sidewalk inside the close heading for Philip's house. Philip stopped at his door, unlocked it, and ushered Kwan in. Without preliminaries, without even a cup of tea or cocktail, Philip and Kwan adjourned to the master's second floor bedroom.

Later, Philip and Kwan were on the bed. On the wall was a picture of a nude man standing in an athletic pose. Philip and Kwan were still fondling one another. Philip was playing with Kwan's generously sized member. They had just completed a hectic sex act. There was a certain languidness, a lack of urgency, a deflation of expectations lingering in the air. Philip turned fully to his bed partner.

"That was rather delightful, Kwan."

"Remember, I still work for you. I don't want fun and games to interfere with job at sauna."

"Heaven forbid. I think it will improve morale in the workplace."

"Whose picture is that?" Kwan pointed to the nude portrait gracing the wall.

"Oh, a sometime friend of mine in the Philippines."

Kwan stared at the figure, rose from the bed, stood by the mirror near the painting, and compared his body with the one on canvas. "Did he, the model, pose for it in the altogether like that?"

"Yes, a painter acquaintance of mine captured his youth and vitality quite well."

"Would you like me to pose in the nude for you?"

"I'd love it, but I would have to get a painter as good as that one, and I'm afraid no one in London would be as reasonable as he was."

"The boy, and he's only a boy, does have a nice body."

"Kwan, *you* have a beautiful, muscular body."

"Thank you. I work on it. Do you have a lot of Asian boy friends?"

"No, not many at all."

"Not yet anyway. Wait until the sauna gets rolling. Then you'll be swimming in them. You'll be the belle of the ball, as they say."

Philip reddened. "Oh, I hope you don't think I'm a lothario."

"A what?"

"A serial seducer."

"No. I think you are, when it comes to the sauna, an opportunist."

"You're very well spoken."

"I did go to London University, you realize?"

"What were you studying?"

"Economics."

"That seems to fit. I know why I like to have a sauna, but why do you want to work there?"

"I like men, too, but I have a much wider range than you do. I like white men, too. I'm working there because it gives me a kick to work there. But, you Philip, you look so happy when you have Asian boys around you."

"Oh, I am. I think my life is enriched when I'm with wonderful boys like you."

"I'm really a man."

"To me, you're still a boy."

"Love me some more, Philip."

Philip and Kwan embraced and kissed. Their hands caressed one another. Blood swelled penises, and the afternoon went on apace.

The date with Kwan turned out to be merely a fling for both of them; neither one was about to make a commitment. Perhaps from time to time they would manage to get the odd one on, but both had too much fun playing the field.

The spring and summer flew by for Philip. It was like working in a candy store. Randy young Asians, looking for older Caucasian companions seemed to be swarming that spring and summer, and Philip took full advantage of his opportunities.

He had dates with several of the Asian young men who showed up at the sauna. He and Archie made frequent inspection trips throughout the sauna supposedly to supervise but really to be voyeurs and occasional participants. Philip found he could mix business with pleasure, but it didn't often follow that the sauna profit stream was enhanced by dalliances.

26

London's Wardour Street on a warm afternoon in September, 1975, was quite busy. Some film people were hurrying to the screening of a new movie. Wardour had a number of movie companies that maintained offices on the street. People walked by the doorway of an unremarkable office building that looked like many on the street. Two young Asian men stopped and looked at a sign at the entranceway. The sign read "East Meets West Sauna, second floor."

On the second floor, from the hallway, one entered a small reception room with a window opening cut in the opposite wall. A counter ran along the bottom of the opening. Binky had just entered and was at the counter trying to peer beyond the opening into what he hoped would be the changing room.

He was nattily-dressed, distinguished-looking as usual. From behind the counter, Philip spotted him and was barely able to greet him when a client entered. Binky stood aside as a young Asian man came in from the hallway, went up to the counter, was greeted pleasantly by Philip, signed in, given a towel and ushered into the inner precincts of the sauna. As he went in, another young Asian walked into the foyer in a towel. Binky looked him over and indicated in dumb show to Philip his satisfaction with the sight.

The young man smiled at the two older gentlemen, the OPs, the older people, chose a magazine from the reception room table and disappeared back into the bowels of the bathhouse.

Philip greeted his old friend, "Binky, I'm happy you were finally able to come."

"I'm always glad I'm able to come. When I get too old to come, life will really be awfully dull and not worth living."

"Welcome to our little divertissement."

"The other night a young stud said to me, 'You should be out looking for a cemetery plot rather than out looking for a one night stand.' But I still can't imagine staid old Philip Croft operating a gay sauna. What is the world coming to?"

Philip, the proud parent, beamed. "I'm sure you'll find entertainment and diversion here."

"How does this work then?"

"We sell memberships for three months, six months, or a year. One can also buy a one-day pass. The clients come up to the window, show their memberships or buy one. I give them a towel and a lock and key for their lockers."

"Valuables will be safe, will they?"

"Oh, yes. Quite safe in this place. Clients go into the locker room over there, disrobe and enter the sauna area. We have showers, a steam room, sauna, and ten cubicles where people can rest on cots. Also a lounge area where they can buy refreshments."

"And in the cubicles? A bit of this and that going on?"

"As far as we know, everything is on the up and up. But if one gets the urge, one can close the door, and confer with a consenting adult. A consensual situation, one would rather hope."

Binky rose and peeked around the corner beyond the counter to see if he could catch some action. "Do I hear the pitter patter of little feet scurrying from shower to sauna to cubicle to lounge to steam room to shower to cubicle again?"

"Something like that."

"And profit from the sauna?"

"So far it doesn't seem to be generating much of a profit stream. We seldom break even, and sometimes we have a few precipitous dips into the red."

"Any new chappies for you to report on? Anything special you aren't sharing with Uncle Binky, eh?"

"Kwan, my helper here at the sauna, and I had a brief fling, but he is too interested in quickies. And perhaps I sense he's a bit more adventuresome than I'm accustomed to. I'll introduce you. You two may hit it off. Who knows?"

"Bring him on. I'm just back from a world tour so I'm ready for the wilds of London again. I think I'd like to try your facilities. Please sign me up for a short term membership."

Philip was encouraged. "Good. I'll have Kwan show you around."

Philip turned and shouted into the inner sanctum, "Kwan!"

After a few moments, Kwan entered, muscled, firm pecs thrust out, a towel wrapped around his waist, big smile, sexually provocative and intimidating.

"Kwan, this is Mr. Binkstone. If he likes you, he may let you address him as Binky."

"Yes, by all means call me Binky. Hello, my dear boy. I love your pecs."

"Thank you, Mr. Binky."

"Just plain Binky, love."

Philip explained, "Kwan is our Kwan of all trades. He's our locker boy, our masseur, our host, cashier, desk clerk, and canteen server, and I really think he's the brains of this whole firm."

Kwan nodded his agreement. "Philip, if I left everything to you, the sauna would go broke. Or worse, raided by police."

Philip loved an opportunity to be self-deprecating for the sake of bonhomie. "Yes, he says I have no business sense, which I'm afraid is very true. I was never taught that in government service."

Kwan interjected, "Philip is kind, a good man, but he lets every good-looking young Asian chap have run of place."

Philip laughed merrily. "That's the truth. I'm a pushover for that fold around the eyes."

Binky added, "I've also heard that Philip is a wonderful lover. I wouldn't know because I'm just a brawny Caucasian, though I've been told that I'm rather well endowed."

"Oh yes, Philip is good lover, the best. I can swear to that. He likes to play whole field, but he is very loyal."

Philip agreed. "I have been known to be very loyal to

people who are loyal to me. At any rate, show my friend here
to a locker."

"Lead on, Kwan. I love your towel."

"I bet you say that to all your masseurs."

"Oh, you said the operative word, masseur. I could really
use a workout and a soothing, long-lasting massage."

As they went out, Binky pulled at Kwan's towel. It dropped
revealing Kwan's perfectly formed buttocks. Binky
exclaimed, "Oh, those beautiful buns."

Binky followed him into the inner rooms.

Shortly after, Binky was face down on a massage table.
Kwan, in a Speedo, was giving Binky's back and rear a vig-
orous rub-down. Binky was joking, and Kwan was laughing
at his jokes. Both were having a good time. Binky shivered
with delight.

Still later, a nude Kwan was face down on the massage
table while a smiling Binky was rubbing cream on Kwan's
muscular back and buttocks.

27

The Shorn Sheep, had a faded crude sign creaking above the door. It depicted a terrified denuded sheep. The pub had seen better days, probably fifty years in the past. It was in the Isle of Dogs section of London. For years, there had been talk of tearing down these shabby buildings with their airless flats and putting up something worthy, but it remained talk. These dockland areas along the Thames remained a neighborhood for many working class families, as well as a liberal sprinkling of the down and out.

Each corner had its neighborhood local pub. To call the Shorn Sheep a neighborhood pub for the working class would be too generous since most of its imbibers were on the dole and receiving rent subsidies. Inside it was shadowy, grimy, smoke-encrusted, and smelly. Sometimes the odor of stale beer would overpower the smells of nicotine, sweat, unwashed clothes, vomit, and urine.

Trimmer hated the place, but it was where Whaley chose to spend his off hours. Whaley avoided most of the regulars and spent his time in his favorite corner reading the tabloids. More than a few of the regulars shunned him because of his reputation as a drunken blowhard.

He'd ask Trimmer to join him occasionally for drinks even though it was miles away from Trimmer's stomping grounds in Islington. Trimmer had a hard time refusing because Whaley was still nominally his boss. A boss that stepped over the line a bit too often for Trimmer's tastes.

At his isolated table, Whaley, hunched over a pint, vented his spleen to a patient Trimmer. He was disgruntled and bitter, and Trimmer sat quietly enduring the Sergeant's gripes and collection of supposed injustices.

"Christ, no sooner did I get the names of those queers from the poof Croft than Sir Bloody Charles starts in on me for me methods. 'Inhumane,' he says. 'I should've used psychology and persuasion,' he blubbers. I bloody did use persuasion. I put boils on his arse, and he talked, didn't he? That's what the fuckers wanted. For him to talk. I got him to talk, and then they bloody turn on me like jackals."

"You did your job, Sarge. No one can fault you for that."

"You're bloody fuckin' right I did my job. What Sir Charles is forgetting is that I got Croft to admit from the first hour that he was a bloody poof. That alone disqualified him from being an operative. What the hell more did they want? They had him dead to rights. The man's a cocksucker. Case closed. Then as a dividend I got them the names of two other poofs."

"They have no gratitude."

"And the gall of Sir Charles. He's barely in the top job a month, and he's on my case for saying I used illegal methods and excessive intimidation. What did he think I was going to do, fan his balls with a feather duster?"

Trimmer sipped his lager. *Even the lager here tasted like piss. What a dump.* But it befitted the misfit he was sitting with. "Did Sir Charles really threaten a demotion?"

"Oh, yeah, he said they might have to take disciplinary action. I said I'd take it before the review board if that happened. Make a right old stink. 'E backed down when he heard that. Said I was to be careful in the future. I ain't afraid of that ponce. The two of them, he and Croft, are cut from the same cloth. Old schoolmates. The nobs take care of each other."

"He's out for good now, Croft? He's been eased out, hasn't he?"

"Oh sure. Out. With full pension. A going away party where I heard Sir Charles had the bloody gall to praise the bastard. I've been keeping my eyes on the prick. He went to Asia for the winter. Lives in his nice little townhouse near Marble Arch. What I wouldn't give for a place like that. Worth a bit, I'd say. Then has the bloody nerve to open a queer bathhouse in Soho. Jeez, talk about parading your proclivities before the world."

"Can they get him for that?"

"I don't think so. He's out of service now. What he's doing is, he's sticking his thumb up their nose. Laughing at 'em. I'll tell you one thing, I'm going to get that little twit."

"What can you do?"

"You mark my words, Trimmer me boy, some dark night that bloody little asslicker is going to go down a dark alley, maybe his close, and he ain't coming out."

"What'll you do?"

"Never you mind. He'll be dead meat, that's all."

"But why him?"

"Because he sat there and made my whole life, my years of service count for nothing. A life for naught. That poof has it all, and he laughed in my face."

"Sarge, I don't know. He seemed kinda mild and just trying to save his own butt. He wasn't talking about you or me."

"You missed the undertow, my boy. It was him versus us. I brought that out. He made it a class thing. I'm going to get the fucker. Pay him back. And I'll get that bastard Sir Charles someday too. You just watch me."

Trimmer knew better than to argue with Whaley who was getting deeper into his cups. When he finally left him, he was pretty sure Whaley was unaware of his departure. As he neared the door, he turned. Whaley was talking to himself, working himself up, weaving conspiracies, exaggerating slights, embellishing unreal wrongs, and making delusions and paranoia an excuse for a life.

28

When they went into business together, Philip had made it clear to Archie that he would be making his regular winter sojourns to Asia even though he was a partner in the sauna. He would cut back on the length of the winter trips, though. Archie had readily agreed. The sauna could manage without Philip under Archie and Kwan's watchful eyes. In fact, Kwan had turned out to be not only the brawn of the outfit, but to a considerable degree the brains as well. He was competent in all areas and a drawing card to the sauna so Philip could leave for his Asian interlude knowing that the Kwan could handle things.

Philip had written to Reynaldo and told him he was planning an extended stay in Manila. At home in Sagnes Close, he stared at Rey's nude portrait and couldn't wait to renew the relationship. Despite all the contacts he had made at the sauna, Reynaldo was still his only heartthrob.

That second winter in Asia in 75-76 after his retirement, Philip planned to stay at the same hotel in Manila, and indeed the management had given him the same apartment as the year before. Rey was waiting for him when he arrived at the airport. Philip had informed him of his arrival time. What he didn't tell Rey was that he had spent a month before the Philippines' arrival in Malaysia, Sri Lanka, Indonesia, and Hong Kong doing his rice queen rounds. What Rey didn't tell Philip was that a few days before his arrival, he had seen off his Dutch older gentleman with whom he had stayed for a month. Luckily, Rey and his Dutchman had spent their time in Bacolod on another island so Rey had not been seen in Manila's gay circle.

That winter, Binky skipped the Philippines. Craig was still there but talking more about leaving the Philippines for good. Philip made one long weekend trip to Pagsanjan on his own because Rey refused to go.

He saw Paul Rowan and Hal Turner, Craig's American friends. They had begun making two trips to the Philippines, one in the winter and one in the summer. Paul and Philip took long walks through the city, and during the walks Paul continued to show great interest in Philip's life, pumping him for details about his bio and career.

Was it Philip's imagination or did Rey's lovemaking seem a trifle more perfunctory than last winter? Rey was gone most days. He said he had classes at college, and he did have a composition book and two textbooks in his knapsack, though he never seemed to do homework. Sometimes when he came home, he had had a few beers and was not inclined to do cartwheels. He took long naps and there were times when he seemed exhausted.

Philip had his own circle of gay friends to see. During the day, he would be busy with his walks and his lunches with Craig and others. The circle kept widening as he met fellow seekers. The winter raced by and before he knew it, Philip was winging home to his sauna honey pot.

29

It was early afternoon, a June day in the year 1976. Sir Charles Monmouth had walked along Wardour Street several times, passing the entrance to Philip's sauna. He stood at the street entrance to the sauna, reading the sign, deciding whether or not he should enter. Finally, he made up his mind, steeled himself and started up the steps.

In the sauna reception room, Philip was at the counter, fussing with some bills. The door opened and Sir Charles entered. He was in leisure clothes carrying an umbrella.

Philip was genuinely surprised. He came out from behind the counter to shake his hand.

"Sir Charles, Good Lord . . . What a surprise. Good to see you here."

"Hello, Philip. I thought I'd come up and see your retirement vehicle. We've missed you in the club of late."

"Well between the sauna and getting reorganized after my trip to Manila, I've had very little time to get to any of my regular haunts."

"I wanted to talk to you some months ago, and then you disappeared."

"Well, welcome to my little den of iniquity."

Sir Charles glanced around the room. "Quite nice."

Two Asian young men in towels went by the counter, waved and smiled cordially.

"Sir Charles, I've heard you packed it in. Retirement suit you?"

"Yes, quite a bit. It was getting worse and worse in the Service. In the old days, we ran our own ship. But then more and more we were controlled from outside. Even the palace was interfering."

"Yes, everyone thinks he's an expert on intelligence matters. Everyone who has been spying on his neighbors and friends for years feels qualified to give advice."

Philip returned to the counter when a client requested a towel.

When the man had moved away, Sir Charles continued. "People don't realize that it's mostly high-tech now, bugging devices, satellites, computers, new gadgets every year. The old days of spies hiding in the closet are long gone."

"Yes, I can attest to the years of hiding in the closet. You just get dusty and moth-eaten hiding in there. No more the closet for me."

Sir Charles looked somewhat embarrassed by this frankness, but it was part and parcel of the new Philip.

"Yes, well taken. But, Philip, my life wasn't my own. New governments, new brooms, witch-hunts, inquisitions. God, what we've gone through."

"You should be glad you're well rid of the Service."

"By the way, our old friend, the trainer Whaley genuinely has it in for you. My sources say he still goes on about you. I reprimanded him severely for his treatment of you. It set back his so-called career."

"Whaley, my nemesis. I'll never be able to figure out that nutter. Took a real pleasure in his sadistic practices. Inevitable when you put a sadist in such a position, eh?"

There was a mild hint of criticism in Philip's observation.

"I've always regretted my part in your ouster, the horrors they put you through."

"My present life is going too well for me to keep reliving the past, though I can never forget those days. The memories still haunt me."

"Life has a way of filling in wounds."

"The raw open wound heals, but the ugly scar remains forever. I look at my bottom in a mirror, and that purplish scar reminds me of my reward for years of service. I admit to more than a touch of bitterness. When you've been deliberately given boils on your rump, platitudes never relieve the pain or the embarrassment."

"I am truly sorry about the whole thing. You know, or at

least I hope you know, all that was beyond my control. By the time I took over, the old regime had marked you down. It had gone too far for me to intervene."

"Whatever." There was a long pause between them before Philip resumed speaking. "Incidentally, Binky is in there, inside the sauna. You remember Binky. Always irrepressible and uninhibited."

"Oh, yes. One cannot forget Binky."

"He's become a frequent visitor here. Good old Binky, an equerry or whatever his current title is in the royal household. How about you, Sir Charles? Care to try out our facilities?"

"I suppose you guessed?"

"When we were at school and at university together, I heard whispers about you and Cunningham."

"Ah yes, Cunningham with his enormous member."

"I've always thought there was something in the eyes that gave gays away. And often you notice a gay man's glance lingering overlong on another male. I don't know why, but I have always suspected you were a club member. I was spying on you. Even then I was a snoop, though without portfolio."

"But you never said anything."

"How could I? I didn't know what the whole thing meant myself. I'm constantly being surprised as various old friends and acquaintances drop their beads. Ah, the dropping of the beads, as Binky says. How horribly I had to drop my beads. And now your beads."

"Yes, I guess here I, too, am more or less out from under the rug."

"Whenever I saw you with your wife, somehow I knew there was a distance between the two of you."

Philip walked to a cupboard and took out a cigar box of receipts, which he spread out on the counter.

"Marriage was my cover, but I wasn't happy being married. Now she's in the country house year round. Our marriage is a sham."

"When I was in the service, I forgot about it, you being gay, but just recently, someone told me you were probably part of the fraternity. The straights better watch out. Our numbers seem to be growing."

"Have your tastes always been toward Orientals?"

"Yes. I've never regretted my preference."

"I've always had a thing for big strapping Brits, soldiers. The butcher they were the better. Rough and tumble laborers and working class louts. I think I was influenced by D.H. Lawrence. His gamekeepers with oversized members. Sometimes I've been turned on by the odd dustman. I suppose I'm predisposed toward rough trade."

"You've never been drawn to the odd Asian?"

"Too delicate for me. Too small in the genital department."

"You'd be pleasantly surprised at times. They come in all sizes."

"The men to me are not enough to hold onto. Too wispy, too willowy, too vague."

Philip had finished with his receipts. He placed them back in the cigar box. He took some pounds from his wallet, shook his head and placed his own money in the till. He said to Sir Charles, "Everyone to his own taste."

Sir Charles shook his head. "Your type, tiptoeing around, smiling, kind of tricky, slippery those wogs. I have always found them manipulative, clever at working their wiles. Batting their little slanted eyes like geisha girls."

"That's part of the charm. Some Asian boys do flirt and act coy."

"Give me a brawny British yeoman any day."

"Ah, yes, the smell of mutton. Tattoos. Mindless profanity and cursing. Swilling down ten pints of beer."

"You are really down on us white men."

"Mainly the Sergeant Whaley type. Gay haters. But Charles, with Asians, small penises are not always the case. I have seen some Asians with large organs, and I can remember some Brits with small ones."

"Yes, but what are the odds of finding a well-hung wog?"

"I've never been what Binky calls a size queen, but the

Asians do seem to be growing bigger members nowadays. Maybe it's those McDonald's burgers they sell worldwide that's equalizing penis size."

One young Asian man peeked around the counter, smiled and winked at Philip, appraised Sir Charles, and disappeared into the inner depths of the sauna.

"I'm afraid I like a bit of the rough," said Sir Charles. "But, Philip, I hear you are practically living in Asia."

"I have been starting to go there for the winter. I've always hated being in London for the holidays."

"Christmas, Boxing Day, New Year's, Dickensian bonhomie?"

"It can get depressing, and also it can become very dull. The cold and damp. The lack of sunny days. Gloom. It gets into my psyche and makes me depressed."

"Don't you feel isolated and lonely out there?"

"Oh, God no. Over the years, I've built up a large circle of friends. Binky goes regularly. I've met men of all ages interested in the same things I'm interested in. Rice queens. Australians, Americans, other Brits, Japanese, Germans, all kinds of Europeans. We're a fraternity. All smitten by that fold over the eyes."

"The Rice Queen Ring?"

"As well as a circle of young Filipino men. They are very available there. All over the place. I have a boy, a young man really, that I met a few years ago. I had his portrait painted, and I have it on the wall in my bedroom."

"I'd like to see that someday."

Philip didn't follow this up with an invitation to his home. He still didn't quite trust Sir Charles, nor had he forgiven him for his part in his disgrace.

Philip went on. "Right now in London with this sauna, I have an inexhaustible supply of very nice, cultured, young Asian men. That is, I will have, if this place doesn't bankrupt me first. My partner and I may have to reassess our future course. A fling is one thing, but going into debt over a few flings is an entirely different matter altogether."

"Philip, I'm still very happy for you. Whatever got you hooked on Asian lads in the first place?"

"I think because my first was an Asian. I was going to say my first conquest, but with my innocence and naïveté I think I was his conquest. I've always loved Asians: hairless bodies, silken smooth alabaster skin, almost translucent . . ."

"And their little puff farts that have hardly any offensive odor."

". . . Their perfectly shaped ivory buttocks with those tiny rosebud anuses, their boyishness. The lads are, in general, small in stature, manageable, not threatening or intimidating."

"You almost sound like a publicist for cohabitating with the young male Asian population."

"I am. I'm deeply attracted to them. They seemed gentler in their dispositions. For some of us gays, it was as if we were safer with them."

"Why safer?"

"I'm bigger than most of them. No, really, some of the rice queens I met in Hong Kong and elsewhere would tell stories about the nasty young Caucasian men they had met, about the robberies, the almost evil nature of boys and men they had picked up in Britain and the States, the viciousness. Not that Asians can't be crooks."

"There are thieves of every stripe and color."

"I guess rice queens do feel less intimidated by their boyfriends' statures. And not being able to speak the language can sometimes be a great advantage. It prevents negotiating and nastiness. But I think there is also the Madame Butterfly syndrome. It's an aesthetic thing with us."

Philip walked to the counter, adjusting his soaps, towels, and toilet articles as he talked. He was anxious to keep everything on track. And he was also anxious to discover what Sir Charles truly intended.

"Are there male geishas?" asked Sir Charles.

"In a sense, there are. Can you imagine the Scots having the equivalent of geishas?"

"Or the Welsh or Irish?"

"Imagine diminutive, gentle, submissive, perfectly polite and subservient Anglo-Saxons or Celts?"

"You know, Philip, I'd like to try out your place here. Can I use a nom de guerre?"

"Yes, do try out our facilities. I'll sign you up as John Le Carré."

"No, sign me up as Bond, James Bond. Double 0-7."

"I'll give you a towel and a lock and key. Not all of our clients are Asians. You may find a brawny Caucasian. Remember, Binky is in there. God knows what he'll be doing. He may have a heart seizure when he sees you, but he'll soon get over it. Let me get my assistant. Kwan!"

Philip went to the inner sauna door and shouted again.

"Kwan!"

Kwan, muscles buffed, pecs assertive, entered in his Speedo and appraised Sir Charles. They exchanged approving glances.

"Here's our masseur now. Kwan, this is James Bond."

"Good day, Mr. Bond. Let me show you around."

"Wish me luck, Philip. Lead on, Kwan."

30

The summer of 1976 in London brought a series of flings, dates Philip would not have had without the sauna. Financially, the sauna was barely breaking even. In the fall, Philip returned to Asia for the winter of 76–77. He made stops throughout Asia and ended up in Manila with Reynaldo for most of his holiday. Philip's life was falling into a pattern that was to continue for most of his life.

Philip was back in London for the summer of 77 and was attending a social function of his East meets West group. Knickers was a small basement club on Shaftesbury Avenue in Soho. Every other Wednesday night, it was lent out to the Long Yang Club for one of its socials. The music was not so loud that it drowned out conversation. Disco lights flashed, and a few male couples danced.

Philip was seated with Binky at a small table. Some tables were full of young Asians laughing and talking loudly. Other tables held rather forlorn looking older Caucasian admirers. And still other tables were made up of a mixture of the Asian boys and Westerners. Binky and Philip were wearing old-fashioned traditional suits. They looked as if they had just stepped from one of London's private men's clubs, bastions of stodginess and the tradition. They indeed had been to Binky's club.

Binky looked around and commented to Philip. "By God, you were completely right. Strictly young Asians. And older Caucasians like ourselves. Good name, the Long Wang Club. The name is pure irony."

"I keep telling you it is the Long Yang Club, not Wang. I've belonged for years. The purpose is getting Asians and their admirers together at social functions to meet one another."

"Drinks seem reasonably priced to me, for a club, that is."

"Yes, they are. We insist on that. It keeps forcing the club's officers to change club venues. It's quite a good organization. I know a few of the lads. Here's Kwan from the sauna."

"Oh, yes, wonderfully versatile young man. Gorgeous pecs."

Kwan wore neatly pressed jeans and a tight polo shirt that accentuated his well-developed upper body. He leaned down, pecked Philip and Binky on their cheeks, smiled broadly at Binky and saluted him.

"Mr. Binky, you are looking well."

"Just plain Binky, Kwan, dear. I feel I am going to need another massage. Very very soon, darling."

"I'll give you good one. Call sauna. Philip, will you be at the sauna when I open in the morning?"

"No, I'll be a little late tomorrow."

An older distinguished-looking gentleman passed Kwan and brushed his buns as he passed. Kwan turned and smiles were exchanged.

"Excuse me, I have to talk to this gentleman. See you later."

Kwan followed the man into the crowd.

Binky asked, "How has the sauna been doing financially of late?"

"I don't know how long I'm going to be able to keep it going. We keep running deeper in the red, and the landlord just went up on the rent. A ruinous increase."

"I hope you can keep it going as long as possible. I've had some good climaxes there."

"We'll try to keep it going as long as we're able."

"And how is it going with you and your beloved in Manila?"

"Reynaldo seems at times to be distracted. I think it's largely due to the fact that he's basically straight."

"Philip, you are not demanding enough of your cherubs. With me it's either perform or perambulate."

"I cannot say Rey is one of those young men who is instinctively attracted to older men. I fear he may be drawn to older men's pocketbooks; his sexual preferences lean more in the heterosexual direction, but I still find him a lovely companion and bed partner. I can count on him."

"Good actor, is he?"

"At times, I think so."

"What you have to do is find yourself a boyfriend who will meet and reciprocate your romantic fancies."

"It's not that I haven't been looking."

Binky, while talking, was cruising. He attracted the attention of a hunky Korean lad. He and the young man were soon chatting, and Philip could see the telltale signs of a one-night stand in the offing. He excused himself and was soon headed home on the underground. He thought what he needed most was a reciprocal London boyfriend.

*   *   *

Philip had been in contact with Tom, his Singapore lover of years past. During Philip's winter sojourn of 78–79, the two had agreed to meet in Singapore. Philip took a room at Raffles, and they had a week of bliss—another honeymoon. Of all of Philip's affairs, the one with Tom had been the best. They were lovers who knew intuitively each other's desires and needs.

At the end of Philip's glorious week, Philip said, "We would make a wonderful pair. Why don't we become fulltime lovers?"

Tom answered, "You know me. I can't commit to one man, even one as wonderful as you. My job takes me all over the world, and I just can't have someone else counting on me, hanging on me. In the future, we'll meet either here in Asia, in London, or somewhere on the globe from time to time, but that's all I can offer any man, I'm afraid."

Philip knew that since he had severed his ties with the Service, their relationship was more tenuous. Neither of them wanted to mention the whys of it, the stress that had been put on their relationship by some co-equal duplicity.

When they parted, Philip spent a week in Malaysia, another in Sri Lanka, and a third in Taipei. Then he went to the Philippines and renewed his strained relationship with Reynaldo. Philip thought it was an easy pairing for both of them, that Reynaldo was there when he needed him, and that he was still attracted to the youth. Or was he just attracted to Asian male youth in general?

31

That September day of 1979 was a sad day for Philip. The sauna was closing. Archie had bailed out in the spring, leaving Philip as the sole proprietor. There had been no hard feelings. Archie signed over the papers to Philip, and Philip assumed the debts. Archie wrote off his share of the partnership to a few years of good times; money, as he said, well spent.

So the closing was a mixed blessing, the hemorrhaging of money spent to keep it going would end, but so would Philip's relationships with a steady flow of young Asians. He thought , *Oh well, I can still see many of them at meetings of the Long Yang Club.*

At the street entrance of the sauna, a workman was unfastening the small sign at the office building entrance that advertised the name of the bathhouse. Two movers came out of the building carrying a set of lockers.

Upstairs, the reception room was bare of furniture. Inside the sauna proper, one workman was dismantling equipment while two others carried a bench out the door. Philip and Kwan were standing in the empty reception room. Both had grim faces as they watched the dismantling of a dream.

Philip groaned. "This is a sad day for me."

Kwan looked around. "I'll miss it."

"It proves how hopeless I am as a practical businessman."

"This recession hit everyone, Philip."

"I'm sorry for you. It's my fault you are unemployed."

"You couldn't have kept the sauna going, could you?"

"No one was willing to buy it. Red ink wasn't much of an inducement."

"You would have lost a lot more money?"

"I would have had to continually take money from my savings. That's not business; that's sheer folly."

"No good."

"Throwing good money after bad."

"I have to go now. Have interview. I'll never have boss as good as you."

"Oh, I'll miss you. Please stay in touch."

"We'll see each other at Long Yang gatherings, and I'll be calling you up to keep you up-to-date on my social life."

They hugged and said a tearful goodbye. Kwan hurried out the doorway and down to the street. Philip took a look around the bare room, walked over to the window, looked out and saw Kwan marching down the opposite side of Wardour Street. He knew Kwan would do all right for himself.

Once all of the closing details for the sauna were out of the way, he was anxious to make plans for the winter in Asia. That would be something to look forward to. The sauna had been fun while it lasted, but life went on. He hoped that Reynaldo would be there when he got to Manila.

If Philip ever chose to write his life story, he had decided to title it *Phases*. His life had been a series of phases with definite starting and ending points that served to define his life's journey. The sauna period was one of those phases—a decidedly pleasant era, a sexually bountiful period, and one in which he had surfaced as a gay entrepreneur, unafraid and sure of himself. He was proud of that phase and was ready for the next one.

Philip wintered in Asia in 79-80. In 1980 just before he was due to go back to his life at Sagnes Close, he was talking to Paul Rowan and Hal Turner in the Lifebuoy. Rey was in class as he seemed to be more and more often.

Philip told them about his sad news, of having to shutter the sauna. Paul said, "You may have gotten out at a propitious time. Back in New York, there is a great deal of talk of a strange and deadly disease that seems to have broken out among the bathhouse set. Doctors have no idea what it is, but it seems to affect only gays. Some are calling it the gay plague because it is killing only gay people.

"It's a dirty little secret among some New York doctors. It's an opportunistic virus that seems to destroy the ability of mostly gay young men to fight off rare cancers and any number of things. These were healthy young men who took care of their bodies."

Philip was aghast. "What is the medical name for it?"

"They haven't been able to isolate it yet, give it a name, but, believe me, this gay plague is going to be an enormous problem in the future. One doctor told me it strikes and kills clusters of friends and acquaintances and may threaten a whole generation of us."

32

Philip's winter in Asia followed the usual routine, but this time he did not have to worry about the sauna sapping him of his retirement funds. In Manila, his relationship with Rey seemed to be operating on automatic pilot. Some of the excitement had worn off, and he and Rey seemed to be seeing less of each other. Earlier than he had planned, he decamped for Sri Lanka, had a pleasant interlude there, and returned to London.

It was a pleasant afternoon in June of 1980. Philip had agreed to walk a dog belonging to his friend, Graham Lasserby. It was a Jack Russell that Philip was minding while Lasserby was in the country for the weekend. He stopped off at Lasserby's flat on Hyde Park Street to pick up the dog. The little dog was delighted to see him and had his leash ready in his mouth. No question of what he wanted. His little rump and stub of a tail wagged wildly.

In the early part of the walk, the Jack Russell, whose name was inexplicably Crinkle, was a little martinet going where he wanted to go, sniffing everywhere and peeing frequently on any object with an intriguing smell in his path. After he had left his scent in a dozen places, he settled down to see where Philip would take him.

Philip began one of his Sunday walks strolling through the lawns of Hyde Park, enjoying the rare sunshine. People were seated in the rented chairs scattered around the grass. He headed across the park toward the Serpentine, the park's large lake. He decided he would start at the eastern end of the pond and walk completely around the perimeter of the waterway until he was back at his starting point. Crinkle paid little heed to the hundreds of birds wandering around; he had grown up with them.

Philip was strolling at a leisurely pace near the restaurants

when he saw heading toward him a young Asian youth. Philip
slowed; the young man decelerated; their eyes met; they
exchanged smiles and nods. As they passed each other, their
paces slowed almost to a halt. Both turned at the same time.
Philip approached the lad in a friendly but diffident stance,
and said, "Hello. Beautiful afternoon, isn't it?"

"Yes, splendid."

"Are you enjoying the sunshine after our week of rain and
showers?"

"Yes, very much, sir. And you?"

"Oh yes, I'm a sunshine person. Where are you from, if I
may ask?"

"Oxford."

"Very nice. You go to university there?"

"Yes. I am studying English."

"Well, you speak very good English indeed."

"Thank you, sir."

"My name is Philip."

"And my name is difficult for people to say, so I ask everyone to call me Robin."

They shook hands. He was shorter than Philip's five-nine
by about two inches, had thick coarse black hair, a wide,
welcoming face, sincere eyes, beautiful white teeth, a somewhat flat nose, high cheekbones and a quick smile. Philip
found him sexually attractive. He was young, Asian, good-
looking, and genial. Philip's loins began to quiver with excitement. *Could he possibly?*

The young man seemed eager to talk. Philip learned he
was Cambodian, had escaped from there with his family,
ended up in Paris, and then come to England.

Crinkle had carefully sniffed the Cambodian's trainers
and was now waiting to see what Philip would do next. The
young man squatted down and gently scratched around the
little dog's ears, which Crinkle tolerated. His little tail
wagged, but not overmuch. He shook his tiny head and
looked up at Philip as if to say, "Don't make this overlong.
We're here for a walk, you know."

"You have a nice puppy."

"Oh, he's not my dog. He belongs to a friend of mine. I'm just caring for him for a few days. He's full grown, not a puppy. His name is Crinkle."

The dog looked up sharply, ears attentive when he heard his name.

"He's very well-behaved."

"Smart as a whip. Too smart for his own good sometimes, though I've found he's not as smart as he thinks he is."

"I've seen dogs like that in the circus."

"Ah, yes, circus dogs."

Philip steered Robin to a nearby bench. He picked one that hadn't been desecrated by the bird crap that defiled much of the area bordering the Serpentine. His sexual yearnings told him he should hurry Robin across the park and attempt to bed him, but his lifetime in intelligence somewhat feebly told him to suss out the handsome young man first. Philip, in general, was too trusting, too quick to rely on first impressions, the words and actions of the new sexual partners he met. He was of "the glass half full" persuasion.

It turned out Robin was due to return to Oxford by train that evening to resume his English classes at the extension school. He liked the idea of going to school in Oxford even though his classes were only nominally associated with the university. He had been eligible for some stipend given by the government to people with refugee asylum status.

Philip pointed out the intrepid swimmers that swam in the Serpentine year round. "How they can swim amid all that bird crap and feathers is beyond me," he ventured.

Philip began setting the stage, carrying out the props, rearranging the set before the curtain's rise. "My neighbor has just given me a tin of homemade shortcake biscuits. Rather delicious. Would you care to come to my place and have tea with me?"

"Where do you live?"

"Across the park."

"Yes, that would be splendid."

Robin followed up that statement with a word that sounded to Philip like *kosher*, but Philip wasn't too sure what it was. He didn't want to ask him. Might embarrass him. His accent was at times slightly strange and his pronunciation of a few words was off the mark. At other times, his English was more precise and more posh than any upper-crust British speaker.

Before he raised the curtain on his matinee playlet, the Philip who had gone through the interrogation wringer in the Terminal, wished to clear the air. "I think I feel compelled to tell you that I am gay."

For a few seconds, there was a puzzled look on Robin's face, then the dawning. "I thought you might be, sir."

"Is that a problem?"

"No, not at all. Splendid. I like old men. I don't like males my own age."

Philip, crestfallen, answered, "I'm not an old man really. More middle-aged."

"No, not old like old. You look fine to me. Just right."

"Let's go then, shall we?"

"Yes, splendid."

Philip had raised the curtain on his playlet. They walked across the park to Lasserby's apartment building on Hyde Park Street. He left Robin standing outside next to the black wrought iron fence and hurried upstairs with Crinkle who was deposited along with a bowl of fresh water. He'd be fed in the morning. Philip left a few dog biscuits on the floor to tide him over.

It was always dangerous to leave pick-ups out of sight as he had just done. Sometimes they bolted, but Robin was there smiling when he returned. They walked to Albion Street and into Sagnes Close. They walked up the cobbled street of the mews, and Philip pointed out his little narrow house.

Robin commented, "It would look beautiful with a big mass of potted plants out front."

Once inside the house Robin was thrilled by the idea of the small private house. Philip showed him the cluttered lounge.

Robin questioned, "The whole place is yours? You live here alone?"

"Yes, mine such as it is, and I live here all alone. Before I start the tea, let me show you the upstairs."

Philip thought, *Now is the time.*

Philip led him upstairs to his small bedroom. *Thank God I made the bed this morning.*

In his bedroom, Philip tentatively reached out for Robin. He pulled him toward him. They hugged each other, and then Philip poised his mouth close to Robin's. They kissed. Philip's kiss was more fervent than the response he received from the young man. Perhaps he was just shy, unsure of his emotions.

Philip started to unbutton Robin's shirt. Robin smiled nervously. He seemed to be shaking. The shirt was off, then the singlet. Philip caressed the soft, silky, hairless skin. Leaning over, he kissed the rose-tinted nipples. Philip was quickly erect, his penis straining at his trousers, a demi-spear longing to be free. Philip stripped off his cardigan, his shirt, and undershirt.

Robin sat to remove his shoes and socks. This was a good sign. When the lad stood again, Philip loosened his and the boy's belts. He unbuttoned Robin's trousers, slid them down to reveal well-formed legs with muscled calves and thighs.

Philip praised Robin's body. Robin gave a quick smile and said, "I do swimming, jogging, and play football."

"Very nice indeed."

Robin wore bikini-type briefs, and there was a protrusion in his crotch. He slid off the briefs and his penis, from a small nest of black hair was hard and was pointing toward Philip. Philip very quickly removed his drawers, and they were soon on the bed embracing. Philip held Robin tightly with their erect penises brushing one another. Philip caressed the smooth silken body and his hand grasped Robin's maleness.

Philip drew Robin further toward the foot of the bed and then spun around into a sixty-nine position so his face was at Robin's dick, and so that Robin's face was greeting his erection. Philip licked Robin's testicles, held them in his mouth gently, and then very softly started to lap at the head of Robin's penis.

Robin had Philip's penis in his hand and was slowly massaging it. Philip thought, *This will have to do at present. I'm having too much of a thrill with his penis.* Philip sucked the head of it, rotated it slightly. Robin's body quivered. Without warning, Philip took the whole penis in his mouth and sucked it hungrily. Robin's body shook from the sensation. Philip was careful not to be too frantic. He didn't want his young visitor to shoot his load too precipitously.

As Philip's mouth dove down on Robin's penis in a new assault, Philip suddenly felt his penis being enveloped by Robin's wet, warm, willing mouth. The two were sixty-nining quite effectively now, finding rhythms, and discovering patterns of sexual arousal. Robin fondled Philip's balls, and Philip couldn't remember being so thrilled in a long time.

Robin came first. Philip's mouth was filled with cum. Soon after, with Robin providing slightly more suction, Philip shot his load into Robin's mouth. He could hear gagging. Robin leaned over him to the Kleenex box, and Philip could hear his manhood being spat into a tissue.

Philip turned around so that he was again face-to-face with his delightful visitor. They lay together for a time on the coverlet, Philip running his hands over the silken flesh. Philip's attempts at kisses were answered with a lessened enthusiasm. He thought Robin was reluctant to exchange kisses because their mouths had been in strange places.

About an hour later, they were at it again. Philip was as motivated as he was during the first bout, but he sensed a slight tenseness and a more tentative response. Both came again. Philip was very satisfied by the encounter.

Philip suggested they go down to tea. Robin dressed himself, and Philip put on a large robe over his naked body. He knotted the cord and accompanied Robin downstairs to the lounge.

He put on some music, a Mozart symphony, and showed Robin his latest magazines. Then he went down to the basement to brew tea. When he came upstairs with a huge tray, Robin jumped up and took it from him. Philip cleared a place on the cocktail table, making the mounds of stuff on the table's ends even larger.

They ate ravenously, finished off a pile of tiny sandwiches, ate all of the shortcake biscuits in the neighbor's tin and polished off the big pot of tea. Philip kept looking over at Robin. He seemed to fit in. Philip felt comfortable with him. Perhaps this might develop into something. Later, the two watched television. At seven, Robin announced he would have to leave at eight-thirty so he could catch his train back to Oxford. Philip asked if he would come up to the bedroom again. Robin assented, but he asked to take a shower first.

When he came out from the shower, his nude body still glistened with a few drops of water. Philip sat on the edge of the bed and maneuvered the young Cambodian to a position in front of him. He ran his fingers over the smooth skin and abruptly popped the semi-erect penis into his mouth. With his right hand, he manipulated his own penis as his mouth stiffened Robin's penis. After a short time, they both ejaculated again.

Later in the hallway, when Robin was leaving, they hugged, and Philip kissed Robin on his forehead and cheeks. Robin agreed to come to the house again on Friday at seven to stay with Philip for the weekend.

That following Friday night, Robin spent it with Philip, and both enjoyed the sex. On Saturday, Philip drove Robin out to his friend Anthony's country cottage. On the way there, Robin asked Philip to teach him how to drive, which he agreed to do at a future date. At the cottage, Philip had to make it quite clear to Anthony that he and Robin were a couple, and there was to be no sharing. Anthony, always one to try and horn in on his friends' companions, realized Philip was serious about this one, so he decided to back off, at least for a time.

33

Philip and Binky were walking along the Thames Embankment a few months later. Binky said, "I've been so out of touch in the wilds of Central America. How did you and Robin meet?"

"Well, one day last June, I was minding Graham Lasserby's dog. You know that cute little Jack Russell. I took him for a walk around the Serpentine. A long walk, a long ramble. The longer the better for that little devil, great staying power. While I was strolling around, this Asian lad gave me the eye."

"Or you gave each other the eye?"

"About right. It turned out he was a delightful Cambodian. He and his family had fled the war when he was about twelve or so. They had been in several countries and ended up in England. He was taking some special courses at Oxford. He's twenty-three now. Back at Number Thirty-one Sagnes Close, we talked about a number of things."

"Talked? And?"

"Had tea and shortbread biscuits."

"How charming. How typically British of you. And?"

"We kissed and fondled each other."

"Before or after tea?"

"Before tea, actually."

"See, I keep imploring the Royals. Always tell your stories in sequence, and then the press won't be up your twats about being open and honest. So you had it off with each other?"

"Yes. And I quite like the lad. Nice at cuddling. And now we've been seeing each other as often as possible. He stays at my home for long weekends. Quite wonderful. Very loving."

"Well, jolly good for you. Cheers, my friend."

"I may have him move in with me and live here in London. I'm getting him a position in Lasserby's firm."

"Does he want to date? Any sharing possible?"

"Absolutely not. He isn't someone to be passed around. No. People will have to understand that, or they'll be unwelcome in my home or as friends. While you were away, I made that clear to Anthony. You know what a leech he can be."

"Message received, old chap. He shall be forbidden fruit as far as I am concerned. I completely understand."

Philip knew that once Binky had been forewarned, he would be true to his word and not go after someone Philip fancied.

34

A hot, humid July day, the kind Londoners crave and then bitch about when they finally get it. Philip with a newspaper under his arm, was off on a park walk. He shambled in that sort of drunken gait of his down Albion Street to the corner and crossed over into Hyde Park. He started down one of the pathways. Women were pushing prams. Some young men were self-consciously propelling strollers with young tykes aboard. Frisbees were being tossed. Squirrels were running about, stopping, waving their tails like flags. Children were running and screaming, screeching as if they had just discovered their voices. Many dogs bounded about without leashes.

Philip eventually came to a shaded bench where he sat. His eyes closed. His newspaper fell off his lap. His mind traveled back, as it often did, to a room in the Raffles Hotel. It was an afternoon. Had he summoned up the year 1970, or had it come unbidden into his mind?

Excruciating bright sunlight everywhere streaming into the room. The young Asian man, Tom, was wearing a pair of white shorts. He was seated in a peacock chair, which dwarfed him, working on a big file of papers. Philip entered the room, an incredibly handsome Philip, glowing with health, wearing a singlet and shorts.

Philip said, "Tom, we are going to have to celebrate. We have gotten through these years successfully, still part-time, infrequent lovers."

Tom looked up and answered in his clipped English, "I think we've made love in most of the cities in this part of the world, haven't we, dearest?"

"But I still like it here in Singapore at Raffles, our first trysting place."

Philip leaned over and kissed Tom who returned the kiss.

Tom rose and embraced Philip. They engaged in a long passionate kiss. Then they caressed and fondled each other.

Philip whispered, "I love you very much. You have made
me a fulfilled, loving human being, rather than the thing I
was before, existing on the fringes of real life."

"You are my expert lover."

"Let's go to tiffin and have prawns and champagne, and
fresh strawberries and cream if they have any left."

"Strawberries, prawns, salmon, gin and tonic. You British
bring Britain with you everywhere you go. Before we go
downstairs, let me get my notes in order and clear up a few
things."

Tom picked up his stack of papers, took a pen, and put on
a pair of reading glasses, which made him look like a successful businessman.

He questioned Philip. "The Berlin station. How did you
make contact with the runners? What was your code procedure? Who was the lead runner? Where were the drops?"

"Well, up until a few months ago, and I believe it still may
be true, an agent would pass by Strenger Strasse about eight
o'clock on alternate nights every other week."

"The same agent?"

"No, it would vary. He'd park near either the Diana or the
Werbler Cafés, go in one or the other depending upon where
Freda was, sit in a quiet corner, and order coffee."

"He'd pick up one of the newspapers off the rack?"

"Yes, then slip a small label on a predetermined page and
return to the table with another newspaper."

"And who was Freda exactly?"

"Freda was the sister of Walther, a runner. She would pass
by and pick up the label. The code procedure was to use yel-
low and then blue."

"Who were the runners?"

Tom was making entries in his notebook. He looked over
the top of his reading glasses at Philip, who seemed bored by
all of this shop talk.

Philip offered. "Our lead runner was Hastings at first, then it became a German named Thorsten. You have the names of the Brits who were involved."

"The codes?"

"I gave you the codes before when I gave you the tunnel locations."

"How often were the codes altered?"

Philip reached down and caressed Tom's chest. "Tom, you're such a handsome Mata Hari."

Tom was persistent. "But how often were the codes altered?"

"Roughly every third week."

"Now about the tunnel. From the wires you had tapped into their headquarters, did you ever intercept a full alert?"

"Twice, dear Thomas. The time of that Russian colonel's defection. And when the second tunnel was discovered. When they shot our radioman."

Tom was busily taking notes.

Philip had other things on his mind. "C'mon, love, we can cover all these mundane matters after lunch and a bout of lovemaking."

"God, I love you, Philip."

"You are the great love of my life. Hurry, tiffin awaits us."

Philip awoke with a spasm, a transition to wakefulness. He looked around, aware that he had nodded off. He picked up his newspaper, rose, and moved off, walking stiffly.

It could be dangerous to dip into the past. You never could be sure what would bubble up to the surface and, indeed, boil over. Better to stick with the present without journeys into the ambivalent past; stick to his current springs, summers, and falls with Robin, and his winters sampling Asia and culminating with his dalliances with Rey in Manila. Yes, better stick to the present, a safer perspective.

35

The Nelsonian Club, a private men's club, is housed in an imposing Georgian building that sits back from Piccadilly. Its crescent driveway leads up to an entrance with a portico and columns. On a fall evening in 1981, unusually cool for the season, the windows in the building looked inviting with the bright lights radiating from within. Through the high windows of a first floor sitting room, Philip and Sir Charles could be seen talking.

Dressed for dinner, Philip and Sir Charles were seated in Windsor chairs preparing to have cocktails. A fireplace blazed at each end of the large sitting room. Members were seated around the room chatting or reading newspapers in the very male, privileged atmosphere.

Philip leaned back and said, "It's pleasant getting together here in your club for cocktails and dinner. But, Charles, your message on the phone yesterday infuriated me."

"I wanted to speak to you about my decision."

"I cannot comprehend your going back into the Service, even if it is only on a temporary basis. God, haven't you had enough of the bloody games and deception. Little boys playing at being men. The endless purges, witch-hunts and betrayals."

Morris, the old retainer-waiter at the club, shuffled over to Sir Charles and Philip and placed drinks on the table between them. They nodded thanks, and he shambled away.

Sir Charles declared, "They say they need me. The Prime Minister herself met with me. The intelligence network in Ulster is lamentable. Look at the mess there in the North. Our lads being ambushed and picked off. Senseless bombings."

"*They* always make it sound earthshaking and urgent."

"All that is needed is a year or two of tight restructuring. How can I say no? I can go back to my own life in two years at the most. I think I can help. They can be persuasive when they want to be."

"Oh, yes, the almighty *they* again. Surely they can get someone else to do what is largely an administrative reformation. Charles, you've done your part. You've paid your full share."

"Philip, I know you're right."

"Now it's time to serve yourself. You've bought a few years of happiness, and you've been honest about your sexual nature. You've lived a little."

Morris silently picked up Sir Charles's ashtray and scuffled off.

"Of course I'm going to miss my gay existence. These have been very happy years. Honest years. I've faced life full on."

"Don't go back in. You returned from the dead, the land of the closeted, to the land of the living."

"I think if I were in a committed relationship with a man, I wouldn't consider going back, but because of the type of bloke I like, I don't think that is ever going to happen."

"All the more reason for not going back—the danger of exposure if you slip and seek out a sexual encounter."

"All I seem to want now is a quickie and anonymity, not to form a bond. I think that my long marriage, those stultifying years, keeps me from wanting a relationship."

"Now that you've had a taste of the open life, closeted life will destroy you. Don't give them a chance to do to you what they did to me."

"God, Philip, that was awful."

"I hope you didn't know what they were going to do in advance. I wanted to die. The pain was unbearable."

"Enough of this. Let's repair to the dining room."

Philip and Sir Charles drank their final gulps, rose and walked to the dining room. They sat at a table with white linen, crystal water and wine glasses, formal dinner settings. The room was another male bastion with men seated at the various tables, old waiters shambling in and out. The waiter brought them a round of drinks.

Sir Charles said, "I've always deeply regretted the part I played in your ghastly interrogation."

"Charles, they almost ruined my life. They tried to destroy me. And they almost succeeded. Look at the way they used you to get to me. They made me shop two people I barely knew, two people I thought to be gay because they were effeminate and were gossiped about as being gay."

"But they were gay, roaringly so. They didn't make any bones about it."

"But it was only office chatter. I didn't know if they were or not. Like everyone else, I just thought they were. What I did was unforgivable and an act of extreme cowardice."

"You couldn't help it. I could tell your pain was unbearable. I heard your screams. But when the two, Tomlinson and McCall, were called in, and were vetted, they freely admitted they were gay."

"Whatever happened to those poor men?"

"Both were pensioned off. One lives in Brighton, the other in Mallorca. They were always camping it up in the Service. They were no loss."

"Maybe they were no loss to the Service, but what gave me or you the right to end their careers? Their being gay didn't make them disloyal or traitors."

Their waiter bustled around the table. The two friends were not paying much attention to their menus; they were not yet ready to order.

Sir Charles offered a suggestion. "The lamb here is always good. But Philip, those two flaming queens. It probably freed them from the few constraints they felt anyway. Both are probably in seventh heaven telling about all their spy exploits. The closest either of them got to an operation was in the archives."

"Not only was I betraying fellow members of the Service, I was betraying fellow gays. I still have nightmares of Whaley and the others squeezing those boils, squeezing out the names."

"You did what any sane man would have done."

"I would have done anything to make them stop. And it turned out that I did do the ultimate. God, what a traitor I really was."

"Don't keep blaming yourself."

"I knew Billy Sadler was gay. I didn't shop him. He was and is a rice queen. Now he's out of the Service honorably. I wasn't about to throw him to the wolves."

"Philip, there comes a time when . . ."

"I protected a friend and sacrificed two acquaintances. I saved my own kind of gay and destroyed two other gays. Betrayal upon betrayal."

"Blame the Service, not yourself."

The waiter approached their table again, saw that they were not yet ready to order and backed off.

Philip's expression was grim. "They infect you with the boils, squeeze them until your whole body shudders with pain, and then lance them so that offal oozes and spurts from the boils *and* your mouth. God, what a country, what an excuse for civilization. Does a country like ours deserve loyalty?"

"In my case, Philip, I have to go back. Partly duty, partly the feeling I know I can do some good in Ulster, and partly because I've still got some good years left to have my fling when I'm out again."

"God help you. You may live to regret it. I wish you well."

"What was strange, Philip, was the way Whaley held such a personal grudge against you, how he blamed you for his problems. And, of course, he blamed me for reprimanding him about his over-the-top interrogation tactics."

"Poor nutter. Not all there. The Service drove him over the top as well. But enough of all this nattering. Sir Charles, here's to good luck and success in the Six Counties."

36

One morning at dawn as Philip lay in bed, unable to get back to sleep, he could hear a soft childish cry. Out of the darkness, a tiny vulnerable voice whispered, "Move my bowels?" Another pleaded, "Shower, sir?" Still another persisted, "Please, sir, let me in." Other sounds, other whisperings. Philip's eyes teared as he thought back to that tropical night. A ceiling fan whirred inside the room. Water splashed on the floor of the public shower beside his cabin. The scratching at the screen, the plaintive pleas, then those wide pleading eyes looking at him from behind the bushes.

His own body issued a sudden frightful spasm. Next to him, Robin awoke and, leaning on his elbow, looked down at Philip's tearing eyes.

"A nightmare?" Robin blotted the tears, reached out and gathered Philip to him. Philip clung to his lover, his body shivering and shaking. They held each other closely, and Philip, in his mind, lingered a while at the cusp of a private hell, then relaxed slightly, aware of how close he had come to the abyss, how tempted he had been to cross over to the forbidden territory. Tempted, tested, had he failed or passed the test?

Three sets of eyes still haunting him, whispering, imploring. It would have been so anonymous, so daring, so utterly damning. He knew he would never go back again to that place on the river, to that bank of an interior river one would cross only at the cost of losing one's soul.

37

Philip and Robin's relationship was going well. Robin had become an essential part of Philip's London life. Robin hadn't moved in partly because Philip still took his long winter Asian trips and partly because he felt he had to spend considerable time with his mother and sisters in a flat in Camden Town that Philip subsidized. Philip and Robin went often to the mother's flat. Robin's absorption with his family and his job at Lasserby's firm in the City gave Philip time for his walks, his luncheons with friends, his attendance at lectures, his visits to the Long Yang Club, and for writing letters to his network of friends around the world.

The last week in October of 1982 was a cold one though it was warm and cozy inside Philip's Sagnes Close home. Philip and Robin were seated in the lounge. The room as always, looked well-lived in and homey. Philip was seated on the sofa. Robin was clearing away dinner plates from atop the magazine and book pile on the cocktail table in front of Philip.

Robin had obviously been able to make use of the services of a bespoke tailor. His suit was perfectly tailored to fit his thin frame. Robin had been working on his English, and he spoke almost impeccable English, finely enunciated. There were a few lapses now and again and a touch of accent, but he had become more British than the British in manners and speech.

"That was delicious," said Philip. "I really didn't know exactly all of the delicious ingredients, but it was very tasty. Thank you."

"Gramps, you old ninny, can't you tell one food from another?"

"No, not in one of your delightful Cambodian concoctions."

"Well, it was shrimp and chicken with lots of fresh veggies

on a bed of Thai rice, some shredded coconut, with a soy and ginger sauce."

"Mmmm. It was heavenly. You are a wonderful chef."

"You are easy to cook for."

Robin smoothed down Philip's hair and wiped his chin with a napkin. If Philip had known what was transpiring outside, he would not have been so comfortable and at ease.

Philip's old interrogator, Whaley, was boldly walking in front of the mews houses. He stopped and stood a short way from Philip's house. The curtains were drawn so no one could look in or out. He passed the house, glanced at the windows, and then retraced his steps. He was disheveled and had had one too many drinks. Slowly, he made his way out of the mews, muttering under his breath. It would take a brilliant analyst to ascertain why Whaley had fastened on Philip as the bête noire of all his problems. It was a single-minded persistent hatred that seethed in his disturbed brain.

His Service file described him as "highly aggressive, apt to carry irrational grudges, homophobic, delusional, easily provoked, obsessive, impulsive, and a man who suffered from symptoms of depression." Nevertheless, he was judged not to be disqualified for the duties assigned to him. Crackpots often did fall between the cracks in his line of work, and were, at times, needed for the dirty jobs.

Inside, oblivious to any danger or possible threat, Philip was listening to Robin, who was being playful as he said, "You really do drool at times. I have to keep you neat and presentable."

"Just keep mocking me, laddie."

"Philip, if other people could see your tenderness, the way you love to cuddle with me, your displays of affection, they'd envy me."

"My fellow rice queens do envy me, I'm sure."

"You are like a father or grandpa to me; loving, caring, and real. And a little bit absent-minded. I think all Englishmen your age have some of their marbles missing."

"A marble here, a marble there, I suppose. Do you mind being called Robin?"

"No, not all. It sounds very British. I picked the name from *Winnie the Pooh*. How much more British can you get than that? Much better than having people mangle my Cambodian name."

38

Robin and Philip had just finished dinner and were listening to some Mozart. Robin said, "Oh, I almost forgot. That awful Simon Tharpe called up again this morning while you were out. I refused to talk to him."

Robin busied himself around the room, trying to make the piles of magazines and books neater, fluffing up pillows. He always tried to bring some order out of the room's chaos.

Philip, annoyed, answered, "Good for you. His supposed research for a book about spies is pure tabloid rubbish. He's looking for more dirt on the intelligence service that he can peddle to the gutter press. Imagine after all these years, they are still digging into my past. It's all those spy novels and films that have appeared lately."

"People like him keep trying to rake up your past. Do you regret your career in the spies?"

"No, not in the slightest. Except for that interrogation and the awful torture I went through at the end, I have never regretted my actual years in the Service. It was a useful life. I am proud of what I did for God and country."

He was pestered by people from the tabloids and so-called biographers who wanted some dirt on MI6. People called up, came to his house, met him in clubs, wanting to write about him, his experiences in the Service, and use him as a source. Some, in tabloid fashion, would unmask and lay bare the secrets of the Service. Few knew he had been eased out.

Books had come out. His name had been mentioned. In one book, they named some agents who had been outed. His name appeared in a nearby paragraph as an operative who had been eased out for murky reasons, not reasons of disloyalty, but for reasons left up in the air. There was the hint he might have somehow compromised the Service. He was rather lumped with people who had committed indiscretions, were security risks, drank too much, gambled, were woman-izers or people who were indiscreet.

Nothing was actionable under libel rules. These writers skirted around the edges of legal liability. Other books in a paragraph or two did trumpet his achievements, in propaganda work, in Geneva and Lisbon during WWII and his work in Berlin during the Cold War, particularly his tunnels, and his surveillance of East German intelligence.

Robin goaded him, "The life and times of a master spy? Philip, why don't you write your own memoirs? Get a jump on these vultures. You write the book, and you make the money from it and get the credit you deserve. Your book could be more authentic. Make it a 'tell-all' without giving away any state secrets."

"I've often thought of that, but I just don't seem to have the ambition to sit down at that old typewriter and bang out my story. It would take years of hard work, and I'm just not up to that. Lazy, I guess."

"Pity, you could scoop them all."

"*Scoop.* You *are* picking up your English rather well. No, I'll never get around to writing my own story. You know, my life seems to have been sketched out and defined by two things: loyalty and betrayal. My life has asked of me, 'Will you ever betray or be betrayed?' Enough of that. What I like is my present life with you."

"Are we a good pair, a good match? A Scot and a Cambodian?"

Robin took a pile of books from the floor by the television and put them on an already overloaded table by the rear picture window.

"Yes, indeed. A good match. Let's watch some telly. Oh, and by the way, Gramps as you refer to me, is not entirely absent-minded and addled, and all of his marbles are intact even though they are somewhat scattered about up there."

Philip lightly tapped his head. Then he added, "Is it a good arrangement do you think for you to spend three nights here and the rest of your time with your mother and sisters in Camden Town?"

"I have to be there to watch over them at least four nights a week, and I'm here when I can. Someday perhaps you'll let me move in full-time."

"The choice doesn't seem to be up to me when you spend so much time with your family."

"You know I have to do that. It's my duty as a son."

"Yes, I fully understand."

Robin worked on a festering sore. "And it isn't as if we are full-time lovers anyway. You'll be going on your Asian trip in a few weeks anyway, and I'll be left here in London for months by myself."

"When you've worked longer, you'll be able to come with me for a month or more in the winter, but right now you can't afford to take too much time off. Lasserby needs you at the office."

"While you're in Manila with that tramp that has his nude body hanging in your bedroom. He isn't even good-looking."

"I won't be spending that much time in Manila. I'll be traveling quite a bit. Malaysia, Sri Lanka, all over."

"Don't forget you've promised to bring me to some of those places when I can get time off."

"Don't worry. I shall, but first you have to build up some seniority on that job. After all, that's why I have paid for those beautiful bespoke suits of yours. You have more expensive clothes than I have. My stuff is off the rack at Marks and Spencer."

"You still wear some of the jackets you had from before the War. But, Gramps, there's a good program on Germany that starts shortly. I'll take this tray of dishes down to the kitchen, do a bit of washing up, and then we'll watch the telly."

Robin took the tray of dishes down the steps to the drab dining room and kitchen in the basement. He had spoken to Philip about the need to modernize and redo the basement kitchen and breakfast nook.

39

That evening, Philip sat gazing off into space remembering his past. His mind wandered back to his days in Berlin. He fastened on a scene he had visited in his mind before. It was night. The Wall dominated the landscape. It had become the most important physical presence that overwhelmed the city physically and mentally obsessed the residents.

Philip closed his eyes. In his mind, a car drove up to a devastated, heavily bombed building in West Berlin close to the Berlin Wall. A younger Philip got out and walked quickly to a cellar way, then down a set of broken stone steps to a basement doorway. He knocked lightly on a door that looked as if it hadn't been used in years. Clara, a harried woman in her thirties, opened the door and led Philip into a dimly lit room.

"What's been happening, Clara?"

"All hell breaking loose. Their radio operators signaling their code has been broken. And it sounds as if they want us to know about it."

Philip hurried with Clara to the entrance of a tunnel that had been burrowed under the wall. Philip and Clara, their backs stooped, crept through long passageways and tunnels held up by makeshift posts. Clumps of dirt fell as they passed. Philip had a small penlight.

At a wider section of the tunnel, a radio operator was seated at a packing crate on which radio listening equipment had been set up. The tunnel continued on beyond this wider area, and beyond was an abandoned sewer main. There was a dim lantern that threw shadows on the walls.

The radio operator had a headpiece on and was listening. Philip picked up another headpiece and listened. No one spoke. Philip listened for about a minute. All of a sudden, he dropped the earphones and whispered urgently.

"My God, they're on to us. Quick. Leave everything. We've got to get out. Run for it."

The radio operator queried, "The equipment?"

Philip said, "Just give me the rucksack of tapes."

Philip slung the bag over his shoulder and whispered urgently, "Leave it. Run. Now. Schnell!"

Clara, the radio operator, and Philip ran from the spot. Philip and the operator had penlights. There was scuffling and shouting behind them. From the sewer main, East German soldiers were running with machine guns and dogs. The soldiers saw the three fleeing people. They started firing. The noise in the confined space was deafening. The dogs howled. Dust was erupting. Dirt fell from the tunnel roof and walls.

The radio operator was hit and fell. Philip took out his automatic and fired at the pursuers. Cries of pain; some soldier had been hit. Part of the tunnel collapsed between the three and their hunters. Philip dragged the radio man with him. An Alsatian had been set free to chase them. Clara shot the dog as it was about to leap.

They reached the basement on the western side. Philip, gasping for breath, was leaning over the radio operator. Clara had her automatic ready and was prepared to fire if anyone came through the tunnel. Philip raced to a detonator mechanism in the corner. He pushed the plunger and the planted charges exploded with great force deep within the tunnel, trapping anyone within and destroying the listening equipment.

Philip returned to the operator and said to Clara, "It's his leg. Help me get him to the car. Hurry."

The two helped the radio operator up the stairs to the basement entrance.

Philip heard a sound. Robin had come into the room with a tray holding two cups of tea and some cut-up fruit. He asked, "Daydreaming?"

"I was thinking about an old movie called *Betrayal in Berlin*."

"Never heard of it."

"Like a lot of things, it was way before your time."

Robin sat down next to Philip on the sofa. He had the remote control in his hand, adjusting the television set for a night of viewing. "I've heard this is an exciting movie about Germany."

"Robin, one thing I can't wait to see is a thriller about Germany."

40

The Eight Ducklings was a charming, inviting name for a pub. If one did not know the disreputable-looking pub itself and the grungy street in Belfast where it stood, one might think by its name it was an up-market establishment in some gentrified suburban hamlet. Northern Ireland in March of 1983 was not a kind place to be. The factions were in a twilight war. The streets were dangerous.

It was evening. On the street in front of The Eight Ducklings, a British army lorry rattled by. The interior of the pub was dimly lit. It was an old-fashioned pub bar built in the Edwardian era. It was a neighborhood place, but few locals were in the pub at the time.

Sir Charles was at the bar talking to a tall handsome young man in his late teens, good-looking in a rough masculine way, well-built in jeans and flannel shirt. Two men were seated by a table in front of the loo. They furtively watched the older and younger men at the bar.

Sir Charles spoke to the young man. "Here, let me buy you another pint."

"Cheers, mate. I'll take you up on that."

"You lads have had it rough here in Ulster. It's not easy pulling duty where everyone is a suspect. No one you can really trust."

The soldier inhaled deeply from his cigarette and took a gulp of the dark ale. "Even the little ones give us a lot of shite. Women spit at us. People swear at us. If I had my way, I'd give up the bloody place."

"It's thankless duty."

"Let the micks and the Orangemen kill each other off instead of killing our boys with a shiv in the back or by setting off a cowardly bomb."

"The most hazardous duty you chaps can pull."

"Bloody idiocy, I call it."

Sir Charles asked, "How long have you been posted here?"

"Eleven months, ten too long. I didn't sign on to become a bloody nursemaid. Are you a businessman then, sir?"

"No, I'm part of our government trade mission. We're trying to encourage industry to move in."

The soldier stretched and flexed his shoulders. He was proud of his build. He looked as if he worked out. He looked earnestly at the older man as he asked, "Why should any industry move to this bloody hellhole, this piece of shite?"

"We're hoping to stabilize things. Get the economy going so that people will want peace. It isn't easy." Sir Charles changed conversational lanes. "You look fit enough. Do you play a bit of football? Sports?"

"I used to, but since I've been here, not much. I've had no inclination. I work out in our gym a lot. Keep myself in shape. Trying to give up smoking. The odd pint or two is my only other vice."

"Are you married?"

"Oh no, sir, too young for that."

"Have you met any girls here?"

"No, it's too hard getting acquainted. In the clubs you don't know who's who. They have a sanctioned dance once in a while, but they get some ugly ones."

"The girls are real pigs, eh?"

"Mostly my mates and I get together for a pint. Some darts, snooker, watch some raunchy videos. Are you alone then? Is your wife here with you?"

"No, she's back in England. At any rate, we've been separated for quite some time. I'm a bachelor all over again."

The soldier stood back from the bar. "Excuse me, mate. Nature calls."

The soldier walked over to the small loo and entered the grimy, dirty space, with its two filthy urinals and a tiny sink. He faced a urinal, unzipped his fly. In a few seconds, Charles followed him into the loo and joined the soldier at the next urinal.

Lamely, Charles said, "I realized I had to go as well. Can't seem to hold it like I used to."

"Room for all. Join in."

Boldly, Charles looked over at the soldier's penis. "Whew, I don't think any girl is going to turn down that equipment. You are certainly well hung, uh, well endowed."

"I guess so."

The two men who were seated outside the W.C. door had stolen up by the loo door. The soldier, having finished urinating, was shaking out his penis. Charles reached over and touched it.

In a loud voice the soldier asserted, "Whoa there. Uh uh. Careful, Mate, I ain't into any of that."

The two men were now in the loo standing behind Sir Charles.

The first man identified himself. "Police. Sir Charles Monmouth, I would call that a lewd and indecent act. We are placing you under arrest. Constable Lewin, did this gentleman place his hand on your member?"

"Yes sir. He did. He made advances and then fondled my privates."

The second man, also a policeman, crowed, "Sir Charles, I guess you got your hand caught in another man's fly. We've been onto you for sometime. Been doing a little too much open cottaging for a man that knows all Her Majesty's secrets. An out and out homosexual, I'd say."

The young man trumpeted, "God, another bloody poof. What is the world coming to?"

Sir Charles was silent. He knew that his world had just been destroyed. Philip's warnings flew into his mind. *How could I have been so bloody stupid. And why did I even think I could get away with it?*

41

The Terminal, the Service's interrogation center, hadn't changed in the intervening ten years since Philip's humiliation, except for more signs of neglect and a failure to maintain the structure. It was a bleak March afternoon in 1983.

From behind the same shuttered window, one could hear a familiar deep male voice thundering. "Faggot. Queer. Cocksucker. Asslicker. You are nothing but a fucking faggot."

It was the same interrogation room Philip had endured. A more potbellied, more dissolute Whaley, old-looking beyond his years, was bleating, "Pervert. Poof. Homo. Bloody scum. Shitlicker. Ass reamer. Sodomite. Sissypuke. Bloody cunt."

The lights blazed in the second floor room. Seated at the table was Sir Charles Monmouth. He looked exhausted, drained. He was unshaven, wearing a white shirt, no tie. Standing to one side of the table was Sergeant Whaley, balding, with coarser features. He was in shirtsleeves, no tie. Drink had played havoc with his face. A slightly younger man, not Trimmer, stood silently in the corner of the room, trying to distance himself from the man being interrogated and the inquisitor, Whaley, who seemed unbalanced at best.

Whaley gloated, "Sir Charles, welcome! If I'm here long enough, I'll be interrogating every bloody one of you poofs."

Charles knew his interrogator all to well. "Whaley, cut to the chase."

"Is there a real man left or has everyone turned into a bloody cocksucker? I can remember you telling me to vet certain people, to find out if they were queer. Now you."

"Let's get it over with, man."

"What the hell did you come back in for anyway? We were well rid of you, and then you show up again like a bad penny, a bent, poofter penny."

"It was stupid of me to come back. I thought I could do some good."

"You thought your bloody position could give you access to some loose cock, that's what you thought. This is a criminal charge, and, thanks be to God, it's going to give you hard time to serve. It's not a question of the Service hushing it up. Oh, I love it. Finally one of you swells pays the piper."

"But he wasn't a minor."

"Oh, but he were, you see. That's how they set you up."

"He looked to be in his early twenties."

"Did that give you the right to fondle his cock? But he weren't in his twenties; he were closer to seventeen."

Whaley's face was a few feet from Sir Charles's. He was angry, and his spittle was landing on Sir Charles. His beer breath stank.

"How could he be so young?"

"That's why they chose him, you see. So you'd think you were safe, a bit of the consensual you thought, but the boy were a copper. Jail bait. Not a consenting adult at all."

"That would be entrapment."

"Entrapment, shite. The boy were wired, don't you know. You never ascertained whether he was a copper. If you see a boy, or a pensioner for that matter, in a loo, does that give you the right to fondle him? Sometimes I wonder what makes you poofs think you have the right to do anything you feel like. Bollocks on your rights. Now, to business. The usual folderol. Who in the service is a homosexual or lesbian?"

"I do not know of anyone. That's the truth."

"I seem to remember a hardened case, your mate, Philip Croft. Miss Croft. She used to run a gay sauna in Soho. The bloody nerve of that poof. It went bust. Served her right. The cheek of the bastard."

Almost to himself, a chastened Charles stared down at his hands. "I should have listened to Croft."

"I seem to remember carbuncles on his arse. I seem to remember lancing. I seem to remember pain and suffering, and finally a confession. Why not start at the inevitable end result and give us what we want before we have to resort to all that claptrap and nonsense?"

"Why are my testicles swollen? You didn't . . ."

Whaley's unwilling accomplice in the corner had rolled out a stainless steel cart. He started snapping rubber gloves, clinking and clanking metal instruments in metal trays. Loud guffaws issued from Whaley, and his triumphant laughter thundered through the room.

42

As well as being one of Sir Charles's clubs, the Nelsonian on Piccadilly was a club to which Binky belonged. When Philip returned from his Asian trip in April of 1983, Binky invited him to a welcome-home dinner. Winter that year had hung on rather longer than it should have. In the club sitting room, two fireplaces were roaring. Binky and Philip were seated in Windsor chairs surveying the passing parade on the busy street. It was late afternoon. Several geezers were seated in quiet areas enjoying the warmth of the fireplaces.

Binky arranged the crease in his trousers and spoke softly. "In the wilds of the Orient, did you hear the news? They bagged Sir Charles in Belfast, caught him in the loo with some underage lad. He's in for it now."

"Yes, I heard. How awful for Charles. I warned him. I told him, 'Don't go back in. They'll destroy you.'"

Morris, the old, doddering waiter, who was not fond of Binky, tried to ignore him. Binky enjoyed playing cat and mouse games with him and signaled to him for a drink.

Binky said, "Sir Charles could be a cocky, arrogant bastard. Seemed to know it all. You still don't know what part he played in your ouster from the service. He could have been the one who shopped you. He could have engineered the whole thing. The outing. The easing out of the Service."

"True. I'll never know. No one deserves to go through what I did. I'm sure the word was out that he was actively gay since his retirement. He was playing the gay scene pretty heavily, even the leather scene. He made a big mistake going back into harness."

Binky signaled to Morris again, who pretended not to see him. A loud shout from Binky. "Morris, dear man!" Finally, the ancient retainer creaked toward their chairs. He grudgingly looked at a smiling ingratiating Binky.

"I'll have a gin and tonic, please. How about you, Philip?"

"Scotch and water, please."

Morris drifted off, moving slowly. Binky watched him putter off, and he smiled. It was a charade, and a contest of wills between the veteran combatants. Then Binky turned back to Philip. "According to you, Sir Charles went after a bit of rough trade."

"Yes, unfortunately he did."

"They say he's going to pull a considerable amount of jail time from this escapade. I've heard he's a beaten man, lost a lot of weight, very depressed. Prison may well kill him."

Morris sauntered by without drinks. Binky looked at him, but Morris studiously ignored him. Binky muttered, "That old fucker. It does little good to report the old bastard to the club secretary. I'm not greatly liked here. I have the audacity to bring my young conquests here."

Philip was more interested in Sir Charles's predicament. "Will it never end? This Spanish Inquisition of homosexuals?"

"When they've finally eaten us all, pooficide, I guess. Burn the faggots, crush the perverts. Stamp out the lavender queers."

"How can one be loyal, patriotic, when they try to destroy one's soul? It sorely tests a man's loyalty. What does loyalty to one's country mean anyway? Isn't it a sham?"

"Just a little boy's game."

Philip asked, "Shouldn't our first loyalties be to our true sexual natures?"

Finally, Morris set two glasses and serviettes down in front of them and tottered off. Binky smiled, a minor triumph.

Philip went on, "When the last gay person is standing, who or what will it be? Any animal that eats its young or its own kind is a beast of the basest sort."

"Remember your experience. Lance the boils. Squeeze the pus out. Make it drain. Get rid of the contagion."

"I still have nightmares, wake up in a sweat. Someone is squeezing my buttock, and the pain from the boil is excruciating. I'll never forgot what they did to me."

Binky rose and retrieved a bowl of crisps from a nearby table. He offered some to Philip, who declined.

Binky sighed. "Enough of this wallowing in self pity. Say a prayer for Sir Charles. His reckless behavior has damn near done him in."

"I'll pray for him."

"I'm still sorry you had to close the sauna. I had some very good times there. Do you miss it?"

"Not really. It was getting to be an awful financial drain. An expensive sex hobby. Some men collect cigarette cards or lead soldiers. I opened a gay sauna for my amusement."

"And, may I add, the amusement of many others."

"It would have been a lot cheaper to collect music boxes. I do miss Kwan, though, and some of those lovely Asian lads."

"How on earth did you become exclusively a rice queen?"

"I'll tell you my Thailand story some day."

"And how is Master Robin? Is that love affair still clicking along?"

"Yes, doing very well. He's been a wonderful find. We really enjoy each other's company. We make a good pair. I think he's the one I'd like to be there to turn out the lights when I go."

Morris stopped at their table, picked up the half-full crisps dish and walked off with it. Binky's eyes followed Morris as he shuffled off. He shook his head in disbelief.

Philip mused. "Now I laugh when I hear I am called a rice queen, and someone else is a potato queen because he likes whites."

Binky added, "Or someone else is a dinge queen or choco-holic because he likes blacks."

"Awful names! I'll never forget my first crush. I had crushes in boarding school looking at some upperclassman or the coaches. When I was young, I fixated on handsome Caucasians, but didn't act upon my desires."

"Philip, my escapades began when I was still in the cradle. My mother stopped breast feeding me when I became so voracious. But before we get too wound up in reminiscences, let us retire to the dining room. I have selected a fine wine to go with our roast. Let's leave Morris to his efficient waitering duties and see if we can fare better in the dining room."

As he passed Morris, he whispered something Morris could not catch. He was left muttering, exasperated, "Eh? Eh?"

43

The American, Craig, was a fanatical letter writer. He relied completely on mail and didn't use the telephone except in dire emergencies. He barraged his friends with long, newsy letters. Most of them dealt with the details and complaints of his daily life. Philip found them interesting, and he, too, was a letter writer, though less intense than Craig.

In the days of running the sauna his time had been limited, but afterwards he had more leisure time for letter writing. Philip and Craig exchanged their missives; usually one or the other would type his letters. Craig gave him news about his retirement in Pensacola, in Florida's panhandle. He had retired there because of its facilities for retired service personnel: medical facilities, commissaries, PXs. Craig had friends in the Philippines who sent him the latest information on the gay scene, but he relied on Philip to fill him in on the latest news he wasn't getting through his own sources.

Craig asked Philip what the political situation was like and if there had been police crack-downs. Philip gave him reports of his latest trips. Craig had no intention of ever returning to the Philippines. When he said goodbye to a place, that was it.

Craig was coming to England. He had never been to see Philip in London, never seen Philip's narrow mews house. He said he would like to make a car trip with Philip from Land's End at the southern most tip of England on the coast of Cornwall to John o' Groats at the farthest end of Scotland's northern coast.

Craig planned his vacations like military campaigns. He had envisioned a three-week trip, a leisurely one where they would stop at historical sites, castles, famous cathedrals, some coastal towns. Philip was thrilled. He warmed to the idea at once. He liked elaborate car trips, and he enjoyed company on his trips. He studied the Royal Automobile Association car guides assiduously and loved plotting a trip. It would be a lovely trip, to him a challenge. He volunteered his car. Every few years, he bought a new car so his cars were always in good condition. Both were C of E men, so they would enjoy seeing cathedrals, churches, and abbeys and attending Anglican services.

Craig arrived in London. He was disappointed when he learned Philip wouldn't be putting him up in his house. Robin was staying there most of the time then. With one bathroom, it was too small for three. Craig loved to freeload off other people. Philip shunted Craig off to a cheap B-and-B a few blocks away near Marble Arch. Craig thought it to be quite expensive, but by London standards, it was dirt cheap.

Robin couldn't take off such a large block of time from work, so he was not going to be making the car trip with them. He would rather tour the continent, take a skiing vacation, or serve as cook on one of his wealthy friend's yachts as it cruised the Caribbean or the Greek Islands. He had already taken off a great deal of vacation time and was skating on thin ice at work. Philip had used his connections to get him the position, and Robin didn't want to disappoint his boss, Philip's friend.

Robin was welcoming and affable when he met Craig for the first time. Robin was an excellent cook, and he prepared a delicious dinner for the three of them with a tasty salad and barbecued shrimp. For dessert, Robin prepared a cake covered with newly cut fresh fruit and a liqueur. They consumed two bottles of wine. Robin had outdone himself and was a charming co-host. He made cooking seem easy and didn't disappear in the kitchen for long periods.

Later, when Philip and Craig were alone, Craig made some disparaging slighting remarks about Robin, which Philip did not appreciate. They were not uttered all at once, but were dropped in at odd moments in their conversations. "Isn't his face marred by a rather flat nose?" "Isn't he awfully slight?" "Doesn't he try to be a touch too British, and exude a tiny bit of British snobbishness, which seems unjustified coming from an Asian lad who is lucky to have been admitted to England at all?" "Isn't it uppity for him to affect a posh accent when he's a Cambodian refugee?"

These remarks annoyed Philip. He countered with an offensive. "He has worked so hard trying to improve his English, and has done wonders. I don't think he should be criticized for being overzealous in trying to imitate an educated English accent."

Philip meant it to sting, but it only resulted in a minimally chastened Craig. Craig was so devoted to his own ego and inner being that it was difficult to pierce his thick, insensitive, bitchy skin.

Philip resented the remarks, but said little in direct rebuttal. He did go overboard in his praise of Robin though. He said many complimentary things in Robin's defense; not in direct response to Craig's snide comments, but just as part of a general offensive.

Philip realized what it was. Craig was alone, and was jealous of anyone who had a lover. Philip did not convey any of Craig's remarks to Robin. He didn't have to. Robin sensed things. He realized that Craig didn't like him. He thought Craig was mischievous and wouldn't mind splitting them up if he could. Craig was nosy and lingered in places where he could hear Philip and Robin talking.

Robin later told Philip he didn't particularly like Craig. Robin didn't turn cold or show any animosity, but there was a certain light chill in the air. He did not bend over backwards to prepare elaborate dinners. Philip didn't blame him one bit. Craig went down a couple of pegs in his estimation, and Robin started avoiding Craig whenever he could.

He told Philip, "I love Anthony and Binky and your other friends, but I am not fond of Craig. I'm sorry, but I cannot abide him at times."

Philip nodded and agreed. "Yes, he can be trying. I think it's a good idea you're not doing this Land's End to John o' Groats odyssey. I may turn out regretting it myself."

Philip and Craig spent a good deal of time planning their itinerary, what they wanted to see. Craig had traveled through various parts of England when he had been in the army, but he deferred to Philip for the best sites.

He said, "Someone has to be the man in charge, so I yield to you. You shall be the leader." Would this were true. Philip later learned Craig never ceded command in any situation.

They started from London and headed west through Devon and Cornwall to Land's End.

Philip insisted, "These two counties are among the most beautiful in the land with many quaint seaside towns, great pubs, and fine beaches to visit."

They went to Clovelly, St. Ives, Land's End, Plymouth, Exeter, Torquay, and back through London and north to Cambridge. Philip showed him his old stomping grounds in Cambridge, the emblematic punting on the Cam; then up to Nottingham, York, a stop at the seaside town of Scarborough, and in Scotland visited Edinburgh, St. Andrews, and Philip's birthplace in Dundee.

On a number of occasions, the troops (Craig) got restless, and the troops were not so compliant. Craig could be obstinate, and if he got a bug up his ass woe betide the commanding officer.

During the trip, Craig continued his digs about Robin (*God, the man could be insufferable,* thought Philip). Most of the time, Philip enjoyed his company. He was funny and did have interesting stories, some quite hilarious. They shared the same sightseeing zeal and the same interest in the C of E.

Craig proved prickly on a few other things, though. Often it was either his way or the highway, even though earlier he had said, "It's your car, I'm your guest, it's your country, and since someone has to be a boss, I defer to you as our chief."

Philip was easy-going, slow to take offense, but sometimes he had to put his foot down, hopefully not in some form of animal shit.

Later in one of his long missives Craig told Paul and Hal in the States that Philip never paid any attention to where he was walking. He had an unerring ability to find and step in cow flop, sheep dung, dog poop, any kind of animal waste. He was an absent-minded walker. The car stunk from manure. Craig had to make sure Philip cleaned his shoes before he got in the car, entered a pub, restaurant, or hotel.

Craig liked expensive and good restaurants. They both enjoyed good wines and liked their booze, but Philip could eat in a pub, a fish and chips shop and be happy. Craig, on the other hand, could sleep in a dump, a cheap share-the-bath place. For sleeping Philip wanted a private bath and a comfortable hotel, preferably with a swimming pool and amenities.

Craig was not comfortable and complained about his night's sleep unless his headboard faced north, and he refused to eat with three-tined forks. Craig could be, Philip later said to Binky, a royal pain in the ass.

Because Philip was easy-going and malleable, and because Craig conceded on the good hotels and Philip on the fine dining, the trip turned out to be a limited success.

Prickly authoritarian Craig and pliant good-soldier Philip went from one end of Great Britain to the other without a serious quarrel.

At times, Craig, a spoiled only child, an ex-army officer used to getting his own way, a loner, and a man who had lived alone and apart most of his life, sometimes lost his temper when he didn't get his way. Philip won on his choice of hotels so he took afternoon swims and could enjoy pools and hotel saunas which gave him a chance to look at nude or semi-nude young men.

After the trip, when Craig had returned home, his letters became less frequent, and the relationship cooled until finally after a year, Craig stopped writing altogether, dropped completely out of sight, and refused to answer any of Philip's letters. A year or two after the end-to-end British Isles trip, Craig dropped all of his Philippines connections. He dropped Paul and Hal at the same time as he made Philip a non-person. Binky and Robin were not heartbroken by the schism since neither of them were fond of him anyway.

44

Paul Rowan and Hal Turner were visiting London in the summer of 1985, staying at the Blaineville Arms Hotel at Marble Arch, four or five blocks from Philip's mews house. They had an itinerary mapped out: ten days in London, a train trip to Edinburgh where they would rent a car and tour Scotland, a ferry to Belfast, a train trip to Dublin, and a flight back to New York from Shannon. While in London, Paul would check on the status of one of his plays that was about to be produced in an Off-West End theater.

Paul and Hal would pursue their overheated theatergoing and probably see a dozen plays. They'd have time for city walks and visits with Philip, whom they had not seen on his home turf before. On previous visits, he had been out of town. Paul called Philip the first night, a night when they were due to see "The Mousetrap." Philip suggested the following morning he would pick them up in his car at the Blaineville and take them on a tour of his alma mater, Cambridge University.

The next morning, they were on their way in Philip's car. Philip explained that Robin, his flame, was working, and that they'd meet him that night for drinks and dinner at Sagnes Close.

Just before reaching Cambridge, Philip stopped at the Rupert Brooke pub. It was a charming, old fashioned public house named after the World War I poet. They sat outside and had pints of lager and pub grub. After lunch, Philip led them to a meadow behind the pub. There were cows tranquilly feeding in a pasture. Philip pointed out the towers and spires of Cambridge in the distance. A path led to the university town through the fields. Philip said he sometimes walked from there to the town.

Philip walked a short way down the path in his usual

absent-minded weaving manner, and stepped into a cow flop patty. Paul and Hal laughed because Craig had told them in one of his last letters that Philip had an unerring ability to step in animal waste. Philip took a branch and wiped as much of the cow dung off his brogues as he could, but the smell of it lingered in the car afterward.

They parked in Cambridge, and Philip served as their guide around the town. He pointed out the various colleges, including his own, Corpus Christi. He showed them the Bridge of Sighs, the Round Church, and they wandered through college quads, went through the King's College Chapel, and the Fitzwilliam Museum.

Philip brought them to the Backs, the grassy areas facing the River Cam where young men with straw boaters were actually punting on the Cam. Hal and Paul, knee-jerk Anglophiles, were enchanted. Hal's respiratory problems were kicking up, so they decided to call it a day. They had seen a great deal of Cambridge with the best of guides, an enthusiast who had spent years there.

When they returned to London, Philip drove his car right up to his front door. Robin came to the door to meet them. Hal and Paul were charmed by him. He graciously served drinks in the cluttered lounge. After spending some time with them, Robin decided he liked Hal and Paul much better than he did Craig. Neither one had Craig's pomposity and dismissiveness. The two Americans seemed to go out of their way to ingratiate themselves with Robin.

As they sat with their drinks, Paul asked about the name for the neighborhood. Philip said, "I've never been quite sure of the name for our district. Some call it Marble Arch; some call it Bayswater because of Bayswater Road; some Paddington. I prefer calling it East Mayfair because I think the name Bayswater sounds too plebian, too down-market."

Paul thought there had always been something of the closet snob about Philip. He was a nice snob, not a bitchy one, but still a snob nevertheless. His snobbery reared itself only occasionally and was not pervasive. Craig was far more of a snob than he.

One night, at a dinner hosted by the two Americans, Paul mentioned the spend-down plan he and Hal were practicing. They had gone to a financial advisor who developed a plan for them. All of their assets were added together and estimates were made of the funds' appreciation. Then the advisor took into account their ages and expected needs.

When they reached age ninety, they would have just enough to see them out. Since neither one had any significant close relatives, and since they did not want to leave any money to any other persons, the advisor gave them a figure they should allot to spending down each year. They were now engaged in spending down their assets by taking expensive trips, and by buying whatever they felt they needed or wanted.

Fascinated, Robin exclaimed, "See, Granddad, I told you that you shouldn't hoard your money like Silas Marley."

Philip retorted, "Marner."

"Whoever. Do what Paul and Hal are doing. Spend it now when we can enjoy it."

"*We?*"

"Follow a sensible plan like they do and allocate so much on expenditures."

"Yes, Robin, I can see how you'd love this scheme."

Each time Robin saw the two overseas visitors, he continued to pump them on the intricacies of the plan, its practicality, and its efficacy for Philip's nearest and dearest.

Robin was intrigued by this revolutionary concept, while Philip was decidedly leery of it. After all, if they pooled their net assets, Robin would have little to bring to the table. The spend-down scheme became a running joke during their London stay. Robin praised it highly. "It's a capital idea," he trumpeted, while Philip maintained, "Yes, it's my capital we're talking about."

By the end of their stay, Robin found he got along very well with Hal and Paul because they treated him as an equal. They were not condescending, whereas Craig had treated Robin as a trick, an inferior, and had belittled him. Paul and

Hal embraced him, empowered him because he was dear to
Philip. Paul made no disparaging remarks to Philip about his
lover, probably because he was used to dealing with a long-
term partner and lover of his own.

When they left, the four hugged one another. Paul knew
which buttons to push to make Robin feel good about himself and his relationship with Philip. Neither Robin nor Philip
suspected Paul might have long-range ulterior motives.
Craig had said you could never trust a writer to ever be completely magnanimous. "You were apt to turn up as grist for
his mill," he had said.

45

Binky was seated in Philip's enveloping and comfy couch in Sagnes Close with a gin and tonic in his hand. Philip was in his easy chair across from Binky with his scotch and soda. Between them was the Mount Everest of books and magazines that formed the great mound on the cocktail table. Small enclaves had been cleared in front of each for his glass. A large bowl of nuts sat perched at the summit of Publications Everest for their use. Both had had several drinks over the course of a few hours. Darkness had fallen outside, and they were losing count of their drink intake.

Binky was slurring slightly, but Philip was in no condition to notice. Both had happily passed the stage at which the buzz kicked in. Their buzzes were in high gear.

Binky asked a question of Philip. Perhaps he had heard the answer years before and only wanted to keep the conversation going and the drink flowing. He often did that when he was in his cups. Perhaps Philip knew this, but perhaps he was unaware that he had answered the same question before. Or perhaps he just enjoyed recounting the story.

"So, Philip, how did it happen that you chose the avocation of being a devoted and unvarying rice queen?"

"My first time, my first sexual encounter hooked me for life."

"Yes?" Encouraging.

"It was in Thailand."

"Yes, I've been there many times. Charming. Beautiful place."

"It was afternoon. I recall lush greenery, stunning mountains, an idyllic setting. A hotel or spa roosted on a hillside overlooking a lake."

"Yes?"

"I was twenty-two. I'd finished university. I was visiting Chiang Mai in northern Thailand. I went to this place in the mountains that had mineral springs and a spa."

"Ah, yes, Chiang Mai."

"At the desk, they asked me if I wanted to partake in a massage. I said yes. Why not? It was a spa. My muscles were tight. I seem to remember being tightly wound in those days."

"Aha."

"I went to the massage room, a small room with a table, a window with a view of the mountains and the gorgeous scenery beyond. A young Thai about eighteen wearing a Speedo was smiling winningly at me."

"Oooh. Nice." Binky was aroused.

"This young man, my masseur, was very handsome. He had a smooth hairless body. He was wearing only that brief bathing suit. I undressed, lay face down, completely nude, on the table. Almost immediately I had an erection . . ."

"Oh my God, no . . ."

"But I felt no restraint and no shame. As I lay on the table, he covered my body all over with a soothing cream. He gently rubbed it on. Every part of my body tingled. It felt glorious. The cream he worked over the buttocks, around the anal aperture."

"I wish you would tape this. I can use it at home. It's better than phone sex."

"His exploring hands were so provocative. He removed his skin tight trunks. He had an erection as well."

"Oh, I love it! You're so poetic and pornographic. Go on, Philip."

"He got up on the table and knelt over me. He had a beautiful penis, but immediately I was smitten by his testicles . . ."

"His balls. It sounds sexier. More earthy, less clinical."

Philip was enjoying his own narrative. "His scrotum sac. I reached over and touched it, silken, smooth like a silken purse with two beans within. We were gentle, touching, caressing and fondling one another. We both had very busy hands."

"Oh, God, this is heavenly."

"His chest was above me. His pink areoles around the nipples were so delicate and beautiful. We kissed each other all over."

Philip rose somewhat unsteadily, picked up their two empty glasses, and shambled to the drinks cabinet in the hall. A clink, another clink. One ice cube in each glass. A quantity of gin, then scotch in the other glass. A dash of tonic, a splash of water. He returned, handed Binky the gin and set the scotch down in front of him in his tiny clearing, grabbed a handful of nuts, and continued his narrative while Binky sat with his mouth still agape.

"I kissed his tiny nipples. He lay on top of me, our penises rubbing together. We kissed passionately. I hugged him to me. I started moving my body against his."

"Oh my God, keep going. You are a pornographic poet."

"Our bodies were undulating and entwining about each other."

"Of course. Brilliant! Yes."

"Our bodies were touching everywhere. We were like one, one entity melded together. I was passionate. We kissed and hugged. Our tongues were tracing inside each other's mouths, every inch of our skin touching. Bodies tightly interwoven."

"I can't believe you ever have to go to the cinema with your imagination. Go on."

"I moved my body frantically against his, and I had an enormous ejaculation, my sperm . . ."

"How graphic! Your cum, your load . . ."

"My ejaculate covered his body. He laughed and kissed me. Then we showered together. Today, when I think about that shower, everything gets very gauzy and foggy, diaphanous in the steam. I felt no guilt. Relief mostly. I realized then I was truly homosexual."

"Indeed. I don't know what else you could feel at that point."

"And I thought, God, this is the most beautiful experience of my life."

Binky looked elated by the story he had just heard. "You
have a wonderful memory, much more vivid and erotic than
mine. But, Philip, why always Orientals?"

"I cannot even remember desiring a Caucasian after that.
I was hooked, really blessed with my love for Asians."

"Philip Croft, The Rice Queen Spy!"

Philip asked, "Your gay life experience has been so different, hasn't it?"

"Much more open than yours. I've loved being gay and
talking about it. My life would have been horribly dull without my gayness. But if I ever bore you with my gay enthusi-
asms, and you want me to talk about embroidery or bridge,
or growing roses, I can, you know."

"That won't be necessary."

"But, seriously, Philip, on another topic, are you still
insistent on going to the Philippines even with all that trouble brewing there between the Aquino and Marcos factions?"

"Oh, yes, I'm going as usual. I'll have my Reynaldo to look
after me. He's always loyal, loyal to a fault."

46

The Manila of February of 1986 was not a kind, gentle, harmonious time for Ferdinand Marcos or for Philip Croft. Indeed, eras were coming to a close. It was early afternoon. Mobs of shouting people were in the street. A country of what some took to be a docile people was in upheaval.

Philip's boyfriend, Reynaldo, was hurrying through the crowds massed in the streets. Civilians were talking to soldiers in and around tanks, trying to persuade them that their futures lay with the insurrection. Signs in Tagalog and English that read, "Down with Marcos" were poking above the mobs. Rey could hear for blocks around the sounds of demonstrations, the loud-speakers blaring. He was not pro-Marcos, nor pro-Aquino either; he was pro-Rey and for any kind of stability. He was two blocks from Philip's apartment.

In his apartment, Philip was seated across from his American friend, Paul Rowan. From the streets outside they could hear the shouting and the roar of crowds.

Philip seemed calm enough, reassuring, as he asked, "Well, Paul, are you settling into your apartment on Mabini all right? I can't think of a worse time to be here in Manila."

"And we Americans may have a little tougher time of it. Those years of backing the Marcos regime may come back to haunt the U.S."

"I fear the real action hasn't started yet. The irony is that neither of us has to be here. We're on holiday. It's their country that's shredding apart. By the way, how is Hal bearing up?"

Paul said, "As usual the pollution here in Manila isn't good for his breathing problems. He and I have already decided to go up to Pagsanjan, away from all this upheaval."

"I think you're right, but I intend to stay. Reynaldo will watch over me. If I get housebound, he can get supplies and run errands. I can rely on him. He'll be here soon."

"You're lucky to have someone trustworthy like that. I certainly arrived here at the wrong time. It's getting dicey. Mobs surging in the streets. Troops and tanks, protesters everywhere."

"One big group of students has taken over a section of Rizal Park." Philip stood and looked across at the park where phalanxes of students were massing. Paul joined him, shook his head, and returned to his seat. The mobs could be heard yelling. Bullhorns were blaring.

Paul asked, "Do you think Marcos can hold out against Aquino's people?"

Louder shouts and crowd noise erupted outside.

Philip said quietly, "Everyone knows Marcos was behind the assassination of Benigno Aquino. People have rallied round the widow, and Marcos is finished. It's only a matter of time before he has to go. It's people power against a tyrant."

"What does Rey say about all this?"

"Rey? You might as well ask the lamppost. He never had a political opinion in his life. Why should he? Like others of his type, he lives for the day, hour by hour. Whoever knows what goes on in their minds? I don't sit and have political dissertations with Rey. He grew up under Marcos; he knows no other. That doesn't mean he's loyal to him. He's loyal to his next pair of Nikes. Street savvy, yes; political loyalty, no. Not necessary."

"Are you worried about your personal safety?"

"No, but the heyday foreign gays have been having here, I believe, is over. Binky says a dictator keeps the lid on, and that sub rosa gay sex usually flourishes under a dictator. His examples are Franco in Spain and Salazar in Portugal. The trouble here is that sex got out of hand and publicly involved the little ones. That won't go over in a new people's democracy. Puritanism may be the wave of the foreseeable future."

"Finished for all gays?"

"For the foreigners who go after the little kids, I think. I can't imagine that will be tolerated any longer. Those of us who like young men in their late teens or twenties may or may not be able to soldier on."

Reynaldo was pushing his way through the mobs, trying to get to Philip's apartment. In the streets a great deal of yelling, shouting of slogans, "People Power," "Marcos Must Go," and other signs bellowing their messages. Jeepneys and buses were trying to move through the crush of people, but with little success. Crowds surged first in one direction, then another.

In the apartment, Paul was saying, "The U.S. has given the signal they will no longer tolerate Ferdinand and Imelda. They are dead meat."

"People here have been waiting for the U.S. to signal and apparently it has—finally."

"The Marcoses and their cronies have stolen hundreds of millions, probably billions between them. Greedy bastards. The U.S. says Marcos has to go—ironic after all of those years of them kowtowing to him, propping him up."

Reynaldo opened the apartment door and came into the room. Philip rose, cheered, "Oh, here's Reynaldo now."

Paul was immediately envious. Reynaldo was a young Filipino in his early twenties; a lithe, athletic body in white shorts with gleaming new blue Nikes.

"At last, the conquering hero. Hello, Rey. This is my friend from the U.S., Paul Rowan. He's a regular visitor here in the Philippines. He couldn't have picked a worse time to return."

Reynaldo shook Paul's hand. They appraised each other. Under other circumstances, something would surely have developed from this meeting.

"Hi. Philip talks a lot about you. All good things."

"Rey, Paul here writes plays that have been produced in New York and London. Some were very successful."

"Maybe I can be in one of your plays."

"As a character or as an actor?"

This didn't quite register with Rey, and Paul was not about to explain the distinction.

Reynaldo answered, "I love plays. But, Paul, it's very bad

out there in the streets. Be careful."

For someone he had just met, Rey seemed to Paul to be solicitous, caring.

"Yes, I've come at an awkward time."

Reynaldo added, "I've been in Manila for years, and I never seen stuff like this. I'm scared by it."

Paul asked, "Where are you from originally?"

"The island of Cebu. My whole family lives there. I . . ." Reynaldo hesitated; he had something he wanted to say, but held back, looking anxiously at Philip.

Paul continued, "It's certainly an eye-opener for me. Chaos everywhere, roadblocks, mobs of people, protests, restaurants and bars shuttered. Gay bars closed. All gay life at a standstill. Tricks scattered to the four winds."

Philip, somewhat disapproving, said, "Surely no one is thinking about sexual encounters in this upheaval. Oh, I know Binky would, but certainly not less sexually driven, obsessed souls."

Paul reminisced, "Reminds me of one summer week in Acapulco. A cyclone, a hurricane brushed the city. Tricks got blown away for days. We were trapped in our hotel for the week, and only the brave or desperate ventured out. Well, speaking of hotels, I have to get back to mine before I get caught in the crossfire."

Philip got up and tapped Paul's shoulder. "Stay in touch. And for God's sake, take care!"

"I'll call you regularly. As long as the phones keep working, that is. Otherwise, I'll try to send you messages by courier. Goodbye, Philip. And goodbye to you, Rey. Pleasure to meet you. Philip, I'll give Hal your regards."

Reynaldo gave Paul a hug and a peck on the cheek, which pleased him no end. "Be careful, Paul."

Philip showed Paul to the door where the two shook hands and said their goodbyes. When Philip turned, he didn't like the crestfallen look on Rey's face. Something was up.

"Philip, I can't stay."

Reynaldo started pacing around the room like a caged

tiger. He couldn't stay still. Philip craned his neck trying to keep up with Reynaldo's frantic circling.

"What do you mean, you cannot stay? I need you this afternoon. For God's sake, stay still, stop circling. Sit down. You're driving *me* crazy."

"No, I mean I can't stay here in Manila. I have to get back to my home, to Cebu. My family needs me."

"Surely your mother and father can get along without you."

"I've got to get back to my wife and baby. I can't leave them alone."

"Wife and baby? You never told me you were married or had a child. This is the first I've ever heard about them."

Reynaldo was a caged animal. He was orbiting the room, frenetically moving about, impatient and frightened.

"I never told you a lot of things. My daughter is four now. I didn't tell you because you guys don't like it if we have wives and kids."

"What do you mean *you guys*? You act as though I'm just one of many. Are there more men that visit you here in the Philippines?"

"Philip, sometimes you are so dumb about things."

"Dumb? How dare you call me dumb. The gall of you."

"I mean, you don't know the real world, my world. I have to go today, the six o'clock ferry. Already it's almost sold out. Everyone from the provinces is trying to get out of Manila. I've got important stuff to do at home in Cebu."

"Sit down. You're driving me crazy. You have responsibilities here with me. You promised to look after me."

"I can't stay here. You can go back to London anytime you want. This is my country. I have to be with my family, my wife and baby."

"Wife and child. You really sprang that on me."

"You're here on holiday. You don't have to be here. Go home where you'll be safe. Where you belong."

"You, young man, belong here with me."

"I don't belong here, and I don't belong to you or anyone

else. My family comes first. Go back to your London. Your home and friends and clubs that you talk about. Nothing ever really changes for guys like me. For a while with you I think I'm getting ahead, then I slip back."

"Rey, I always wanted the best for you."

The ferocity of Reynaldo's pacing had increased. He was sweating, and he looked like a hunted animal.

"You're here; then you go. Now something like this happens. You guys can always fly away like gods. While you're here, you're playing with us like little toys. Some of you even call us toy boys. You never invited me to London."

"I never thought you wanted to go."

"Take me to London now. Tomorrow. I'll go. I can mail money to my family."

Philip was flummoxed. This had been sprung on him without warning. He was flustered. The last thing he'd want was for Rey to be on *his* home turf. Not anywhere near his London life. Especially with Robin on center stage. All right here in Asia, a semi-serious fling, but not on the sceptered island.

"I can't. You wouldn't be happy there. It would never work out."

"See? I knew you wouldn't ever take me to England. I gotta go back to my province."

"I absolutely need you here. There's no way for me to get food, provisions."

"You're in no danger at all. You can come and go and get food whenever you want. Go out there and smile and wave your arms around in support. They'll love you, and let you go wherever you want. You can even go to the British embassy. They'll let you in. You told me you were one of their spies. They owe you."

"I'll be trapped in here."

"It's not my problem anyway. You always say you're on holiday. My family needs me. No one is going to bother you."

"Please. I beg you."

"Foreigners aren't the targets. It's the Aquinos people

versus Marcos. People power. That's a laugh. The people won't be any better off under Aquino and her crowd. I may end up worse off."

"Rey, stay here."

"You think Marcos had crooks around him. Wait until you see the rich landlords backing Aquino. Wait until you see them."

Outside, a mob of people surrounded an armored personnel carrier. They were waving *Aquino* and *People Power* signs. They implored the soldiers to join them. One soldier climbed down, took off his helmet and was embraced by the crowd. Yelling, shouting, much agitation everywhere. A group of nuns formed a line and were marching. Philip had gone to the window as the shouting increased in volume. He turned to Reynaldo and pleaded. "Reynaldo, I need you here desperately. I cannot be left alone. I need you."

"You're not alone. You've got a whole bunch of well-off Brits and Americans in your gang."

"Rey, I beg you. I promise I'll help you out. You'll be pulling the rug out from under me if you leave me here alone. I'll be deserted. I'll have no one I can trust."

Rey went to Philip and hugged him close. "Philip, I need some money for my family when I get home. You aren't like the other sugar daddies. You haven't given me much cash—ever."

"I am *not* a sugar daddy. I hate that expression. I told you from the start it was not going to be money for sex with me. Dinners, drinks, the hotel, small change, new trainers, yes. Not handouts of cash."

Reynaldo looked at the chaos and upheaval in the street below. Surging mobs, armored personnel carriers surrounded by crowds.

"I haven't complained, but you've always been very tight with me. Please give me a hundred pounds for my wife and baby, my parents."

"No, I need you here. I'll give you a hundred pounds at the end of the week, next Sunday, if you stay."

"I told you. I can't stay. I have to be with them. I called

them yesterday. They are scared to death. Food is getting scarce there."

"Rey, *you* calm down!"

"Everyone is acting crazy at home, my wife says. I've got to be with them. Please give me the money. I've earned it. I gotta be with my family."

"I have very little cash, young man."

Philip faced off with Reynaldo; he was angry. Rey was desperate.

"If you won't help me now when I need it, this is goodbye forever. If you don't give me some money, I'll never forgive you. You're taking bread out of my baby's mouth. Please don't be so mean and selfish, so cheap to me when I'm desperate."

"No, no. Please stay. I beg you. I need you."

This was not one of Philip's finest hours. Inside, he could feel self-hatred growing as he groveled. If he ever told Binky about his groveling, he would be told he was shameless, a disgrace to johns everywhere.

Reynaldo cried out, "Will you help me or not? I'm going."

Philip took out his wallet and threw money across the floor. He held his hand to his head. A kind of wailing sound issued from him. Reynaldo quickly gathered up all the money. Then he reached over, hugged Philip, kissed him and headed quickly for the door.

He said, "When all this is over, I'll come back, and we'll have fun again. I promise."

He opened the door and ran out into the hall.

Philip followed him, shouting, "Rey, Rey, come back. I need you. I can't be left alone . . ."

But quickly, out of a sense of pride, a feeling of shame, Philip's mood started to change. A tougher, inner Philip, a Philip from the past, started taking control. "Ingrate . . . Bastard. What the hell am I going to do now? Alone, here in Manila. Rey, you've betrayed me. Another betrayal. Bloody . . ."

He went to the telephone. picked it up, heard no dial tone, kept tapping the button.

"Oh, shite, the phones are out. Bloody hell!"

Outside were shouts, the noise of tanks moving into position.

Reynaldo rushed out of the apartment street entrance to the chaotic street scene. He was pushed, shoved, buffeted. More loud shouts. An army jeep tried to plow through the crowd. Reynaldo saw Paul standing in a doorway watching the crowds. He went up to him. They smiled at each other and shook hands. They talked together. They walked across the street. Reynaldo put his arm around Paul's shoulder.

Philip was looking out his window to the street below. He saw Reynaldo and Paul walking off together, Reynaldo with his arm around Paul.

He swore, "Bloody hell. Bloody betrayals!"

47

On the flights back from the Philippines, Philip had a great deal of time to think about his future. Now he would have to be shrewd, selfish to some extent, and manipulative. It was 1986. Soon Philip would be seventy-one years old. It was pretty clear to him that even though he would be traveling back to his beloved Asia for future winters, the Philippines would not be on his itineraries.

His last encounter with Reynaldo left a sour taste in his mouth. He didn't want any more of him. And he had pretty much given up on the country in general. It would be different now with the new regime.

In thinking about his future, he took stock of what he had. He had a good relationship with Robin, but there was a danger of losing him unless he paid more attention to him. He decided Robin should move into Sagnes Close. A selfish thought crept in: who was going to take care of him in his declining years? He hoped it would be Robin. He would have to stop taking Robin for granted.

He was ready to make changes. Some he would make on his own; some he was willing to concede to Robin if pressed. He would see how far he would have to give in.

After arriving at Heathrow, he took a train to Victoria and a cab to Sagnes. It was an extravagance, but he had changes to make. Robin was waiting for him when he got to the house. A long hug and kisses. Philip hoped Robin would perceive the kisses were more fervent and meaningful than usual.

Later, Philip was settled down with a light snack and a gin and tonic. He gave Robin a first-hand view of the people power revolution and the overthrow and exile of the Marcoses. Carefully picking his way through a minefield of deceptions, he told Robin nothing of Reynaldo or Reynaldo's betrayal. In general terms, he assayed the new Philippines was not to his liking. He told Robin he was determined not to return. Robin was pleased with this decision for a number of reasons, not least of all because Reynaldo would be out of the picture now.

Robin told about his life while Philip had been away, though Philip knew that it was a sanitized version with all social relationships with older men expunged. Robin said his mother and sisters were soon going to move to Toronto to live with one of Robin's brothers.

Then Philip broke his news. "On those long flights coming home I had a great deal of time to think. Robin, my mind is made up. I want you to come here and live—permanently, full-time, for good. I'm a lonely old man, and I want your company."

"I don't know if I can manage that. Mother, sisters—I don't know if they can manage on their own."

"You could go over there evenings. I already go to dinner there a few times a week. I'd go more often if need be."

This would be wearing on Philip; he found the nights with Momma and the sisters quite boring. But since he was footing the bill for the rent of their flat anyway, he might as well get more use out of it.

"Robin, you're here three or four nights a week now. I want you to move in full-time."

"Why this change of heart, Gramps?"

"I think we should be a couple, as live-in lovers."

"Some of your neighbors think I'm your houseboy because I look the part."

"I shall stand out in the Close and shout, 'We are lovers.'"

"That won't be necessary. I'll think about moving in with you, but I want a change before I even consider moving in. Come on. Get up, and follow me."

"Why?"

"Up, please."

Philip got up slowly, creakingly, a quizzical smile on his face. Robin headed up the stairs. Philip followed Robin up the stairs to the floor above. Robin and Philip reached the doorway to Philip's bedroom on the second floor. They stood in the small bedroom facing the nude portrait of Reynaldo.

Robin was unaware that Philip was looking at the picture with disgust. Truth was, he'd have liked to tear it to shreds and burn it; such was his disillusionment with Rey.

Robin issued his ultimatum. "You may keep the picture, but it must come down before I'd consider moving into this house full-time. It will only be a memory—in the back of your closet."

Philip moved with unusual rapidity. He took down the picture and shoved it unceremoniously in the back of the closet behind some pieces of shabby luggage. He said, "In the closet you go. In the closet. That was the story of most of my life. The spy in the closet."

Robin said, "See, Gramps, that wasn't so difficult, was it?"

"No, indeed, my dear. It takes a burden off my mind."

"Well, good for you. As soon as I can straighten things out, I may plan to move in full-time in the fall."

Robin thought Philip really seemed to have changed. Maybe he was coming to his senses about the Philippines. He thought how easy it was to have him get rid of the picture. Perhaps he hadn't asserted himself enough in the past.

He did want some changes made. The basement kitchen and dining room were a disaster. Modernization of the basement was a must. *If I work at it, I may become more of an equal, less of a second-class citizen in his eyes.* Secretly, he had thought Philip to be too domineering and that their relationship had a tinge of racism or colonialism to it, topics he had never broached to his old-fashioned lover.

Philip thought all his scheming on the planes coming back had borne fruit. Getting rid of Reynaldo's picture was satisfying, but he mustn't let that on to Robin. There probably would be later battles, but this one hadn't even amounted to a skirmish.

48

It was an October morning in 1986. Philip's lounge was getting only a few shards of light from the outside as the sun fought a losing battle on a cloudy fall day. Autumn had conquered summer's frivolousness. Philip was wearing a bathrobe. He has been ill, an illness that had precipitated a bout of depression. Age was creeping up on him, and at seventy-one when he had a bout of flu, he did not recover as rapidly.

Robin came into the room. He was well-dressed, wearing a blue, double-breasted blazer and an ascot.

"Gramps, I'll be off to work in about an hour." He fluffed up the pillow behind Philip. "Look at you. You look so disreputable. I'll have to wipe that drool and snot off your face."

He leaned over with a Kleenex and wiped Philip's mouth and chin. It was a caring gesture, not demeaning.

Philip complained, "I'm famished."

"Would you like me to cook you some eggs and bacon before I go?"

"Yes, that would be lovely."

"Well, come on down to the kitchen with me."

Robin led the way toward the short stairway to the basement dining area. Philip shuffled behind him. Robin walked through the tiny dining room and into the kitchen. Philip slowly maneuvered the stairs.

Philip came into the kitchen nook and sat at the table facing the kitchen. The room was not a pleasant modern area; it was dingy and needed a dressing-up. Robin busied himself in the antiquated kitchen, taking bacon, butter, and eggs from the fridge. Philip, leaning over the table, his elbows braced on it, rested his head in his hands, looking exhausted by the short trip from upstairs. He livened up when he smelled the frying bacon.

"Thank you, Robin, for everything. I owe you my life. If it weren't for you, I would never have gotten over that bout of depression. I'd have been in some nursing home for life were it not for your ministrations."

"Oh, not quite, but I did think for a time you'd never come out of it."

"The way you hounded the doctors to work with me; that's what saved me. You were there every minute when I needed you. You've been magnificent. My Godsend."

Robin was busying himself in the kitchen, frying bacon, scrambling eggs, chopping up parsley, preparing bread for the toaster. Robin was encouraging. "You're coming along nicely now, showing great progress."

"Yes, thanks to you. Now I want that move. I want you to come with me full-time."

"I will move in, Gramps, but only under certain conditions."

Philip's Scotsman's sense of shrewdness clicked in. "What conditions?"

Robin set out on the dining table a plate with jars of various jams and marmalades.

"First, Paul's spend-down plan. If I'm that great, let's start on that spend-down plan Paul Rowan was talking about. You figure out your assets, use a table to judge life expectancy . . ."

"That should be easy in my case with the little I have left . . ."

Robin was on a roll, "Calculate interest, and then allocate a certain amount of money to spend each year, so by the time you pass on, you've depleted a goodly amount of your wealth."

"I thought the doctors were due to get it all."

"Use your money while you can still enjoy it. I can use some new clothes."

Philip was beginning to rethink things. "Well, we'll think about spend-down now. You may be right."

"You aren't going to live forever, even though all you Scots think you will. I want us to sit down and work it out on paper and figure how much we are really going to spend-down each year."

"Spend-down each year. That has a Labour Party ring to it."

"You'd have to stop being so blessedly cheap about certain things. You do spend on travel, the car, and some things, but look at this dining room and kitchen; this place needs modernization and a complete makeover. New floors, new tile, walls redone, new cabinets, modern lighting, new appliances, high tech stuff . . ."

"We've talked about that. Yes, I can see you're right, but . . ."

"You can't be a cheapskate forever."

"Frugal, thrifty, economical . . ."

"Spend some of that money you've got salted away. Exotic trips with me, a new car, clothes for my job, new telly."

Robin placed plates in front of Philip, scrambled eggs, toast, potatoes, thick, crisp bacon. Philip admired the food and dug in with gusto.

Philip, chewing, offered, "New bespoke suits for you, a Woolworth cardigan for me perhaps, or to be real spiffy, a Marks and Spencer leisure suit."

"And a new CD player with a decent sound system. So a true spend-down would be number one."

"And item number two on your list of ways to squeeze poor, indigent, depressed old gramps?"

"We would have to go to your solicitor and draw up a legal agreement, a will that would leave me a sum from your estate, but most of all, this house when you pass on. I've known you for enough years to deserve that, haven't I?"

"Six blessed years."

"I don't mean to sound mercenary, but don't I deserve to inherit rather than some cousins or nieces or nephews. I've stayed here many nights and whole weeks anyway. I don't want to go homeless, Gramps. Can't you see that?"

Philip had almost finished his breakfast. Robin had been clearing up in the kitchen.

"No one deserves this house more than you. You've cared for it for years. And more importantly, cared for me. Loving care. And you've certainly earned what money I have left when I pass on."

"Thank you, Gramps, uh, Philip."

"Of course, with our mutually agreed upon spend-down plan, I may be a pauper by that time. But I agree to your terms so far. I wouldn't want you to file a palimony suit."

"I'm the pal who's earned the money. And, Philip, no more trips to the Philippines unless we go together. And I don't want to go to the Philippines anyway, not the way you've described that place with all those little sex-crazed friends of yours rooting around for pick-ups. I want to go to Sri Lanka, and I want you to go back to Cambodia with me. It will soon be safe enough to go back."

Philip spoke half in jest when he said, "Spend-down, the house, my money, no more solo trips to the Philippines. God, what else are you going to try and squeeze out of me when I am too weak to fight back?"

"Fourth, I promise to stay with you forever, to love you as no one else ever did, even Tom, and to have a rich and abundant sex life with you."

Philip finished his plate of food and was relishing his last sips of tea.

"Why is it that mates promise you a rich and abundant sex life when you are too old and weak to enjoy it? You are the great love of my life. My savior. I surrender. God, now I know what unconditional surrender means. Robin, you should have been a solicitor."

Robin should have quit when he was ahead, because one of his desires proved a sore spot between them.

49

The Long Yang Club was meeting in Heather's Haunt on Dean Street in Soho, another basement club that lent its facilities out to the club on a slow Wednesday. The year was 1987. Music was playing, and the lighting was not bright but flattering for some of the older chaps who needed every subterfuge of vitality they could muster. As usual, there was a mixture of Asian young men and older Westerners. Philip was seated with Binky in a booth.

"Philip, don't you ever get a young strapping guardsman or football yobs at these fetes?"

"No, afraid not. Only my type, which quite satisfies me."

"I still think the name Long Wang is quite ironic."

"Do you say that to top me off?"

"No, don't be silly. Only a bit of levity to break the ice. Perhaps tonight I'll get lucky and meet my Prince Charming, my M. Butterfly. I wouldn't mind seeing Kwan again. Now there was a stud."

"He shows up once in a blue moon."

"Will Robin be meeting us later?"

"Yes, but only reluctantly. He said he'd drop in for a bit. He comes here with me occasionally, but he doesn't like it. Spot of jealousy when he sees me talking with young Asian men. I know a few of the lads."

"Like you, Robin's not much for bars."

"Doesn't feel up to these late nights that get him off his exercise regimen. He goes to the gym early, jogs, and then goes on to the office."

"He looks fit. But isn't it more than his exercises that keeps him from coming to these socials?"

"He really is quite jealous when I'm at these dos. Thinks I'm going to pick up a replacement for him. His latest fixation is to quarantine me in some country cottage where I won't be able to have the odd fling now and again."

Robin entered. He looked somewhat ill-at-ease and dismissive of the surroundings. Binky greeted him. "Ah, here's the young prince now."

"How are you, Binky?" He hugged Binky and saluted Philip, "Hello, Gramps."

Binky said, "I'm fine, young sir. But why ever does Philip let you address him so demeaningly as Gramps?"

Robin's tone was playful, joking. "Because he is getting to be a doddering old pensioner. Doesn't know enough to stay home and stop going to smoky dens like this one. Always out scouting for new conquests."

Philip's expression was not a pleased one. "You'd like me to stay home and take up knitting."

"I've just had a long talk with Anthony at his club about purchasing that little cottage in Devon near his digs with that beautiful garden that I could really make into a treasure. It's going for a song right now, and you know how close it is to his home."

Philip was taken aback by this quick assault in front of Binky. "I love London. We'd have to do a lot of thinking and talking before acquiring a second home."

"Think of how nice it would be to have a country cottage to get away from all the city bustle."

Male couples were dancing in the background. Some pairs consisted of a Caucasian and Asian; others were two Asian young men laughing and dancing together.

Philip asserted. "I adore city bustle. How much time would we be able to spend there in the country? I certainly wouldn't want to be there during the week while you were cavorting around London."

"Think about the lovely garden we could have."

"I have lovely gardens to look at everywhere in London. Beautiful parks. I love going to lectures, to my club, the occasional cinema. Seeing Binky here and my other friends. I love weekdays in the city. The country is all right for weekends if you're working. I'm retired, remember?"

"But the beauty of the country . . ."

Philip was becoming more emphatic, more defiant as he avowed, "And dear Robin, I absolutely refuse to be ware-housed, put out to pasture in some drafty little cottage in the countryside. I fully intend to live and die as a city mouse, thank you, young sir. I appreciate your advice, but I defi-nitely do not concur."

"Anthony said we could get it for a very good price."

By then Philip had become angry, and Robin hadn't been gauging his true mood. "Sod, Anthony! You two do a little too much plotting, too much something behind my back. I am telling you once and forever, Robin, I shall never be ware-housed in some godforsaken bloody cottage in the country. I worked for my whole life with the goal of living in London where there's life going on. I shan't be shelved quite yet, thank you very much!"

"But, Philip . . ."

"London is where I am going to live. That's final. You would love to stick me in some cottage while you had your escapades with your clique of gray-haired admirers."

Binky, ill-at-ease, was very embarrassed to be witnessing this burst of temper coming from a usually unflappable Philip, but he also knew when to be silent and not interfere in a lovers' spat. *Never try to separate two cats in a fight or you might get badly scratched.*

Robin was still at it. "You have me all wrong."

"I know your game, so please don't play me for an dod-dering old idiot. One reason you don't like these gatherings is the fear you might run into some of your patrons."

This was news to Binky.

Robin stuttered, "I . . . I . . ."

"You can take that cottage and stuff it up your rear end. That's final! My last word! Another word about it and we are history, my fine friend. Do you read me loud and clear?"

Robin was crestfallen. "I do. I'm sorry I brought it up."

Binky tried to soothe the troubled atmosphere. He hadn't seen Philip this angry before. He had secretly enjoyed watching the encounter because he liked a touch of drama to enliven a dull evening. The display of raw emotions and venting was amusing to watch. Even Philip looked quite satisfied with himself.

Binky said, "On that rather final, rather decisive note, young lord Robin, will you honor me with a dance?"

Robin, very sheepishly while trying to ingratiate himself with Philip said, "Yes, but don't step on my toes the way Granddad does."

Philip answered sourly, "Yes, you two youngsters have a good time while old gramps sits here drooling into his whiskey. If I have to take a pee, I'll call Nurse. Where did my knitting go?"

The music swelled around them, the lights flashed frantically in psychedelic colors and smoke permeated the atmosphere.

50

Paul and Hal had been settled in their retirement home in Deerfield Beach, Florida, since 1988. The two Americans had visited Philip in the close several times. They had invited Philip and Robin to visit them in Florida. Their house was one mile from the ocean and they had a large diving pool in their backyard.

Robin was keen to go. He liked the beach and swimming in the ocean and pool. He wanted to get some sun. Philip had spent time in Washington, D.C. as a liaison between MI6 and the CIA. He had also visited some of the key tourist spots in the States, but America was never much of a draw to him. He could go ga-ga walking down a street in some Asian town, but for him, the States were boring and expensive. He preferred the antiquities and historical relics of Europe and the sexual excitement of the Orient.

He'd never been to Florida so he'd give it a try. It was in 1990 that Philip and Robin agreed to go. Robin was through with the supervision of the remodeling of the basement. What had in the olden days been a coal bin and a coal chute had been transformed. Robin had redone everything. A shiny modern kitchen with new cabinets and appliances, beautiful tile floors and baseboards, crown molding, recessed lighting, a formal dining room that could seat six, its walls appointed with expensive wallpaper. The dining room furniture was the best he could find. He hadn't skimped, and the basement was transformed into an attractive state-of-the-art showplace. With the renovation completed, there was time for Florida.

Paul and Hal picked them up at the Miami airport and drove them north to their home in Deerfield Beach. The house was a large spread-out ranch home on a hundred by hundred foot plot with three bedrooms, three baths, a large living room, an equally spacious dining room, a newly remodeled kitchen, a dinette, a big Florida room, and a screened porch. Almost the entire backyard was a concrete deck surrounding the pool.

They were given a guest bedroom with a queen size bed. There was also another guest bedroom with a sofabed if they desired it.

Robin spent most of the days out sunning himself by the pool. Occasionally, he would accompany Hal to his gym for work-outs. In the mornings, Philip would take long walks with Paul. They would pop into various coffee shops where Paul had a routine of stopping for a morning bagel and coffee. Sometimes Philip would have eggs and bacon and even developed a taste for grits.

During these walks and coffee stops, Paul would encourage Philip to talk about his life, his career, his outing, his rice queen escapades. Philip liked recounting his stories and Paul was, unusual for him, an ardent and patient listener. Usually he dominated a conversation, and others could barely get in a word. They covered a great deal of Philip's biography.

In Florida, Paul still worked on his plays and taught creative writing, while Hal dabbled in selling real estate and continued workouts at the gym.

One morning, trusting in Paul's discretion, Philip blurted out, "There are times when Robin makes me seethe. I get jealous, annoyed at him, the way he takes so long getting home from work. He's full of excuses. He could be leading not only a double life, but like many young guys who like older guys, a multiple life. These guys were born compartmentalizers. Woe be to him who is in one of the minor compartments, or who lacks the needed virility. From my experience, younger men who like older men have one thing in common; they never like just one older man. They're insatiable."

Well, Paul thought, Philip wasn't a saint after all. What went on below that surface was quite extraordinary, but it was important for Paul to probe it.

One night at dinner in a fish restaurant, Philip noticed dolphin on the menu, and he was shocked. Paul told him there were two types of dolphin, the beloved mammal and a fish that was also called mahimahi. They all ordered broiled portions, and Philip declared it quite tasty.

Paul reminded them that he and Hal were still on their spend-down plan, and though they tried mightily, they were still accumulating rather than spending down their assets. Hal said, "It seems that though we travel freely, spend like drunken sailors on gadgets, books, and videos, we still are behind in our spending. We'll just have to become more extravagant."

Philip responded sourly, "Unfortunately, Robin here has gotten the hang of your spend-down rather too well as his tailor, his travel agent, and his family know only too well. He was made for your spend-down scam, and thrives on it. Meanwhile my poor nephews and nieces may find their uncle has left them bills to pay rather than any small legacies."

One night while Philip was watching television in the Florida room, Paul made a trip to the back guest bedroom bathroom to change towels. As he passed Philip and Robin's room, he saw Robin in the nude with his back toward the door. He couldn't help noticing the firm body, the beautifully proportioned frame, the exquisite small sculpted buttocks. Robin jogged, played squash, exercised, and it showed. It was a glorious body, a treat. Later he told Hal it was eye candy. He didn't think Robin had seen him, but Paul had certainly been aroused by the sight. Philip was a lucky man indeed.

When they left Florida and were winging their way back to a gloomy London,Philip decided that he had enjoyed bathing in the ocean waters, enjoyed his hosts' company, enjoyed the sights, such as they were, but the States were still not on his list of must see or must revisit places. Europe and Asia were in his blood; America was not. Perhaps he liked individual Americans but didn't like Americans in general. Could it perhaps be another example of his mild case of snobbery—a Croftian demi-snobbishness?

51

In August of 1995, at six in the afternoon, Binky met Paul Rowan in the lobby of Paul's hotel, the Blaineville Arms, at Marble Arch. Binky was getting on in years and no longer had his old bounce. His body had aged more than his mind, which was still young and limber. The two had agreed to meet there on their way to a birthday party for Philip at the Close.

They took off walking along Edgware Road at a leisurely pace. Paul said, "It's been great seeing some of the Soho gay bars and clubs through your eyes. I've had a ball."

Binky laughed and said, "Yes, even with these old creaky bones and faded body, I like to get out and make the rounds—occasionally you understand—not as a regular thing. I love to have company when I do my pub crawls. Could never get Philip to accompany me. He's never been much of a bar person, and, of course, none of his type are in those bars anyway."

Paul always seemed to be looking for little tidbits about Philip, and the two had often had long conversations about their mutual friend. Binky thought Paul's insatiable desire to learn as much as he could about Philip could be attributed to Paul's Anglophilia.

Binky was still on about the gay bars. "But the gay places have changed a great deal in recent years. Tipping is rife now in Soho—blasphemy for the U.K. and a damnable custom. And of course all those young bucks look right through old farts like us, but who gives a shit? I just want to keep up with what's going on."

They turned down Connaught Street heading for Albion. Traffic was busy on the street. The high black taxis went hurtling by, making a short cut and a sharp turn at a corner street by Connaught Square.

Paul asked, "How do you think Philip is getting on?"

"At eighty, he's getting frailer, but when I walk with him, I find he has great staying power and stamina. He is as unsteady as ever, staggers like a drunk, but he can wear me out."

"He used to be quite strong. Walked every day for long distances."

"Surprisingly, he still does."

"He seems always to be in good spirits and interested in life and friends. Has his life been a happy one, do you think?"

"Oh, I should think so. He loved his life in the intelligence service. He loved to travel anyway. After they viciously outed him, he was his own man; he led an openly gay life—and thrived on it."

"No great disappointments?"

"His biggest disappointment was the way he was forced out of the Service, disgraced after years of noteworthy service."

Paul, ever the pumper for biographical information, plodded on. "Head of station in several key posts, wasn't he?"

"Yes. He was one of the best field agents they ever had. A damn fine civil servant treated very shabbily."

"Do you think he minds being labeled a rice queen?"

"I wouldn't think he worries much about it. Asian men were and are his passion. He's had his lovers, a mysterious long-running affair with a chap in Southeast Asia named Tom, a short fling with a muscle-man named Kwan of the sauna era."

"And Reynaldo in the Philippines, whom I met."

"His best choice, I think, was Robin who has turned out to be a mainstay in his later life."

Paul said, "I wish he'd let me write his biography. It could be a doozie. Philip has to be understood in terms of his aborted sexuality. Why did he do such an unfathomable and uncharacteristic thing as open a gay sauna at his advanced age and with his aura of respectability and gentility? He was a university man who moved in some high circles."

Binky answered, "He did that seemingly shocking sauna thing because he had become something of a rebel. He had come out. Owning a sauna was a way of thumbing his nose at the establishment when he was no longer a government servant. It also gave him a ready source of young Asian men, don't forget.

"For years he had been stifled, circumscribed by his profession. He had developed a predilection for young Asian men, but this had been kept in check by his job. He came out of his shell with a vengeance even though he didn't see it in those terms. He had been outed summarily and in a quite traumatic manner."

Paul added, "Many gay men come out in late life because they had married and chosen a heterosexual life style. Their children grow up, they announce themselves and move out. Or they just get that urge, feel their life is slipping away and come out. Philip didn't wake up one day and decide to become openly gay. He was forced out. And once out, when he decided to go gay, he went whole hog."

Binky contributed, "He didn't become a drag queen or a leather fetishist; he opened a sauna aimed at young slant-eyes. It was a recruiting gimmick.

"He had chosen as his bride the Service, been wed to it, enjoyed his years of intelligence work, got a kick out of being nosy and scheming. While in the Service, he had to tread very carefully, closeted and undercover as a spy *and* as a gay man, living two layers of deception. He was outed from one area of deceit, and that liberated his second self from an inner core of deceit.

"His liberation and entry into a more gay lifestyle wasn't as discreet or as circumscribed as some might have made the transition, but it had suddenly become his life, his choices, his options. He did it his way and had no regrets. It was typical of Philip, ever the optimist, enjoying his new life fully. The times, the last quarter of the twentieth century, were suited to his new lifestyle and his new found freedoms. He was a post-Stonewall baby in his fifties."

Paul asked, "Isn't there a danger for others to see him as a saint?"

"Oh, he can be and is, at times, petty. With Robin, he can

be willful. Philip almost always does what Philip wants. He can be persuaded to do something only if it is in line with what he wants to do. Robin wanted a country cottage to go to on weekends. Philip had no use for it. He put his foot down. You'll notice that Robin never got that country cottage.

"On the other hand, Robin wanted to redo the basement. Philip agreed. Robin supervised the modernization of the basement with a new kitchen and a dining room. Very contemporary, tiled floors, recessed lighting. Wait'll you see it. Ah, here's Philip's close now."

Before they entered the archway, they went into the wine merchant's store, which guarded one side of the close. They each chose a good vintage wine as a present to their host.

As they turned into the archway of Philip's close, they failed to notice an untidily dressed, looming, red-faced man who smelled of drink and sported a beer potbelly. The man moved away from them. It was Whaley, who still stopped by at times to keep an eye on Philip and his digs. When he was deep in his cups, he would sometimes head for Philip's neighborhood, hoping for a sight of his enemy, still ready to settle old scores.

Whether he would publicly insult Philip or cause him bodily harm, he had never worked out in his alcoholic fogs. He had watched as the two men entered the wine shop. From outside he could see them picking out bottles, gifts for Philip, no doubt. *Two more queers.*

In the close, Binky's walk was more labored than when they had started at the hotel. They passed the row of small mews houses on either side. Most of the houses were painted in various muted pastel colors, though Philip's house was of a slightly brighter hue than the others. It also stood out because it was the one with all the flower pots, huge displays of plants and blooms.

Binky said approvingly, "All of these flowers and plants are Robin's doing. He takes great pride in caring for them. They get a deal of compliments from the neighbors, but it takes a great bit of time, effort, and watering on Robin's part."

52

Binky rang the bell, and the two were greeted by a beaming Philip. To Paul, he seemed older, more stooped than ever, but quite animated. He was dressed, as usual, traditionally in a tweed suit, dress shirt, tie, and a vee neck sweater under his suit coat. It seemed a bit much for a warm August night, but Philip did not mind the heat.

Some distance away from the gateway to the close, Sergeant Whaley watched as Philip admitted his two guests. He knew the house well and knew Philip lived with Robin. Indeed he knew Philip's routines, the routes of his daily walks, his club, and his shopping habits.

In unison, Binky and Paul chanted, "Happy Birthday, Philip."

Each handed Philip their wine offerings. Philip read the labels, pursed his lips and nodded in approval, remarking that the vintages were quite noteworthy.

Philip ushered them into his cozy lounge and placed the bottles next to one of the magazine peaks atop the cocktail table. The room seemed more cluttered than before. A certain air of genteel neglect about housekeeping permeated the room. Bigger piles of magazines, newspapers, books, souvenirs, stuff in general. It was the room of a man of many interests, not that of a recluse. Binky and Paul took up seats on the couch and repeated their happy birthday greetings.

Philip said, "Thank you, dear friends. I don't feel eighty at all. I feel ninety. But remember that both of you are due here on Sunday for my big to-do, which Robin is planning. He's invited more than twenty-five people, and how they'll all manage to squeeze in here is beyond me."

Binky answered, "We wouldn't miss it for the world. I've heard the Mad Hatter and the March Hare, as old as they are, will be here."

"Yes, I understand the two are in town for some Eastern

Asian boy meets Western old man function."

Binky said, "I shan't be wanting to take part in that sort of claptrap."

Philip was still standing. "Paul, I'm glad you and Binky could hook up together and visit some of Binky's disreputable pubs. What'll it be, gin and tonics?"

They nodded in agreement, and Philip mixed them drinks at the hall drinks table. He was stingy with the ice, but not with the gin.

When Paul received his, he asked, "May I have a little more ice, please?"

"Ah, I remember. You Americans like glacial drinks."

Philip returned with a glass of ice and a scotch for himself.

Paul remarked, "Binky is a great guide to Soho gay life."

Philip pronounced, "Always has been."

Paul inquired, "Are you looking forward to your big birthday bash Sunday evening with all your friends?"

"Oh, yes. I love parties, and it will be good to see a lot of friends I haven't seen in years. And, of course, both of you will be there. For our little celebration this evening, young master Robin will be along shortly to prepare our dinners."

Paul complimented Philip. "You're looking quite chipper."

"I'm fair to middling."

Paul continued, "It's good to see you looking so peppy."

"Paul, how has the playwriting been coming along? Anything imminent?"

Paul stammered and stuttered. "Oh, er, nothing in the immediate future. Projects in the fire, but nothing I can talk about right now. I'm in the hatching stage, I suppose. I still can't get over how well you look."

Paul looked discomfited by Philip's question. He seemed evasive and avoided looking at Philip. Both Philip and Binky noticed his evasiveness. Philip, quick to pick up on somebody's shift of mood or equivocation, put it down to an author's unwillingness to talk about a work in progress for fear of talking it out of his system. Sometimes an author's evasiveness could be traced to a recent failure or rejection.

Or perhaps he was having writer's block, Philip thought. Binky thought Paul's feints had something to do with Philip, but he couldn't put his musings into concrete terms.

Puzzled by Paul's evasions, Philip changed the subject. "How has it been in Florida? Robin and I still talk about our wonderful visit to your home. Bathing in the Atlantic Ocean and in your lovely pool."

Paul seemed relieved to have a chance to talk about something else. "The pool is there waiting for you and Robin anytime you wish to come back."

Philip quickly submitted, "Oh, and tell Hal how much Robin and I miss him, and how much we would have wanted him here. We both have great fondness for Hal."

"Hal loves you two. He'd be here if he could make it, but he's tied up with some serious therapy treatments to alleviate his emphysema."

Philip got up and moved a canapé tray from the desk to a spot on top of a mound of magazines in front of his two guests. Robin, a more alert host, would have moved the snacks earlier, but the more absent-minded Philip operated on his own time schedule.

Philip continued his thoughts on his stay in Florida. "And all that fresh, tasty fish in the restaurants. I finally got used to ordering the fish called dolphin and realized it wasn't the mammal."

Binky licked the shrimp paste from his cracker and offered, "Did either of you know that the mammalian dolphins are bisexual and very active sexually? They're at it all the time. Horny creatures, I've been told."

Philip countered, "As usual, you, Binky, are our guide to the sexual mores of all mammals."

Paul asked Philip, "How are things progressing here in the mews?"

"Well, as you've seen outside, neighbors have started copying Robin's flamboyant flower arrangements. Window boxes have appeared at most of the mews houses, and some people have even hired professional landscapers."

Outside on the street, Whaley kept vigil at the entrance to the close. He saw Robin go into a small convenience store across from the mews entrance, and he watched from outside as Robin picked out some grocery items.

Paul questioned his host, "Do you help with the gardening?"

"Not really. Once in a while I'll remember to do a little watering."

Binky added, "You're the envy of the close. The display is très gay. A grand prix of blooms. Where will it all end?"

Paul inquired, "And how are your current walks around London going, Philip?"

"Not so well, I'm afraid. In the last six months, I've taken three spills. Thank God I didn't break anything or get bunged up. All three times, nice people nearby helped me up and got me going again. I must say I've been terribly lucky with these strangers assisting me."

Binky quipped "Ah, yes, the kindness of strangers. Many a time years ago I was assisted in some loo by a kind stranger."

Philip rose slowly, picked up their glasses, and walked unsteadily and tentatively to the drinks table, unconsciously demonstrating his precariousness. He returned with refills.

Philip assayed a new topic.

"Did you hear about the knock for knock experience Robin and I had? While we were in our car on the street outside the close, getting ready to pull out, our car was sideswiped by another car."

Paul queried. "Knock for knock?"

Binky answered, "What you call no fault insurance in the States, we call knock for knock coverage here."

Paul added, "Appropriate name."

Philip, quite perturbed, described the incident. "The other driver was quite abusive, quite nasty, directing some ugly remarks toward Robbie, racist in nature I thought. I wouldn't believe such attitudes were prevalent in London in this day and age."

Binky retorted, "In some ways, Mr. Croft, you are very

naïve. Your knowledge of London, I'm afraid, is limited to your circle of friends and your club."

"Ah yes, I remember being told that by a certain loutish sergeant over twenty-two years ago. A sadist named Sergeant Whaley."

Binky continued, "Many Brits despise wogs. They call Indians and Pakistanis dot heads, towel heads, knot heads or far worse. The Pakis who run many of our convenience stores are not greatly liked."

Binky rose and went to the drinks table. He poured himself more tonic.

Philip nodded. "No, I'm sure you're right. Sometimes when we are in a restaurant, I've seen Robin get short shrift from a waiter, simply because he's Asian, I think, and some anti-gay sentiments too."

Binky agreed, "And for Robin, it can be double-barreled. He's a young Asian with a doddering old man, maybe a sugar daddy arrangement, and just the fact he's an Asian, sounding posh and upper-class, can cause him difficulties. That posh accent Robin has acquired over the years may set some people off, giving them the impression that here is an uppity snobbish Asian wannabe who doesn't know his place. With his blazer, his ascot, and his upperclass vowels, there are many lowly mortals, native Brits, that would get their backs up."

"I never thought of all that."

"Again, The Croftian naïveté."

Paul offered, "I agree with Bink. It could have been a double whammy. That driver could have been overreacting to an Asian and also to an older man with a younger man, imagining a gay liaison. Robin may have had two strikes against him: being an Asian and perceived as possibly gay."

"I have a lot to learn. I think Reynaldo said I lack street smarts."

Paul assured Philip, "But aside from all this prejudice nonsense, Robin has been truly great for you. A blessing."

Binky cheered, "Hear! Hear!"

Philip agreed, "Amen to that."

Philip turned to Paul and jokingly admonished him.

"Oh, by the way, Paul, that spend-down scheme you put young Robin onto? He is eternally grateful to you for introducing him to it. Unfortunately, I was dragged, screaming and kicking, into that infernal plan of yours."

Paul's defense began, "I've been saying for years the armored car with your savings doesn't follow the hearse to the gravesite with the stash to be buried with the body."

Philip laughed. "Thank you for all of your unsolicited investment advice."

Binky walked to the drinks table and poured himself another drink. He gestured to Paul and Binky, but they both begged off.

Paul wondered, "How are things in Manila these days? We haven't heard a word. What about the crackdown?"

Philip said, "I heard reports of Pagsanjan raids. They rounded up some gays; some were detained, some were deported. Authorities cracked down on the pedophiles. They have been driven from the country. A different climate. During the crackdown, there were protest marches by some of the townspeople in Pagsanjan. Their livelihoods were challenged; the little ones could no longer bring home the bacon. Some saw their economic situation decimated.

"It's very different from before. A few gays are left, the discreet ones. The ones who like eighteen-year olds and up aren't bothered as much. But many have been scared off. Manila, where the more secretive ones stayed, is still active.

"There are still periodic purges of the gays who prey on little boys. And to some extent, the other gays don't feel as comfortable there. I haven't been back since the Aquino people took over. As far as I can gather, they certainly turned off the spigot on unfettered gay life. I've heard the Lodge in Pagsanjan has been shuttered for some time."

Binky asserted, "Everyone got what they deserved out of that mess. The pedophiles were put to flight, the townspeople had to make do with what was left, and life went on."

Paul contributed, "The sex situation had gotten to be too

flagrant, too over the top to survive; the excesses had become so blatant. The islands were attracting more and more pedophiles. The pedophiles there had to flaunt their obsession. Few were discreet about it. They helped drive out those who were having sex with the young men of legal age. The Philippines became a tighter place, less gay-friendly."

Binky said, "I frankly tired of a bunch of pedophiles excusing, rationalizing their bizarre tastes. 'They love me.' Puulease! What does a five-year-old know of right and wrong, good and evil?"

Paul added, "The families were economically distressed. Their offspring brought in a lot of money."

Philip said, "After the crackdown, I heard that the boatmen became more venal in dealing with the tourists. Some had lost their sideline incomes and became more desperate. There were too many boatmen anyway. They forced tourists to pay more, demanded larger tips, used extortion techniques."

Binky said, "Now I hear there's a crime wave of pickpockets and bag slashers in Manila. The jeepneys and cabs have become unsafe for tourists."

Paul asked, "Any word from Craig? Hal and I never hear from him anymore, though we're sure he's still alive."

"After my epochal Lands End to John o' Groats trip with him, I think he wrote me off. No great loss. I think I said or did something he didn't cotton to. But I did not like the way he denigrated Robin every chance he got."

Paul queried, "Any word from Reynaldo?"

Philip addressed Paul rather pointedly, almost sternly, as if his remarks had some hidden import. "I don't think we will ever fully know the extent of Reynaldo's betrayals, eh, Paul?"

Again Paul avoided looking directly at Philip, and said in a low voice, "I suppose not."

Philip was wistful as he spoke. "He certainly pulled the rug out from under me. Just looked after himself. Haven't heard from him since. Talk about betrayal."

Paul said, "I thought you'd go back."

"Robin won't allow it. After my bout of depression last

year, we made a pact. If I expected him to live here, have him take care of me, I wasn't to go back to the Philippines on my own. And that's when your damnable spend-down came into play. But it was fair what we agreed to. He saved my life, I believe. He deserves whatever I can give him."

Binky, slurring slightly from overstepping his drinks quota, remarked, "Robin rightfully wanted a loyal Philip. He wasn't about to be cuckolded. Not by a creaky, rusty, old dodderer like Philip."

"He was jealous of my other life. A guy in every Asian port sort of thing. He put his foot down. Right in the middle of my privates."

Binky added, "Robin has been a good influence on you."

A bit of doubt and regret crept into Philip's voice. "Uh huh. But I still yearn for those good old days."

The front door could be heard opening. "Ah, here's the young master now."

Robin came into the lounge, back from the office, wearing a black bespoke pin-stripe suit and an expensive regimental tie. He greeted Binky and Paul and hugged both of them warmly and affectionately. He leaned over Philip and wiped around Philip's mouth and chin with a Kleenex.

"Here, Gramps, let me wipe that drivel off you. As usual, you're drooling. You'll be frightening our guests. Grandpa, G.P. as I sometimes call him, looks in great shape for his age, doesn't he, gentlemen?"

Binky and Paul assented in a good-humored manner.

Robin said, "Paul, in your honor, we are going to have a real treat, an English dinner of bangers and mash, but cooked Oriental style with a few variations thrown in. I have prepared some lovely prawns for starters."

Paul congratulated Robin. "I can see that you have taken wonderful care of Philip over the years."

"Oh, he's easy to care for. He's a cross between a big spoiled baby and a lovable, sometimes absent-minded, old Granddad. We have great fun living and traveling together, don't we, Gramps?"

"Indeed. You are the great love of my life."

"I think you have said that to all of the loves of your life."

Robin hugged Philip who seemed mightily pleased by the show of affection, like a needy child.

Philip held up the two wine bottles he had placed on the cocktail table. "And look at the wines these kind gentlemen have brought. This is from Paul. And this one is from Binky. Do I have time to get our two esteemed guests another drink?"

Robin announced, "Thank you very much for the wine, gentlemen. Gramps, serve them another round. Get them properly sloshed so they can enjoy my cuisine. But let's all repair down to the dining room so I can talk to all of you while I'm preparing dinner."

Philip agreed. "Yes, please. Go ahead with Robin. I'll bring the drinks down."

With Robin leading, Paul and Binky followed him through the hall and down the stairs to the remodeled basement dining room. Robin carried the two gift bottles of wine to the kitchen counter between the dining room and kitchen. Paul and Binky took seats at the dining room table, which was set lavishly. Robin used the dimmer switch to brighten up the festive dining room setting. Moments later, Philip shuffled into the dining room with their drinks, which he placed before them. He lit two candles.

Robin, corkscrew in hand said, "I'll open Paul's wine first. Ah, it's a white Bordeaux. Then we'll go to Binky's rosé, and if need be, I have our red. Oh, but first . . ."

He quickly darted up the stairs and came back with a big wrapped present saying, "Philip, love, this is for you from the three of us."

Philip oohed and ahhed. "I love presents."

Paul, Binky, and Robin in unison shouted, "Happy Birthday!"

They started to sing "Happy Birthday." Philip was overjoyed; his face glowed as he looked at his lover, his old British comrade in arms, and his American friend.

53

Philip had decided to visit the British Museum in Bloomsbury on a May afternoon in 1996. In the forecourt of the museum, a group of senior citizens, pensioners, with Philip among them, were leaving the building after attending a lecture. Philip, using a cane as he often did to steady himself, said a few words to a man at the bottom of the stairs, and then walked to the gate and took a right.

He walked in a rather haphazard fashion, first veering a little to the left, then to the right. He walked at a fairly brisk pace for a man of his advanced years, but he seemed to be off balance, rudderless at times, almost like a drunk.

About a block behind, following him, was Whaley. A close view of him revealed a man who had known alcohol too well and too unwisely in his lifetime. He had also had a few drinks that day. As he followed Philip, he did not have to be evasive or mindful of discovery. Philip was oblivious to anyone behind him. He was lost in his own world, thinking about the lecture.

Philip wandered back toward Marble Arch and his home. For over an hour, Philip was trailed by Whaley. Both men were walking in a somewhat drunken, unsteady fashion. Whaley at times was muttering; he seemed to be a man on a mission. When they approached Marble Arch, Whaley tired of his cat and mouse game. He would choose another time and place to get his prey. He veered off and headed for a pub while Philip stumbled on alone, heading home.

54

It was in April of 1997 that Hal and Paul's fateful and tragic visit to London took place. People would later read about it in Hal's book, *The Daemon in Our Dreams,* in which he had stitched together his narrative from Paul's extensive notes, and from the memories of Lloyd Carr, which Lloyd had gleaned from his wife, Fran, as the eerie experience unfolded. The niece of the third victim, Dr. Ably, had made available to Hal her uncle's diaries and journals. Paul, Fran Lloyd, and Lee Ably had been the victims of the tragedy.

The horrible assassinations of the three people in the Blaineville Hotel had shaken Great Britain, the United States, and indeed the whole world. The sensational headlines in the tabloids had gone on for weeks in Britain.

Paul and Hal had planned a short stopover in London after a land and ship tour of the Far East. Paul was to have a short visit with the producers and director of his upcoming play. Nothing had hit the media by then regarding the play. And, of course, it was imperative that Philip hear nothing of it. Had Philip known the play was about his life, he would have hit the ceiling. For him, it would have been the ultimate betrayal.

The real title of the play written by his friend Paul Rowan would have set off alarm bells. There was no question that Paul's unauthorized use of Philip's life story would have caused seismic tremors at Sagnes Close. The story he had been guarding so faithfully and militantly for all of his adult years was for Philip alone to reveal—if he ever chose to do so. A dummy working title had been used, but when the time came, Paul would insist upon the title he had planned on all along—*The Rice Queen Spy.*

Paul's horrible death may have been the workings of some force akin to the working of Fate that the novelist Thomas Hardy often expounded upon, but as for Philip, he played no part in the tragedy: his role was only that of a shocked spectator.

Paul and Hal were rabid theatergoers. On some trips lasting ten days, they might see a dozen plays. London was like a second home to them. They could wander all around the city and feel they were on familiar ground.

When they arrived in their London hotel room, Paul telephoned Philip. Paul had not seen Philip for two years, not since the birthday celebration. Philip talked to Hal briefly. He hadn't seen Hal since Robin and he had had their Florida visit. Philip invited them over for tea.

That afternoon, Hal, suffering more from his debilitating emphysema, was going to take his time walking over to Philip's house so Paul said he would go ahead and stop in their former local, a pub near their old apartment and meet Hal at four at the close archway. Paul stopped for a drink at the Duke of Kendal on Connaught Street, a short distance from Albion Street and the archway leading into their friend's close.

Hal was waiting for him when he got to the gateway to Sagnes Close. They walked in the mews area together. They could always tell Philip's house because it had the most flower boxes and big pots with blooms and shrubs.

Philip shuffled to the door to greet them. As usual he wore a tie and sport coat or suit and in cooler weather, layers of sweaters and waistcoats. While inside the house, he wore his carpet slippers. He was then a spry eighty-two year old.

"It's good seeing the two of you. Robin and I always recall our lovely visit to Florida with you two wonderful hosts."

While serving them their tea and homemade shortbread biscuits made by the woman across the close, Philip told them about a trip to Malaysia and Singapore he had just completed only a few weeks before. By coincidence, Paul and Hal on their trip had been in Kuala Lumpur in Malaysia about a week after his visit.

Hal said, "We were amazed by India, particularly that bus trip from Delhi to the Taj Mahal in Agra. What sights along the way."

"By the way, young Robin, the princeling, won't be available until tomorrow night around eight, so we hope you can manage to come over here tomorrow evening for a light supper, maybe his famous Oriental version of bangers and mash again."

Paul and Hal agreed to come over, which meant they wouldn't be seeing a second play. That night they were to see the play *Fate* at Wyndham's Theatre with the couple they had become so intertwined with.

Paul valued Philip's opinion and advice about most things. He decided to tell him the story about the strange things that had happened on their trip.

"I have a strange and disturbing story to tell you about our journey. A few months ago, Hal and I decided to take this trip that consisted mainly of a long cruise. The trip was called 'Passage to India.' It was on a ship called the *Global Quest*. The cruise began in Singapore where we were put up for a night prior to the cruise. Gave us a chance to reacquaint ourselves with Raffles, now newly redone and quite spiffy."

Philip footnoted as Paul went along. "Ah, yes, I have some quite sensual, pleasurable memories of rooms in Raffles."

"We boarded the ship in Singapore and stopped twice in Malaysian ports in Kuala Lumpur and Penang, then Phuket, Thailand, and a stop in Sri Lanka."

Philip appended, "I had the pleasure of introducing young master Robin to Sri Lanka, and we spent a month there on holiday only recently."

Paul continued. "The ship went on to India, with a stop at Cochin, thence to Bombay where the cruise ended and where we spent the night aboard ship. Early in the morning we were flown out of Bombay . . ."

"Again called Mumbai to confuse things."

"Landed in New Delhi where we spent a night in a hotel. Then that fascinating bus trip from Delhi to Agra to see the Taj Mahal. Overnighted there in Agra. Bussed back to Delhi, another hotel night, sightseeing, and then an eight-hour night flight here to London."

"Quite a trip, I'd say. You covered a lot of territory."

Hal interjected, "Now comes the spooky part. Go on, Paul."

"I was really looking forward to the trip. Maybe too much. Never been in India before this. Well, before the trip in Florida on three separate nights, I had a dream about this dark-complected guy, an Indian, young, clean-shaven who seemed to materialize out of nowhere and who just stared at me in the dreams. Seemed threatening, menacing in an ineffable way. Couldn't fathom him."

Philip offered, "An old flame, perhaps?"

"No, nothing as easy as that. A stranger. A scary, alarming person. When we were in the San Francisco airport waiting for our flight to Singapore, we met a couple there, the Carrs, Fran and her husband Lloyd. I hit it off with Fran. We got friendly. Something seemed to draw me to her. We talked. We seemed to have a lot in common. Somehow I knew she was a soul mate in a sense. I sort of hinted about my dreams, which seemed to shake her up."

Philip said, "This is getting quite intense. How about gin and tonics to wash down your tea?"

The two Americans agreed. Drinks were served, and Paul began again. "In Singapore, she had a quite frightening experience. She told me that before the trip she had had three dreams similar to mine. That day, she actually saw the man in her dreams, in the flesh, in a Hindu temple. She described the man. It was the same one that had invaded my dreams. I told her about my dreams. The two of us were deeply worried about her sighting. I felt at that point that I would see this person in the flesh, and that she would see him again. And that's the way it happened.

"Even before we boarded the ship, we began to suspect some other people might have had our dreams as well. We hinted around at our experiences and could tell from the reaction of one of our tablemates that he, too, was in on our secret. Incidentally Hal and Fran's husband, Lloyd, hadn't had any manifestations."

Hal said, "Lucky me. Lloyd and I thought Paul and his wife Fran were bonkers."

Paul continued, "The third person, the tablemate, was Dr. Lee Ably, the ship's lecturer who is, by the way, in London now staying at the Blaineville Arms Hotel along with Hal and me, as are the Carrs."

Philip sounded skeptical. "It seems to me, as a former intelligence operative, far too coincidental that you would meet this Fran in San Francisco, and coincidentally a third so-called victim would be at your table. How many of you dreamers were there?"

Paul answered, "Just the three as far as we know. All three of us began seeing this apparition in real life at various ports, an actual person, as the sea and land tour unfolded. Believe me, it was frightening to see him in the flesh, a threatening, menacing figure. Dr. Ably never really let on that he was seeing the man; in fact, he vehemently denied it. But we learned he had seen him, and had named him Ramesh."

Philip was admitting some confusion as he said, "Pardon me, but again putting on my spy cap, if he denied seeing the man, how did you know he was in fact seeing him, and that he called him Ramesh? How could you and this Fran creature possibly know all this if he denied everything?"

Paul sheepishly replied, "Because Fran with our complicity broke into his room and read his private journal."

Philip was aghast, "I can't believe this. You participated in this assault on private property and someone's right to privacy? I can't believe it."

Hal was red with anger. "I agree, Philip, this whole thing is sheer madness. This woman is a real bitch as far as I'm concerned. I can't believe Paul talked me into taking part in the break-in."

Philip said, "I've never heard of such goings-on. Criminal behavior if you ask me."

Paul said, "I value your opinion. What do you think about the dreams and the sightings and about Fran and Ably?

Philip's reaction was sympathetic but skeptical.

"I can't see how one man, this Ramesh, could get around

like that. You say the three of you saw him in different cities, different countries hundreds of miles apart. Just keeping track of you and getting from place to place would be a logistical nightmare. I rather think that it was either more than one man, or that your eyes were playing tricks on you altogether. Some strange things happen in the Orient. I can't figure out the meaning of those dreams at all.

"And this Fran sounds like a real strange bird breaking into someone's cabin. She sounds to me to be rather batty and reckless. What if she had been caught? She took an enormous risk. Could it be hysteria, hallucinations by the three of you? I think now that you are in London, you are well out of it. The dreams have stopped, haven't they?"

Paul nodded. Philip continued, "When you get back to Florida, I would say your chances of seeing a menacing Indian there were rather slim, if not altogether impossible.

"And your dreams weren't very detailed were they? A man staring at you. Anybody could dream that any night. Three people having similar recurring dreams doesn't seem so odd really. I would be positing group hysteria as an explanation. Your friend Fran could have induced you to have these sightings. If I were you, I'd forget it. It's just been a bad dream in a way. This Fran sounds like a right nutter to me, and the sooner you're clear of her the better. Look at old reliable, sensible Hal here. He isn't seeing Indians coming out of the woodwork."

55

After tea, Paul and Hal walked back to the hotel where they met the Carrs. The four were to have dinner together and then attend a performance at Wyndham's Theatre of the play *Fate*. That night, they had dinner at a traditional fish restaurant.

The four later saw the play. In the audience was Dr. Ably with a London friend. After dinner, they repaired to their hotel bar, Peter's Lounge, where a tipsy Hal lost his temper and let loose an all-out attack on Fran saying her violation of Ably's cabin and private papers was inexcusable.

The next morning at breakfast Hal mentioned, "Tomorrow is St. George's Day, and we'll be heading home, Thank God."

They planned their day. Paul would take a long walk through London. That afternoon they would see the Globe Theater reconstruction. Around six, Paul was scheduled to meet Fran in the Blaineville's Peter's lounge for drinks. Hal wanted no part of another meeting with Fran. At 7:30, Hal and Paul would go to Philip's for drinks and a light supper.

They would try to make it a fairly early night. On returning from Philip's, they might hit the gay pub next door if they had time. The next morning, they were to get on the van for Heathrow. Paul and Hal were going to Miami; Fran and Lloyd would be returning to New York on a later flight.

After breakfast, Paul had some business to conduct before his morning walk. At ten a.m. he met in a conference room on the second floor of the hotel with his two producers and the director of his new play. The four men talked over the preliminaries. Casting was well underway, and a theater had been let. Stage and lighting designers had been chosen. It was decided that in July, Paul would return and rehearsals would begin on *Betrayals*. All of them agreed this would be the working title, and no one would reveal the real name of the play, *The Rice Queen Spy*.

Herbert Crashaw, the senior producer, a tall, gangly man famous for his string of West End successes was still leery about the provenance of the central character, that he might be based upon an actual person. He asked, "Paul, can you assure us this character is not founded upon the life of a real person? The last thing we want is for the play to open, and to have someone step forward and say that it is based upon his life. The charges would be actionable, and we'd be embroiled in a serious libel suit."

Paul was adamant. "It is a work of imagination. The character and events are fictional. There was no model for the work. Rest assured, I'm not that dumb."

Paul knew he was taking a chance by lying, but at this point in his career, he needed a success. Money was starting to leech out. Spend-down had spiraled out of control. He thought he had changed events sufficiently to fight off any attempts by Philip to bring suit. He also believed the last thing Philip would want to do would be to bring attention to himself.

The meeting broke up amicably at noon. The text was complete. Plans were well underway for a fall opening.

Paul started out on an afternoon walk while Hal stayed back in the room. He would be taking a walk, too, but not until a couple of hits from his puffers. On Charing Cross Road Paul went in and out of bookstores and bought a copy of *Fate* because he wanted to read portions again, particularly the last speech. After his walk, he rejoined Hal in their room.

In the middle of the afternoon, he and Hal took a cab to Southwark on the other side of the Thames where Sam Wanamaker, the late American actor, had started the reconstruction of Shakespeare's Globe Theater in a spot near the original one. It was still under construction and was scheduled to open in May.

In their hotel room later, Paul and Hal got ready for dinner at Philip's. At six Paul went down to the bar to meet Fran while Hal went over to the City of Quebec pub for a pint.

Paul joined Fran in Peter's cocktail lounge. Fran and Paul took seats at the bar, Fran facing the entrance and Paul facing her. She lit up her cigarette. As they were talking and drinking, Dr. Ably came into the room and stopped to talk to them. It was a crucial conversation in which he finally admitted that he had dreamed about Ramesh and seen him in the flesh. He left them and sat in an armchair off in the corner.

Fran had a look of triumph on her face. Over and over again, she said, "Yes, yes. Yes, yes, at last."

After Fran and Paul had acknowledged their moment of triumph and the long-awaited admission from Ably, they still tried to grapple with a logical explanation for the Ramesh phenomenon. Fran lit another cigarette. In mid-sentence she stopped talking and seemed to be staring at something or someone by the door. She had a look of concern on her face. "It's him, Ramesh, look."

Paul started to turn in his chair. Fran's hand was poised over the ashtray ready to flick the ash in the ashtray. Facing the lounge entrance, her head craned slightly to the right, as she tried to get a better view of the entranceway. Ramesh was standing by the lounge door with a gun in his hand. Shots echoed in the low-ceilinged room. Fran was struck by three bullets that came in rapid succession. Her death came instantaneously.

Paul had turned toward the doorway. He heard the blasts and was convulsed by the explosions. He was unaware of Fran's condition. He felt liquid and some matter splattering against the back of his neck. As he caught sight of the man in the doorway and recognized him, his mouth gaped open, then he was hit by three bullets. The impact drove him back. He felt himself falling backward into Fran's lap as life passed out of him.

Ably, seated alone at a table far to the side heard the deafening blasts, a staccato of three and then three more. He had been reading a copy of the periodical *Granta* with Indian women in saris on the cover when Fran was hit, and he had not seen her being shot, but he saw Paul get hit and slump back. He looked toward the door and the shooter. A shocked look of recognition came into his eyes. The man beside the door focused on Ably and realigned his weapon.

Ably crouched down like a small child in the large club chair, trying to make himself look and become smaller. The portly man's eyes locked onto the assassin's eyes as the relentless and cool killer steadied his hands around the gun and assumed a firing stance. Again the assassin took careful aim and pumped three more bullets into his third target, Lee Ably. The shots were thunderous within the confines of the low-ceilinged room. Blood spurted onto the cover of the magazine, spattering on the photograph of the women in their colorful saris. Ably's last gasped words were, "He Ram," an echo of something he had read and heard many times, Indira Gandhi's last words before her passing, "Oh God."

56

Philip was in his bedroom getting ready for dinner with Hal and Paul. Downstairs in the basement, Robin had come home from work early to start preparations for the night's dinner party. He was watching the small television set that had been set up on brackets in a corner of the small dining room.

He watched and listened with horror to the news bulletin. Immediately, he bounded up the stairs. When he reached the hall leading to the bedrooms, he started shouting.

"Gramps, on the television news, something horrible has happened."

Philip went out in the hall. "What is it?"

"There's been a shooting at the Blaineville Hotel. A young gunman, Asian-looking, has killed three people in the hotel bar. Two men and a woman. Americans they're saying. Aren't Paul and Hal staying at the Blaineville?"

"Yes, my God, they are. Oh, I hope this doesn't involve Paul and Hal. It might have something to do with that story about the man who seemed to have been tracking them. I'll call their room and find out if they're all right."

Philip hurried as best he could down the stairs. He used the front hallway phone and called Paul and Hal's hotel room. Robin had followed him downstairs. After a few moments, Philip said, "No answer."

Robin said, "Do you think I should go over to the hotel and check to see if they are all right?"

"No. Let me try the hotel desk." Philip looked up the number and dialed. "No answer. Only a busy signal. They must be swamped with calls."

"Why don't I hop over there and see?"

Philip answered, "No, I'll do it. It will be a mad house over there. Swarming with police. You stay here and see if one of them calls. I want you well out of this. Don't go anywhere near there. I'll go over. If it is too difficult for me walking, I'll take a cab."

In a short time, Philip was ready, bundled up. He took his cane. Robin stood at the front door watching him hobble out of the close. Philip was used to long walks. The four or five blocks to the Blaineville wouldn't be that much of a strain for him.

When he was within a block of the hotel, he saw the flashing lights, the armada of police vehicles. Some streets had been blocked off. Philip went to the Oxford Street entrance to the hotel. A constable stopped him and asked him if he were a hotel guest. Philip said yes.

The policeman said, "You'll have to show me your key card, sir."

Without hesitation, "My wife has it. She's inside. Room 643. I have to get in to get my medicine."

The policeman signaled to his mates inside, and Philip was allowed to pass through into the lobby. His age had won the day. Inside, the lobby was swarming with police and Scene of the Crime people. Philip stood off to the right near a theater booking agency office. Then he took the elevator up to the eighth floor to Paul and Hal's room. He knocked on their door. No answer.

He then went back to the lobby where he tried to stand as far out of the way as he could. People were being herded around. After fifteen minutes and several close calls when he was told to go up to his room or leave the lobby, he spotted Hal with two large men in suits. He yelled out to him. Hal saw him and hurried over. His face was ashen. Philip knew the news was not good.

Hal, his voice breaking, tears in his eyes, said, "Some madman shot and killed Paul; Fran Carr, the woman from our trip; and Lee Ably, the ship's lecturer. They were the three who kept seeing Ramesh. God, I should have believed him. I was so skeptical. Now I believe it was Ramesh who killed them. Witnesses said it was a dark-complected Indian or Pakistani."

Philip and Hal hugged one another. The policemen accompanying Hal said they needed his help, and he was led away. Philip was distraught, not knowing what to say or do.

He walked slowly back to his house. Robin was waiting at the door. Philip told him the bad news, and the two stood holding each other in the hall.

The next days were agonizing for Philip. He saw a great deal of Hal as Hal tried to deal with the tragedy, the loss of his long-time companion. Robin and Philip absorbed everything they could read in the papers and everything they could see on television. The murderer had vanished. The police had no idea of a motive. All sorts of theories were expounded, but there was such a element of the paranormal involved that it was impossible to fathom much.

Days later the police reported they had shot and killed the assassin in a raid, but no information was given about the killer's motive or any real details. It looked to Philip and Hal as if the police had been under tremendous pressure just to "clear" the case.

57

It was an early afternoon in London in 1999. Philip, leaning slightly on his cane, entered a tube station. He went down an escalator to the platform where he was alone on the end section. Further down the platform from behind a column he heard a voice, not the thundering voice as before, but a strong insidious whisper in male cadences.

"Faggot. Queer. Cocksucker. Asslicker. You are nothing but a fucking faggot. Pervert. Poof. Poofter."

Philip was startled. He thought for a few seconds his mind was playing tricks on him. No, this was real. This was an external source. He looked around searching for the source of the ominous, remembered words and voice.

From behind a column emerged Sergeant Whaley who, twenty-six years after Philip's interrogation, was a man of close to sixty who looked ten years older, his body and mind ravaged by heavy drinking and hard living. It was obvious he had had a considerable amount to drink that day and was unsteady on his feet. He slurred his words.

"Homo. Bloody scum. Shitlicker. Ass reamer. Sodomite. Sissypuke. Bloody cunt."

He approached Philip with a drunken smirk on his face.

"As I live and breathe, Philip Croft, super spy for Her Majesty's government."

"Whaley! Good God, you. What the bloody hell are you doing here?"

Spittle burst from Whaley's mouth as he came so close to Philip that Philip could smell the drink and several days' worth of funk. "The queen of spies herself. The Queen's rice queen. The man who hated his own kind and took up with the slant-eyes. How is she hanging, Miss Croft?"

Philip was angry, deeply annoyed to be addressed by his old torturer. "You're despicable! I haven't seen you in years.

Are you still in the same line of work? Do you still cause and lance boils?"

"In a manner of speaking you could say I'm still doing the odd lancing job. Sort of working off the books. How have you been, Croft?"

"What business is it of yours?"

"Did you get over that spill you took on the steps of St. Paul's last week?"

"How do you know about that?"

Whaley was almost in a stupor. He had been drinking heavily since early in the morning. He was very clumsy on his feet. He rocked back and forth, seemed almost about to fall over.

His eyes were not quite focusing on his prey. He muttered, "You might say I've been doing a bit of surveillance for a number of years. The Service taught me how to shadow people, and you're a snap. Following you has become a bit of a hobby with me."

"What gives you the right to follow me?"

"You are completely unaware of anyone tailing you. You live in your own little ponce world. The only time I see you react is when some young Asian chap comes into view. Then you light up like a bitch in heat."

"The cheek of you. You shadowing me."

"Righto. I decided to even up some old scores. What really riles me up is the reduced pension I'm getting because of you."

"I suppose you blame me for all your woes. I made you into the boozer you are, I suppose."

"After that little session with you and the boils, the management, Sir Charles for sure, decided I had been too harsh, and they gave me a hard time."

"Perhaps a deservedly hard time for your torturing."

"I gave that other poof Sir Charles or better yet, Lady Charles, a hard time before I was made redundant. I got back at that fuckin' queer. The two of you deserve to rot in hell. Bastards!"

Whaley had been coming closer and closer to Philip.

Whaley reeked from the smell of alcohol, sweat, and dirty clothes. There were no other people at this end of the platform. Philip tried to edge away from him. His senses were all on alert now.

"When Sir Charles, thanks to me and my mates, was caught with his hand on the cock of an underage lad, I was back in favor with the new regime for a while."

"So the arrest of Sir Charles was a set-up?"

"Too bad I haven't had a chance to settle with Sir Charles personally, too, but my chance may yet come. Prison didn't agree with him. They finally let him out. Used his connections to get early release. Lot of good that will do him. I hear cancer is doing him in."

Philip was defiant. "He's a better man than you'll ever be."

After he had said it, Philip regretted it. This encounter, he knew, wasn't just about talk. He knew Whaley had more on his mind than a verbal comeuppance. A lonely underground platform. Opportunity, motive. Philip steeled himself for what might happen.

Whaley was still ranting. "Probably for the best that Sir Charles got out when he did. One of the screws or cons probably fell in love with his mean old arse."

"Does your type never quit?"

"Under the new bosses, a lot of old stuff was reexamined, and your name cropped up. Philip Croft, the spy poof who doted on Orientals. You might say I'm working in a consulting capacity these days so I've come to settle some old scores, mine and some others."

"What do you mean?"

"I've never believed all that loyalty crap you tried to sell to everyone. You were Kim Philby all over again. As far as I'm concerned, your day of reckoning has arrived. You're . . ."

A thundering underground train was approaching. It was within seconds of passing the two men. Whaley lunged at Philip, but slipped to one knee as he charged. Philip proved sprier and more agile than he seemed. As Whaley got up clumsily on both legs, Philip feinted to the left, and caught

Whaley's leg with the crook of his cane. The charging Whaley, like a mad bull, was trapped by his own momentum. He hurtled off the platform, crying out in panic. Whaley fell onto the track into the path of the onrushing train.

Philip shuddered and collapsed back against the platform column. He could feel the violent vibration of the train and feel the whoosh of air. He got his wits back, turned and hurried from the station as fast as he could.

58

A month later, Robin and Philip were in their basement dining room. Philip had aged perceptibly but was still mentally able and sharp. His legs still allowed him to take long walks, but it was an uncertain body that could fail him at times and cause spills or prolong illnesses or alternately surprise him with its staying power and spurts of strength.

Philip's favorite theme, betrayal, was uppermost in his mind on this particular morning. He worried about actual betrayals that had taken place and possible acts of betrayal that might lie ahead. The betrayals preying on Philip's mind were deeply felt and related to his very being.

He was not worried about betrayals on the home front with Robin. Like many gay couples who had been together for many years, he and Robin had made some accommodations, some of them silent pacts regarding sexual matters either real or imagined. If one didn't know certain things, one couldn't be hurt. This was a working hypothesis or a modus operandi for their lives. Certain things were not discussed. And at Philip's age, little harm could be inflicted. Consequences would not and could not flow from peccadilloes.

Philip, seated at the dining room table, was finishing a bowl of porridge with sultanas. Robin was cleaning up in the kitchen, talking to Philip as he worked.

Robin asked, "Why did Sir Charles invite you to have lunch with him today?"

"He's recently been released from prison. Also it may be that he heard about a mutual friend of ours who died in an accident."

"Anyone I know?"

"Definitely not. Thank God you were lucky enough never to have known him."

"A gay man?"

"About as far from gay as you can get. Unless he was one of those self-loathing homophobes who repressed their homosexuality and struck out against what they themselves secretly are."

Robin abandoned this subject and went back to Sir Charles. "So Sir Charles has asked you to the Spanish Steps? You'll love it. That restaurant gets great reviews. It *is* good. Combination of Spanish and Italian."

"You've been there, have you? One of your admirers take you? One of your elderly white-haired consorts?"

Robin had been caught off-guard and was uncomfortable. Philip was in an uncharacteristically catty mood. Robin changed the subject.

"Do you think Sir Charles has heard about Paul Rowan's play?"

"I imagine he has. Everyone In London is talking about it. Rowan, that traitorous bastard. Bloody spy, he can rot in hell. I truly feel sorry for Hal, and I deeply regret the way Paul had to die. It was an awful death. A terrible, terrible thing, but the man in life had no right to write a play about me and my life. It was an invasion of my privacy and a terrible betrayal."

"Do you think they really got his murderer?"

"I shouldn't imagine so. Unfortunately, because of the manner in which Paul died, the play is getting more publicity than it normally would. They say it's going to be a hit on the West End. *The Rice Queen Spy* indeed. A name Binky used for me. How a man like Paul could pose as a friend as he was stealing my life to make a few pounds for himself is beyond me. One man has no right to steal the life of another man. Bloody betrayer of every confidence I ever made to him."

"You'd better start getting ready, or you'll be late for your meeting with Sir Charles."

"Yes, Mother."

59

Philip and Sir Charles met in front of the Spanish Steps Restaurant in Soho. They entered the small restaurant with its rough hewn wooden tables, rustic wooden chairs and the wall hangings that blended Spanish knick knacks with Italian memorabilia. They were led to a table for two at the window with a view of the street life.

Sir Charles had aged. His face was gaunt. His head and hands shook. He looked in perilous condition. He still took pride in his dress, but his suit looked well-worn and out-of-date. The clothing hung from his wasted frame.

Sir Charles ordered a bottle of red wine. They sat and sipped as they appraised one another. Both were losing their holds on life. They were both on steep descent slopes.

While they were buttering their rolls, Philip said, "So it wasn't the death of Whaley that precipitated this meeting?"

Sir Charles hesitated. His words had to be carefully thought out before he uttered them.

"No, honestly, I knew nothing about it until you told me just now. As far as I am concerned, the bastard got his comeuppance. I'd have gladly shoved him under a train for what the son of a bitch did to me."

Philip hadn't mentioned his part in the "accident," that he had been present and precipitated the mishap, just that at some past date he had had words with the sergeant.

Philip wondered aloud, "Why that single-minded hatred of me lasted all those years? I'll never be able to figure out why he was so fixated on my case and not scores of others. Simply because I was gay?"

"I think you became all of his hatreds crystallized into one individual. You represented his loathing for gays and his feeling of injustice about the class system. And I suppose I became a target to despise as well. He thought you and I were the cause for his several suspensions, his pay cuts, his reduced pension."

"My God, if it was all that, it's a wonder he didn't come at me with a meat cleaver long ago."

"The dolt focused all his grievances on you and me. Well, we're well rid of the bastard. Good riddance to him."

"I heard you had a rough time of it in prison."

"Terrible. It was ghastly. As a convicted faggot, a former army officer, and a knighted civil servant, I was despised by everyone, including the screws. My health was failing so fast, no one tried to get at me, though I did get kicked and pummeled a little too often. Thank God I was spared the rapes you hear so much about. No one wanted this mean, wrinkled, old ass."

The waiter, Xavier, a handsome Spaniard, was serving their soup course. If he were like many of Soho's foreign waiters, his knowledge of English would be barely adequate for menu English.

Philip asked Charles, "What's you general prognosis now?"

"Not good at all. My doctor says I'm on my last legs. Prostate cancer, bladder cancer, diabetes, heart disease, hypertension. Take your pick, I'm a walking casebook for all the maladies that kill you."

"Treatments?"

"Too far along for chemo or radiation. Doctors say don't bother. If the prostate doesn't kill me on Monday, the stroke and heart attack will get me on Tuesday, the diabetes on Wednesday, and so on."

The busboy was at the table, refilling water glasses, replenishing the bread basket.

"I am sorry to hear that. Truly sorry."

"Thank you, Philip. I know you are sincere. The reason I wanted to see you before I go is to make a kind of amends. I am doing this to ease my conscience, I suppose."

"Amends for what?"

"I'm the one who shopped you. I turned you into internal security and outed you as a homosexual. A friend of mine told me about you, that you were a rice queen."

Philip looked at him with disgust.

"Binky always suspected you of it. Playing royal politics as long as he has, he's a wilier and more astute judge of character than I am. But why me?"

"The pressure was on me to root out some moles. I had no evidence of moles so I sacrificed you, a homosexual, in order to make myself look good. My damnable ambition drove me to it. Can you forgive me?"

"I rather thought you were responsible. I figured it out by a process of elimination. I wish I could give you a bit of forgiveness, a modicum, but I can't. And I shan't forget. I do believe in divine retribution though, so you may not get off easily. What you did is still detestable, despicable. Especially coming from someone I thought to be a friend."

The waiter was serving them salads and spooning out a dressing. He refilled their wine glasses. Philip thought, *why I am acting so civilized with this creature, breaking bread with him. I should walk out on him.* But at the same time he was curious to hear what else he had to say, and after all, the person across the table from him was a dying man.

Sir Charles continued, "The main thing was for me to confess to you."

"I don't give absolutions."

"I never knew what Whaley and his lot were going to do, how far they were going to go. The boils. If it's any consolation, they did the same to me, only it was my testicles."

Philip stared off into space. They were momentarily quiet. The lunch went on. Little was said as they ate their main courses. Charles asked about Philip's life, what it had been like. Philip talked about his life in Asia, the sauna, his life with Robin, his holidays, his meetings with friends while Sir Charles listened.

Philip and Sir Charles had finished their main courses. The waiter cleared away their plates and was serving dessert, a trifle. Philip loved desserts; his childlike delight with sweets came to the fore. Charles ordered another bottle of wine. Philip didn't protest. If he didn't want to drink any more, he'd just stop, and let his host drink it. Philip had determined that this lunch would be Charles's treat anyway. He'd be damned before he paid anything for the lunch.

As he looked at the dessert, Philip purred, "Looks lovely." There was a pause, and then he said, "In one way, I've thought of my life as a series of deceptions and betrayals. Your confession today only reinforces that belief."

"Philip, it was a very difficult thing for me to do today."

"Not as difficult as what I had to suffer on your account, but I feel my life had a new beginning when I started living as an openly gay man. Beginning during that first hour of interrogation."

"I, too, felt relieved when I could go to your sauna as a liberated man."

Philip expounded, "In a way, you did me a favor outing me. Of course, I went overboard and opened the sauna. Looking back, that was really brazen and reckless of me. From one extreme to the other."

Philip's head, at times, bowed toward the table. The daytime wine was affecting him. These were two old men who were both in bad shape. Prepping for their finals.

Charles asked, "So you really think betrayals have defined your life?"

"I haven't told you of one of the worst acts of double dealing perpetrated against me. I don't believe you knew my alleged friend, Paul Rowan, the playwright."

"I've heard of him. But what have I heard?"

"The first thing that may come to mind in his regard is the murder of three people in the lounge at the Blaineville Arms Hotel two years ago."

"Oh, yes, of course. He was one of the three slaughtered along with a woman and a professor. All Americans, weren't they? A horrible, ghastly thing."

"Yes, the fact he was so cruelly and savagely murdered is terrible. I regret his murder of course. I feel sorry for his companion, Hal, who has just written about the strange happenings in his book *The Daemon in Our Dreams*. A strange, bizarre story. But the fact remains that before he died, Paul Rowan stole my life. The man wrote a libelous play about me titled *The Rice Queen Spy*."

"Without your permission? Where did he get the information?"

"Of course I didn't give him permission. He never told me of his intentions. Over the years, I've told him all about myself. He has talked to Robin and Binky, not telling them he was gathering material for a play. Met Reynaldo, my catamite from the Philippines. Observed me. Spied on me. Probably took notes on everything."

"How did you hear of the play?"

"A friend of Binky's told him the play was in pre-production here in London. They used a dummy title for a long time. I think Binky, unknowingly, gave him the title for the play. It's an epithet he's used for me."

"If I were you, I'd have your solicitor contact the producers, and tell them you intend to bring them to court. It sounds fully actionable to me."

"I fully intend to stop the bastards in their tracks. So you see, I am still being betrayed."

Xavier, growing friendlier as tip time approached, smiled and poured them more wine.

"Pardon me, Philip. I, of all people, after what I have done to you, have no right to judge, but my impending death does give me a few little perks—like speaking my mind without fear of consequences. Perhaps this wine is loosening my tongue."

"No, go ahead."

"Aside from this egregious act by a now dead Rowan, I rather think from your recounting of your life's highpoints, that you were not betrayed that much in your various love affairs. At times you often were the betrayer."

"How so?"

"Judging from your love affairs with Tom, Kwan, Robin, and Reynaldo, I would say you were often a user and a taker in those relationships. You were loyal when it suited your purposes. Disloyal and unfaithful when your gonads called for it."

"Yes, Binky says I like to play the downtrodden victim, and it's a part for which he says I am unsuited."

"Because you pick Asians, it is an uneven playing field, and you are always the master and have the upper hand."

"Sounds like my own brand of colonialism."

The busboy cleared away plates. Philip looked very tired, old, and had the demeanor of a man who was heading downhill at a fast pace.

Sir Charles dug in his heels, "It is like a holdover from colonialism, being a rice queen. It seems to me the rice queen cannot be the victim because he makes and enforces the rules. Being a rice queen smacks of Kipling's discredited white man's burden."

"This lunch is becoming like a visit to an analyst's couch. A role reversal. You came to grovel, and now you are taking the liberty of making me seem crass, but I don't mind. I'm interested."

"Had you chosen Caucasian lovers, I think you would have learned what real betrayal could be. The combatants are on a level playing field. You would have been equally matched combatants. Not one inferior to the other."

"You may be right. I wonder if I have treated my lovers as equals?"

"That I have no way of knowing."

"Sir Charles, I have to get going now."

"Philip, I truly betrayed you. That, Philip, was one of the real betrayals of your life that you will not forget. I shall remember I caused great pain and suffering to a friend only because it helped me advance in a profession built on the rotten foundation of betrayal, the spy trade."

Sir Charles made sure a tipsy Philip was ensconced in a cab to take him back to Sagnes Close. He handed the cabbie twenty pounds for the fare, and the two waved a final farewell through the window. A few weeks later, Sir Charles was dead.

60

Philip had taken several small spills while out walking alone. He still insisted on taking car trips by himself. It became necessary for Robin to keep a closer eye on him. The two rode the Millennium Wheel together, and Philip walked across the new Thames pedestrian bridge with Robin holding his arm.

Binky had suffered a small stroke and was in a nursing home in Exmouth where he was visited by Philip and Robin. Philip could barely make it down the hall to his old friend's room. They chatted, laughed, and unspoken was the realization that life was winding down for both of them.

In 2002, Philip's health deteriorated greatly. Philip was in grave condition. Robin couldn't believe how fast he had gone from an ailing old man to a dying man. The doctor told Robin that Philip's systems were rapidly shutting down and suggested that perhaps he should be placed in a hospice.

Robin said no, that he wanted him at home where he could care for him. He took leave from his job to be with him round the clock. Philip had told him long ago no morphine at the end, so he wasn't given any.

Philip lay in bed, not knowing whether he was asleep or awake, or dead for that matter. His mind drifted in and out of awareness, flitted from scene to scene in his past.

He was a child seated in the family pew in Scotland. His father was on the aisle sitting up tall and straight while his mother was next to the father in all her finery looking as beautiful as ever. On either side of Philip was an older sister, one smoothing back his errant hair, the other one straightening his collar, playing with their little boy doll brother.

They faded away and then Charles Monmouth, a big, strapping seventeen-year old, sweaty and covered with mud was walking away from the pitch with his arm around his mate, Cunningham. Both were laughing as they bonded.

In Risal Park in Manila, all decked out in his gleaming new Puma trainers, Rey was imitating the deaf and dumb waiters that worked at the outdoor restaurant. Rey was handsome and vital. A tall gawky, crane-like Craig, wearing a red play-suit, was stepping gingerly into the pool in the Lodge.

An erect penis stood up proudly and triumphantly from an Asian lad in a cubicle in Philip's sauna. A nude Philip was beckoning him and the penis to come closer.

Robin and Philip were first in chaise lounges sunning themselves around the pool at Paul and Hal's house, and then they were prone in chaises at a pool in a Mount Lavinia lodge in Sri Lanka.

Philip was face-down on a surgical trolley, and a doctor was probing enormous crimson carbuncles on his backside while a gloating Whaley pulled out strings of gelatinous goo. Philip squirmed and turned in his bed as a memory of pain shot through his body.

Robin was concerned as he saw the look of pain and severe discomfort that shot across Philip's face.

It soon faded to be replaced by a frown. Philip was in a Lisbon café with another man. They were talking about Nazi gold to be retrieved. The next image was of Philip staring down at the bullet-scarred body of the same man who lay at his feet at the front doorstep of his apartment house in the Portuguese capital.

Philip was walking in the park with the little circus dog. The dog lifted his leg and peed on Robin's trouser as he and Robin laughed. Robin became Kwan in a Speedo, then Kwan became Tom in tennis shorts.

Philip was inside a screened-in porch, reading. A little boy, tearful and sorrowful, scratched on the screen. His tiny mouth opened, and little pleading sounds came out. The screen door opened, and the little boy entered the porch. Then another boy and another until there were five of them. Philip cowered in a corner of the porch. One boy laid his hand on Philip's forehead and comforted him. The boys laughed as Philip entertained them with a circus dog that could do real tricks.

Philip wandered into the food court of Selfridges department store making purchases of fruit and candy and sweets of all kinds. He left the store with these in carryalls. Next he was in a tricycle as it sputtered up the hill, heading for the Lodge in Pagsanjan.

In bed, Philip was either dreaming in a sleep state, or he was daydreaming, or allowing his mind to role play. At times, he seemed delirious; at other times, his mind was severely clear. He was lying on a bed in a room that resembled a room in Raffles but seemingly without walls.

The room was brightly lit, but there was a cloudy, gauzy look to everything; something ephemeral, not quite of the real world was taking place. A big four poster bed with an overhead fan moving quite languidly; the French windows were open; light was streaming in. One young Philip was looking down upon another Philip. He saw a man who looked very old and infirm, near death.

Tom entered, clad only in shorts, barefoot, looking very fit, carrying a tennis racket. Philip's voice was frail at first. Then he became energized as he interacted with Tom.

"Tom, how luscious you look this morning. Just like old times. You were the great love of my life."

"That's one of your favorite lines."

"I never imagined how clever you were when I first met you. How could anyone so devastatingly sexy be a fellow spy? I had so much fun fooling you, didn't I?"

"Yes, unfortunately for me, you were ever the loyal Brit all the time you were in the Service until they latched onto your sexual proclivities."

"They dropped the beads *for* me, pulled me out of the closet."

"Too bad. We seemed to be such a great team. But the real irony was that you were a patriot all along. A triple agent. All of that material you fed me over the years was pure shite. You had reported me to your superiors."

Philip was proud of himself. "Well, I did my best."

Philip reached over to touch Tom's hand. Tom held Philip's feeble hand and nestled it in both of his strong hands.

Tom said, "It took my masters years to figure out that your stuff was pure crap. You were a mole within a mole. You tricked me from day one. Your service knew, and they fed you what to feed me."

"True. It was a confusing time in my life. But my own masters never realized, never suspected it was a gay relationship we were having. They never caught onto the fact that we were gay."

Tom asked, "Why did you do it? Why did you betray me? Was it so you could get the sex? Bartering for our lovely lovemaking, our sexual escapades over all those years?"

"No, my sexual desire came from my love for you. I truly loved you. But why did *you* do it? Why were you gathering intelligence from us?"

"I did it for the money, darling. I never really accepted your explanation for betraying Britain. I should have realized you were too conventional, too Church of England after all."

"I tried to convince you that because British society made me repress my homosexuality, I didn't care a rat's ass about their stupid conventional world."

"And I accepted it because I wanted to believe it at the time."

"I led you on for the intrigue. They taught me to be a spy, and I got carried away with the sheer madness of it. They teach you to lie and deceive and betray so you do it on your own like buttering bread."

"Spying becomes too easy after a while."

Tom straightened out Philip's bedclothes, fluffed up his pillow, rearranged his pajama collar.

Philip said in explanation, "That thing about trying to get back at Britain because of its sexual repression? All bollocks. Tom, my dearest, it never really bothered me pretending to be straight. One pretense or another, what's the difference? But I'm sorry, I really enjoyed leading you astray."

"You were a wonderful liar."

"Tom, it came from my predilection to dissemble as a

child, tell white lies. As a youth hiding my gay nature, I learned more about dissembling. It became second nature. Then the Service reinforced it."

"Black became white, white became gray until all the colors merged into lies."

"With you, I had to mock loyalty and patriotism, but I have always kept my love of country."

"Philip, the Conventional."

Tom gently smoothed Philip's brow. He caressed his face lovingly. He leaned over and kissed him on the cheek.

Philip went on, "As a Scot, I was too frugal and acquisitive to toy with communism in the thirties. I watched many of my generation lose their sense of balance in a strange brew of homosexuality and communism. By staying under the carpet, in the closet, I wasn't really tempted. My music, my faith, my instinctive love of country kept me away from Marxism. And I didn't even know what being gay was until much later."

"We were a great team over the years even if you were a double agent deceiving me. I made a great deal of money with what you gave me."

"Did I ever tell you, dear Tom, that you were the great love of my life?"

"Yes, many times, but did you ever really mean it?"

Tom took up a position at the left-hand head of the bed.

Kwan, the Kwan that Philip first knew, entered the room wrapped in a small towel that revealed more than it covered.

Philip marveled. "Kwan, you look fantastic. Been working on your body, I see. Let me feel your biceps? Mmm, lovely."

"How have you been? I'm sorry the sauna went bust."

"I regret leaving you jobless."

"I opened a Chinese restaurant in Torquay. It's doing very well."

"Good for you!"

"We have great dim sum and those spring rolls you loved. Remember that Chinese place on Wardour Street we both liked so much?"

Kwan smoothed Philip's hair, straightened his nightshirt. Philip loved to be babied and catered to.

"Yes, indeed. And lovely wonton soup. While the sauna was still going, I'm sorry I wasn't able to pay you more."

"That's all right. You Scots are always tight."

"Frugal."

"Pennypinching. I just loved working there. I wish now I could get a tenth of the sex I got when I was working at the sauna. Working for you was a lark."

"Didn't we have a wonderful time? God, the boys that came in. Stunners."

"Yes, those free passes for Asian boys helped a lot. It brought in the boys but not the money."

"After a while, according to dear old Binky, we had every horny Asian in all of Soho."

"Binky would take out his teeth and give fantastic blow jobs."

"Shocking. By the way, did you ever marry anyone?"

"Yes, an Italian. He's a great lover; twenty years older than I am, but he doesn't give head as well as Binky did."

"Kwan, I've got something to tell you."

"Yes, Philip?"

"You were the great love of my life."

"Oh, I bet you say that to all your boyfriends."

Kwan took up a position at one corner of the foot of the bed. Reynaldo entered the room wearing a Speedo. He was wheeling a stroller, which he left by the door. He looked fit and healthy. He did a cartwheel and stood on his hands.

"Rey, you naughty boy. You left me high and dry in Manila. All by myself."

"And nothing happened to you. When I got back to Manila, I found you'd skipped out right after I went home to Cebu."

"Yes, because of you, I had to cut my holiday short. I flew back right after you left. You betrayed me."

"Did I really? Didn't you ever betray me? Cheat on me? I can remember other boys. Didn't you have a lover back in London, a Cambodian boy? And you were perfectly safe in Manila without me."

"I didn't know that then, did I? I was all alone. Isolated.

And telling me about a wife and child when you did. That was unfair, abandoning me."

"You big baby. And you with all your spy stories of the big deals you pulled off. Shooting it out in tunnels. Bang, bang! Hah! You were a baby, but a sweet old baby."

"You abandoned me at a crucial time."

"You were so childish. Nothing happened to you or the other sugar daddies."

"Oh, I hate that—other sugar daddies, as if I were just one of hundreds."

Reynaldo cupped Philip's face in his hands, kissed him, and declared, "There wasn't really much shooting. Marcos was tossed out. They found Imelda's shoes, and you lived through it without a scratch."

"I was so desperately alone."

"You silly old coward. I couldn't have protected you. You were better off by yourself. Knowing you, you went out and got another trick the same day I left."

"No, I suffered all alone, and I never went back to the Philippines."

"Because I was gone or because you had heard the police had cracked down on foreign gays?"

"Because you betrayed me."

"I'm sorry. I wish we could have gotten the old days back."

"You deserted me. You had no right to leave me, but I forgive you, though you never wrote, never got in touch with me."

"I didn't have your address. You never gave it to me."

Philip lamented, "And I think you had a liaison with that betrayer of my inmost life. Paul Rowan."

"He was murdered, wasn't he?"

"Perhaps deservedly so. I still have your painting. Robin, a dear friend of mine, the dearest, hates it. He wanted me to destroy it, but I wouldn't do it. I treasure that painting because you were the great love of my life."

"Then why didn't you ever come back to Manila?"

"I made a pact with Robin. God, I missed Manila, and you. Rey, you know. . . ."

Reynaldo interrupts him. "Yeah, I know. I was the great love of your life."

Reynaldo took up a position at the other foot of the bed opposite Kwan.

Philip's body on the bed shook involuntarily; his forehead furrowed, and then he returned to his dream state with Robin entering the room. He was dressed in a well-tailored pin-striped business suit. He had his briefcase and laptop computer case. He had just come from work in the City. At three corners of the bed stood Tom, Kwan, and Reynaldo watching Robin.

"Gramps, are you resting? You aren't getting yourself agitated, are you? Did you nap, get some rest? Here, let me wipe that drool and dribble off your chin. Always drooling."

With a Kleenex, Robin lovingly wiped the drool and dribble around Philip's mouth.

"I was telling Reynaldo why I never went back to Manila."

"No, you never went back because I wouldn't allow it, not as long as we were going to live together. It was either me seeing you into old age and the state you're in now, or you taking your chances of being able to fend for yourself."

"You were there whenever I needed you. Stood by me, comforted me, got me through the rough bits. If it hadn't been for you, I'd have ended up in a nursing home."

"I made sure you got the proper therapy, counseling, and medication when you had that bout of depression."

"I know. I owe you everything. You are the great love of my life."

"Where oh where have I heard that before?"

"I mean it. You are. You've stood by me. We made concessions. Both of us. I agreed to certain things, and you have been my savior. You are a wonderful cook."

"But you talked me out of that lovely country cottage and my garden.Gramps, you look very tired."

Robin wiped Philip's mouth and chin again. He lovingly held his hand to Philip's forehead.

Philip asked, "Remember our first meeting at the Serpentine?"

"Yes, you were walking that dog. He wasn't even yours. I think he was a prop. You gave me a big smile. The second time you went by, you winked."

"I didn't wink. The sun was in my eye."

"We started to talk, and you picked me up."

"You picked me up."

Robin conceded, "We picked each other up."

"We've had a wonderful life, Robin. I'm very tired. I feel so weak. My eyes, I can't seem to focus. Let me sleep . . . Robin, you were the great . . ."

All four men intoned at once, "We were the great loves of your life."

"Love of my . . ."

Philip fell into a deeper sleep-like state. In his mind he saw them. The four men each unfolded a corner of a Scottish flag in military fashion with military precision, a team effort. They each took a corner, and they placed it over his body, covering it entirely.

Kwan said, "We had such fun in that sauna. I loved those years. I loved you for it. Ta ta, Philip."

The light grew dimmer.

Tom said, "You were a wonderful lover. A traitor of sorts to me, but you were *my* very lovely and loving traitor. Cheers, darling."

Reynaldo declared, "You were a big baby, but a cute, lovable baby. When we were together, I think I loved you like a father. Mabuhay, Philip."

Robin said, "We never did get through all of that spend-down plan, but our years together were wonderful. You always said that whoever was there at the end to turn out the lights deserved everything, but I wish you could have lived longer. We're all here to turn out the lights, dear Gramps. You were the great love of my life, our lives. Goodbye, Philip."

All four men in unison declared, "Goodbye, Philip."

It was dusk. Darkness was coming on fast, so fast. Philip's mind couldn't evoke any more images. He tried to create another picture, dream a bit more, but darkness kept coming on. Darker, darker than any ever before. Soon it ended. The Rice Queen Spy was no more. A light, a life, had gone out.

The Daemon in Our Dreams

Three strangers in different parts of the world each has three nightmares in which a young Indian man stares menacingly at them. The dreams invoke funeral pyres, glaring skulls and feral beasts. On a land and sea tour from Singapore to the Taj Mahal these three people, Dr. Lee Ably, Fran Carr, and Paul Rowan, separately begin to see the threatening dream daemon in real life, in real time. They have given him a name—Ramesh—but cannot find a reason for his pursuit of them. And how does he get from place to place to materialize before them?

The suspense builds as one after the other of the three travelers is confronted by Ramesh in exotic places. They watch in horror as their daemon changes and evolves in successive sightings into a more deadly foe.

When the trip nears its end, the three think they have found surcease in England, but an Indian hijra message causes them to think otherwise.

In a London hotel lounge three assassinations take place. The assassin appears to be the dream daemon. Why has all of this happened? What ties these three people and their ghostly interloper to one another?

We are drawn into this eerie and insightful story as the book's narrative drive propels and impels readers deeper into the labyrinth. It's an unforgettable tale of human beings facing ominous futures.

Previous Book by John F. Rooney

Nine Lives Too Many

This is a violent and unsettling novel about terrorists, a cautionary tale, but also the deeply moving personal story of a conflicted police detective.

Felix the Cat, only nominally Muslim, but fanatically anti-American and anti-Israeli, is terrorizing New York City and Washington, D.C., with a series of bombings. This third-rate screenwriter plants a deadly bomb which kills and maims hundreds in the Main Concourse of Grand Central Station. The FBI seems in suspicious haste to label it a suicide bombing.

Grand Central Station is Detective Sergeant Denny Delaney's turf. Minutes before the attack Denny has been suspended because his drinking is interfering with his duties. His wife Monny has left him. After Denny barely misses getting killed in the bombing, he examines the terminal's surveillance tapes with his wheelchair-bound, attractive coworker Terry, and he and she realize that this is not the work of a suicide bomber. The bomber has walked away unscathed. After Nine-Eleven Denny had been on TDY with the FBI, and he has made a connection to that duty and the bomber. By threatening to reveal what he knows, Denny gets reinstated to FBI duty so he can work the case.

The novel cascades through a series of suspenseful actions: FBI raids, firefights, ambushes, and attempts on the lives of investigators. Felix, the failed screenwriter, sets up a cinematic conflict between antagonist and protagonist by telephoning Denny. They begin a series of cat-and-mouse, insightful colloquies as Felix's deadly acts of violence proliferate, one for each of his nine lives.

After the Grand Central devastation, nowhere and no one is safe including the streets of New York, the Broadway theater district, the White House, cruise ships, hotels, beaches, and bridges.

Denny has to battle Felix and his alcoholism. Will he be able to win in his inner and outer struggles and defeat a terrorist monster?

Printed in the United States
200037BV00005B/103-210/A